Preface

~

I started writing this story for my grandson, Vincent. I now have two more grandchildren, Wren and Aki, and I hope that all three of them will enjoy reading it.

I owe thanks to a number of people. Kirsty Ridge proved to be a brilliant editor, whose suggestions hugely improved the story and who was sympathetic to the fragile emotions of a first-time author. My son, Kenzo, produced the illustration for the cover, which far exceeds my own visual imagination. Other members of my family gave support and encouragement. I must also thank Hannah Dakin and her colleagues at Matador for their kind help and advice with the publishing process.

Alamanda

Alamanda

Graham Fry

Matador
Unit E2 Airfield Business Park,
Harrison Road, Market Harborough,
Leicestershire. LE16 7UL
Tel: 0116 2792299
Email: books@troubador.co.uk
Web: www.troubador.co.uk/matador
Twitter: @matadorbooks

ISBN 978 1803137 131

British Library Cataloguing in Publication Data.
A catalogue record for this book is available from the British Library.

Printed and bound in Great Britain by 4edge Limited
Typeset in 11pt Minion Pro by Troubador Publishing Ltd, Leicester, UK

Matador is an imprint of Troubador Publishing Ltd

Contents

Chapter 1

Drin Breaks the Rules

~

He was a big man with a dark face and a full, black beard, just flecked with a few white hairs. His name was Asterballudrin, but everyone called him Drin. He was strolling by the sheep pens of the great animal market of Banjut, not with the idea of buying anything but because after many days in the city he enjoyed the warmth of the sun on his back and the sight and sounds and smells of the animals all around him. There were sheep of every breed – with short wool and long wool, brown, black, grey and white wool, fat sheep and small sheep, sheep with white faces and black faces and mixtures of the two – and Drin looked at every one of them and heard them bleating and baaing and felt at ease.

He was not supposed to be there in the open market. It was held in a big, grassy field just outside the city, and the rule of the mountain traders was clear: while in Banjut, they should never leave the walled city on their own. But Drin loved the open air and the animals, and he had never really understood why he had to do something just because someone else told him to. That had got him into trouble in the past, and it was soon to get him into trouble again, but for the moment he enjoyed his freedom. He had escaped the confines of houses and walls. Above him was the big, open, blue sky, and from the sea came a gentle breeze. After the sheep he would have a quick look at the cattle and – best of all – the sheepdogs, and then return to the city. None of the other traders who had crossed the mountains with him need ever know that he had slipped away.

Overhead a crowd of swallows was skimming to and fro, catching tiny insects in flight. Drin looked carefully and could tell the parents from their children: the older birds had long outer tail feathers but the young ones did not. They reminded him of home long ago, when swallows had nested every year in the cow shed.

His eye fell on a large tent across the field. Its bright colours of purple, green and black made it conspicuous. He wondered what went on inside. Perhaps that was where the more exotic animals were bought and sold. He had heard tales of a giant bull with a thick horn growing above its nose, of an orange hairy monkey with long arms and a flat face like a man's, and of a huge lizard whose jaws could break a man's body in half. Did the tent perhaps contain marvellous creatures like them?

Curiosity drew him on. Drin walked over to the tent and quietly slipped inside, but as his eyes adjusted to the gloom, he could see no animals of any kind, just rows of seats facing a small stage on which stood a muscular man. His arms and legs were bound together by thick ropes, and he was wearing only a short cloth around his middle. Beside him a smaller man with a loud, high-pitched voice was saying something about how strong the man was and how hard he could work.

Then suddenly Drin felt shocked to the pit of his stomach. This was not an animal market he had stumbled into. He realised that it was a market for human beings. Slaves were being sold at auction. Drin was in the wrong place. He should never have come here. Like all our people of Akond, he had been brought up to understand that every person contained a small element of the divine spirit, and so no person could be owned by another, or be bought or sold. Drin had heard of the slave market, but never in his life had he imagined himself watching a slave being sold. He shook his head in disgust.

The bidding was fast and soon over. Before Drin had collected his thoughts, the auctioneer was announcing that the strong man had been sold to someone in the front row for 210 juts, as the money of Banjut is known.

Drin now realised that he should leave as fast as he could, and he was turning to go before anyone noticed him. But already the next person was standing on the little stage, and this time it was a girl. He guessed that she was no more than fifteen or sixteen years old. The auctioneer was proclaiming her virtues in his piercing voice:

"And now we have the final and finest lot of today's sale – a young girl of surpassing beauty, of an appearance never before seen, even here in Banjut, where all the nations of the world come together. See for yourselves her fair complexion, her high and slanting cheek bones and her long, golden hair hanging down to her waist. Have you ever seen hair that colour before? It has not been dyed: I swear by the God of the Sun that this bright gold is its natural colour, the same colour as the god's own rays. 'Where does she come from?' I hear you ask, and the truth is that nobody can say. Perhaps a distant, mysterious land across the ocean? Or was it the land of eternal moon shine? Imagine, gentlemen, imagine that this girl was waiting at your table or serving as a handmaid to your lady wife – quite a curiosity she would be, wouldn't she? She is quite the rarest item we have sold in this tent for many a month. Now who will start the bidding?"

As he listened to this, Drin's mood had changed from one of shocked disgust to boiling anger. All thought of leaving had gone from his mind. He pushed forward to the front rows of seats. It was bad to see a fit young man sent off to a lifetime of hard labour, but the idea of this young girl being sold off to the highest bidder was unacceptable to him. He had to stop it. Whatever happened, he had to stop it and save the girl.

His first thought was simply to push aside the auctioneer, grab her and make a run for it. But as he looked round the tent, he realised that there were too many men there who would block them and prevent them from getting away. The only result would be that he himself would be arrested and punished for breaking the strict laws of Banjut against disrupting the markets. The girl would still be sold. So he stood for a moment, undecided, determined to save her but not sure how.

The bidding had started at 50 juts and rose quickly to 100, but one by one the bidders dropped out, and soon only two remained. "100... yes, 110, thank you, sir," said the auctioneer. "110 I am bid. And 120 from Lord Nostoc on my left. It is a rare honour, sir, to see you here in person. Do I have 130? 125 even?"

But the other bidder was shaking his head. Drin looked across at the man identified as Nostoc. He was dressed finely in flowing orange robes, and he had a smooth, bald head and long ears. Even his eyebrows were shaved off. He looked well-fed, sleek and oiled, and his lip curled in a complacent smile. The auctioneer was looking round, but there were no more bids.

"130," shouted Drin with all his force. He had hit on a way to save the girl. He would use some of the money he had, to buy her and set her free. He created quite a commotion in the tent. People looked at him and pointed at him. There was a hubbub of excited voices.

"Fresh bidder at 130," cried the auctioneer. "The big man dressed in red on my right. I have 130. Lord Nostoc, sir, will you offer 140?"

Nostoc nodded sulkily.

Then they were off. Neither would give way. The price rose higher. Every now and then the auctioneer looked across at two men dressed in blue tunics and seated at a small table on the other side of the stage, but the Banjuti officials appointed to supervise the auction stared back without expression. The girl stood alone on the stage, with her eyes fixed on the ground. She was dressed in what looked like straw mats sewn together, and they looked grubby and torn at the corners.

Soon Nostoc was bidding 200, and Drin 220, and so on up to 320 from Nostoc, 340 from Drin. They began to slow their pace a little now, and each bid was followed by a murmur of comment among the spectators.

"360?" asked the auctioneer. Nostoc nodded, and all eyes turned back to Drin. The scale of the bidding was beginning to make him nervous. He had sold in the walled market of Banjut all the fine teas which he had brought on his donkeys over the mountains from Akond. Concealed under his red coat he had the money which he had been planning to spend on Banjuti goods to take back and sell in Akond on his return. This was all his wealth, and he had already pledged nearly a third of it in the auction. While he hesitated, the girl straightened her back and looked up. Her eyes met his. He had never seen anyone look so miserable, and yet there was something proud in the way she looked at him, and undefeated. If he had had a daughter, she might have been the same age: would she have shown the same courage? He made up his mind: he could not stop now. He could not allow this girl to be bought by Nostoc as a slave.

"400!" he said.

"400," repeated the auctioneer. "I have 400 from the gentleman in red. Lord Nostoc, will you offer 420?"

This time with a soft, dangerous voice, Nostoc spoke: "Red man, I have not seen you before. You seem to be new to the markets, so let me give you a little advice. Can you guess why the other bidders gave up so soon? My master is Zeno, Great Leader, Marshal of the Souvian Army, ruler of all the countries of the North, and he intends to possess this girl. I can spend as much money as I like. You cannot win. So I advise you not to provoke my master's anger. Give up now, while we are willing to forgive you. I bid 450 juts."

Everyone in the tent was silent as they waited for Drin to react. Even the auctioneer fell silent. Nostoc's lip was curling again as he anticipated triumph: surely nobody would dare to risk the anger of the mighty Zeno? But Drin did not like being told what to do, and he especially did not like being threatened by someone like Nostoc. Any doubts he might have had about the auction were now swept away. He did not care if he spent all his money and had nothing left: he would fight Nostoc to the end, and he would never let him buy the girl.

"500!" he said.

"You fool!" shouted Nostoc. His voice was no longer silky, and he jabbed his finger at Drin. "I gave you a chance to stop, but you ignored me. Now my master will punish you, and the more you persist, the more you will regret it."

The crowd erupted in a fury of excited comment, but when one of the Banjuti officials stood up, they fell silent.

"It is my duty to remind the last bidder of Article 52.4 of the Law concerning the Conduct of Auctions. It is forbidden for one bidder to threaten another with the aim of deterring him or her from participating in the bidding. This is a final warning. If the same bidder breaks our law again, my colleague and I will take the necessary action. Auctioneer – proceed."

This intervention restored calm in the tent, and the auction resumed. An angry Nostoc bid 550.

Meanwhile Drin was furiously calculating in his head how much money he could bid. The penalties for bidding and being unable to pay were severe. He could not take out his money and count it, and so he had to think back through the sales he had made and add them together in his mind. The auctioneer was beginning the countdown: "550 juts. Any more bids? I give you fair notice. Going to Lord Nostoc for 550…"

"600." Drin called out his bid, and the auctioneer turned

back to Nostoc, who gave Drin a long, cold stare before bidding 650. The spectators oohed and chattered. "Six hundred and fifty!" repeated the auctioneer.

Drin had finally worked it out. He had gone through everything twice and then three times in his head and was confident that he had 1,046 juts in total. But would that be enough? If Nostoc really had an unlimited budget, he would be outbid, and then what could he do? But he had no time to worry about that now: he had to keep bidding as long as he could.

"700," he said.

"750," came the reply.

Drin needed to work out the maximum that he could bid. The Banjuti officials would take a tax of one twelfth from the buyer and one twelfth from the seller. What was one twelfth of 1,046? No, that was wrong: it had to be one twelfth of what he bid, not of the total. For a moment his mind went completely blank, but then he heard the auctioneer asking if he would bid 800, and since he was sure the answer was more than that, he did.

There was a long angry glare from Nostoc before he agreed to 850. The crowd was silent. Drin's mind was whirring but he found it hard to concentrate. He could hear the auctioneer repeating the bid and starting again to count down: "Going for 850 juts… going…" Suddenly the mist cleared: eight 12s was 96; times ten made 960; add 80 for the tax; and the answer was 1040. Forget the extra 6, and he could bid up to 960.

So he said: "900!" and he tried to sound confident, but he knew now that he was very close to his limit: he had only one more bid to go, and that would be the end.

Nostoc shook his head with a faint smile, and Drin hoped for an instant that he was admitting defeat, but then Nostoc said "950", and Drin knew that it was all over.

He desperately tried to think of a fresh plan, but none came to him, and so he made the only bid he could. "960." Not 1,000, but 960. Since the bids had been rising by 50 juts at a time, everyone understood that 960 was his limit, and that Nostoc had only to make one more bid to win. A broad smile crossed Nostoc's face, like a snake which has squeezed its prey to death and is about to swallow it whole.

Slowly and quietly he hissed: "I bid nine hundred and seventy juts."

Once again Drin looked at the girl, standing slight and straight. He had done what he could, but he had failed. He had no more money, no bright ideas, no brilliant stratagem. She looked up at him, and again he saw the courage in her eyes, and once again he was filled with a kind of desperate courage of his own. He looked across at Nostoc and felt an urge to punch him on his upturned nose. Perhaps that was the best he could do: start a fight.

"Before I make my next bid," he said, "I have a question for this man Nostoc who is bidding against me." There was silence in the tent, and expectation. "He says that his master is called Zeno. Is this Zeno the smelly, orange monkey with the long arms, or is he the big lizard with the jagged teeth and the bad breath, or is he the round, fat ox with the stubby horn…?"

Drin would have continued, but he could hardly be heard above the hubbub in the tent as everyone began talking and shouting at once. Nostoc was standing up, and five big bodyguards were on their feet around him, and he was screaming insults and threats at Drin. He had managed to control his irritation during the last stages of the auction, but he could not allow these insults to his master. So he yelled at his men to deal with Drin there and then, and Drin squared up for the fight. The rest of the crowd edged out of the way, and Drin saw not just five, but ten, burly men rushing towards him, kicking chairs out of their way. There was no way he could fight them off on his own.

But they were still in a market in the territory of Banjut, and amid the pandemonium the officials intervened again. Both stepped forward and raised their staffs of office. From nowhere five archers had appeared, all in the same blue uniforms, and lined up behind them with their bows drawn and ready to shoot.

"Wait!" said the older official. "We command you to stop!"

Nostoc's men hesitated, and the crowd in the tent grew a little quieter.

"The bidder Nostoc has ignored the final warning we gave him. He is disqualified. His last bid is invalid. This auction is concluded."

"What?" cried Nostoc. "I am disqualified? But he insulted my master. I demand justice. He is the one who should be punished."

"Nostoc, our law ensures the fair operation of the markets. It applies to all equally, including you. You threatened to use violence against another bidder. You broke the law. You are disqualified."

"No!" said Nostoc. "No one has the right to insult my master, in Banjut or anywhere else. I made a fair bid. The girl is mine."

"We have given our judgement. That is all."

"In that case," said Nostoc in a tone of cold anger, "I will leave but I will not forget. The time has not yet come, but soon, quite soon, my master will take over this city of Banjut with its precious markets and its two-faced officials, and when he does, Gadim, your arrogance today will be punished. You will suffer for this, you and all your people. As for the girl, my master will obtain her by other means. He does not have to pay high prices in your markets. He takes what he wants whenever he wants it. Oh yes, and there is the red man. The penalty for you, red man, will be death. You insulted my master, and I will take pleasure in making your death very painful indeed."

And with that, Nostoc turned and pushed his way out of the tent with his bodyguards in tow, and only when he had left did the buzz of voices start again.

But Drin had hardly heard Nostoc's threats. They did not bother him anyway. His heart was full of one enormous fact. His mind could think of only one thing. It made him want to dance and sing and leap in the air. Here he was, with all his money pledged, threatened with a painful death by the agent of a powerful tyrant, but all that mattered was that he had won. By some miracle he had defeated Nostoc and bought the girl, and now he could set her free.

Chapter 2

Paying the Price

~

It is some years now since Marcon, the leader of the mountain traders, brought Drin and the girl to see me in the palace of Kandalore and Drin told me this story, but I can still remember every detail. I was only fifteen then, and I knew nothing of the world except what I had read. Unlike my elder brother Hargon, I had no interest in martial sports or horse races or the other things which young princes were expected to enjoy. I was no good at them anyway. What I loved to do was to study old manuscripts and learn about the deeds of our ancestors and the customs of other countries. My favourite room had once been my grandfather's study, but I had converted it into my own library. The shelves where he had kept official documents now held my collection of manuscripts, and I had spent many happy hours poring over them. Most of them concerned our own kingdom of

Akond and the countries in the broad plains to the west below us, but the ones which most fascinated me were the few which Marcon had managed to obtain for me on his visits to Banjut, the great city on the eastern coast beyond the mountains. These I had read and re-read, and I had pestered Marcon with questions about the many things I did not understand, until he must have been thoroughly fed up with me.

But I had never in my wildest dreams expected to meet someone like this girl. When she was first introduced she gave a nervous smile which lit up her face and made her beautiful. At first I had no idea how I should respond, and I must have stared at her rather rudely. As Marcon and Drin began to tell me a little about her, I noticed that she looked tired and uncomfortable, her clothes were torn and dirty from so many days living rough in the mountains, and her long, golden hair was unkempt. That gave me an idea, and I called the servants and told them to take her away and give her a hot bath, anoint her with fragrant oils, arrange her hair, and dress her in fresh clothes. Marcon and Drin said they were glad I did that; it was definitely the right thing to do.

Then at Marcon's urging, Drin told me his story, which continued as follows.

It was quiet in the tent now. Almost everyone had left. Drin found himself in front of the officials at their small table. The girl was still standing in the same place next to the auctioneer. Two men with ragged clothes and tattooed bodies were lurking nearby. One of them had a long scar on his forehead. They nodded and smiled at him, but Drin did not smile back.

It was time to pay the money. Drin reached under his coat to his left armpit, pulled out a small purse and placed it on the table. Gadim's colleague poured a pile of coins out of it and began to sort them according to their values. Meanwhile Drin reached into his coat again, this time on the right side, and pulled out another purse, which he again put on the table. Then he reached inside under his belt on the left and produced a third purse. The fourth had been hidden under his belt on the right. Once the coins had been sorted, they were counted, separately by each official.

"This is only 860 juts," said Gadim when they had finished.

"Oh, sorry," said Drin. "I forgot." He turned away from them, reached round to his back, and produced yet another purse. "This is the last one – 100 to make up the purchase price, 80 for your auction charge, and 6 left over for me."

Gadim left his colleague to do the count. "Auctioneer," he said, "who is the seller?"

The auctioneer pointed to the two men, who grinned as they came forward.

"Which of you is the owner?" asked Gadim.

"We both are, together like."

"Names?"

"I'm Dubash, and he's Goollen, sir."

Gadim made a note on a register. "Where do you live?"

"Begging your pardon, sir, but we're seamen, and we live on our boat."

"Name?"

"She's the *Octopus*, sir, but we're getting a new boat once we get the money."

Goollen was staring at the money and nodding. He looked like a dog whose owner was holding a meaty bone in front of its nose.

"Can you write?" asked Gadim.

"No, sir," said Dubash.

"Then make your marks here to show that you have both received what is due to you. 960 juts minus 80 makes 880." Dubash and Goollen each scratched an X on the register.

"Can we take the money now, sir?" Goollen asked. He had already stretched out his hands.

"Yes, you may," said Gadim, and Dubash produced an old leather bag and the two seamen swept the money off the table and into the bag. They held it up and began cheering and laughing.

"Thank you, mate," Dubash yelled at Drin. "Y'know what they say – one man's loss is another man's gain. But I never thought anyone'd pay that much."

"Wait!" said Drin. "Tell me who the girl is and where you found her."

"Too late for that," said Goollen.

"Yeah, sorry, mate," said Dubash. "You've bought 'er now, paid the money, too late to start asking questions. We're off, mate, thirsty, time for a drink, celebration."

They hurried out of the tent, with Goollen hugging the bag tightly.

Drin turned round with a face like thunder. He was angry with himself for having paid so much money to men like this, and angry with them for the way they had treated the girl. But there was nothing he could do about that now. He reached into his boot and pulled out the slim knife which he always kept concealed in it. It was time to set her free.

But when she saw the look on his face and the knife, the girl cowered back and raised her hands to protect herself.

Drin was horrified. "Oh no, I don't mean to harm you. Don't be afraid."

He held out the knife to Gadim and said: "The girl is frightened of me, but all I want to do is to cut the rope around her wrists and set her free. Sir, may I ask you a favour? Could you please cut the ropes for me?"

"You mean you've bought her for 1,040 juts and now you're going to set her free?" asked Gadim.

"Yes," said Drin. "In my country our law forbids us to own slaves. The only reason I bought her was to set her free. How can it be right to tie up a young girl and buy and sell her like a cow or a sheep?"

"Now that is remarkable," said Gadim. "I've never seen a man do what you're doing. Quite remarkable, and in a way praiseworthy. Anyway, I don't need the knife. I'll just untie the knots."

Drin slipped the knife back into his boot, and Gadim went over and untied the rope. "There," he said gently, "you are free. This man has set you free."

The girl did not react in any way. He spoke to her again with words which Drin did not understand, but she still looked blankly at him. Then she spoke for the first time, but the words she used were strange, and neither of them knew what she meant.

"She must come from very far away," Gadim said. "She doesn't understand Banjuti. I have tried speaking to her in five other languages, but she doesn't seem to understand them either, and her own words are completely unfamiliar.

No wonder she was frightened of you. She must have very little idea of what's been going on here."

"At least she's free now," said Drin, "and she can go back home to her own people."

He was feeling that he had done what he had set out to do and had better return to the walled town before the other traders noticed he was gone.

"But that's not so easy," replied Gadim. "You can't just leave her now. She's in a strange land where she doesn't speak the language and has no friends. Her home is so far off that nobody in Banjut has any idea where it is. She doesn't even look like any of us. How is she to find her way back without help? It's far more likely that someone will take her prisoner again. You heard Nostoc's threats, and on top of that, every thug in the neighbourhood will soon know how much you and Nostoc were prepared to pay for her. She may be free now, Drin, but she's in great danger. She needs someone to keep her safe."

Drin now understood for the first time the consequences of what he had done. He had given no thought to what would happen once the girl was free, but now he understood that he could not just walk away. Without meaning to, he had taken on responsibility for her welfare. This was the moment when he made a pledge and, without fully realising it, found himself a mission.

"Yes, you're right," he said slowly. "I am responsible for her. I will protect her. I have to finish what I've started." Then he added: "But only if she wants me to. She's free now. She doesn't have to stay with me if she doesn't want to."

"But how can you ask her what she wants if you can't speak her language and she doesn't understand ours?"

"Wait a minute." Drin knelt down so that his head was

slightly below the girl's. He pointed at her, then at himself, and then he acted silently as if he was eating and she was eating too. She stared intently. Then he pretended to go to sleep, and finally he gestured to invite her to go with him. She looked at Gadim, and he nodded as if to say that he approved. She shrugged, and then she nodded too.

"She's agreed," said Drin, and he smiled. Drin's normal expression for his fellow men did not show much warmth; it was more designed to persuade them not to mess with him. But on the rare occasions when he did smile, his face lit up with kindness; and when the girl saw that, she seemed to relax a little.

"My archers and I will walk with you to the gate of the walled town," said Gadim. "I doubt if anyone will dare to attack you if we're with you."

Drin brought the girl to the inn where the men from Akond stayed when they were in Banjut. The city had been built at the mouth of a large river, where a natural harbour had been formed by a high rocky hill which blocked the flow of water into the sea. It was joined to the northern bank by a low neck of land, and the main channel of the river passed round its southern end into the sea. It was on this hill that the Banjutis had built their citadel and fortified it with mighty walls wherever it was not already defended by natural cliffs. Below it along the northern bank of the river stretched a jumble of wharves and jetties crowded with boats, and beyond them were buildings of every kind where people lived and traded and stored their goods. Walls had been built to protect this area, but over time, as business flourished, people had added wharves and buildings outside the walls as well. Only the citizens of Banjut were allowed to enter the citadel, but trusted outsiders were able to enter and stay in the walled town below as long as they were unarmed. The Banjutis did their best to keep order throughout the city, but it was harder to do so outside the walls, especially at night.

The Akondians' inn was inside the walled town, and they were able to do almost all their business in the markets and shops there. Above them they could see the rock of the citadel and some houses on its upper slopes, but not the summit, where there were said to be large temples and other buildings made of white stone and decorated with golden statues. Some of the traders from other countries were jealous of the enormous riches which the Banjutis had amassed from their own trading and from the fees they collected from the markets they controlled, but the Akondians had no such feelings. Banjut was good for them: the markets were fair, and they could do their business in peace. They felt comfortable and safe while they were there.

When Drin and the girl walked into the courtyard of the inn, they found the landlady hanging up washing. "Drin, what've you been up to?" she asked. "Who's this girl?"

Drin tried to stammer out an explanation without quite knowing where to start.

"Oh, never mind all that. She looks half starved. I bet you never thought of giving her something to eat. Come on, my dear. You look so pale. Come inside, and we'll give you some food and make you comfortable."

"Thank you," said Drin.

"And you, master Drin, had better go and explain yourself to Marcon."

The landlady was right. He did have to explain it all to Marcon, and that was not going to be easy. Drin tried to order his thoughts, but the more he tried to get his story straight, the more of a muddle it seemed to be. At length he gave a deep sigh and went inside.

He found Marcon in his private room drinking a cup of tea. Marcon made him a cup too and waited. In the end Drin did not try to justify what he had done; he just blurted out everything which had happened in roughly the right order. As he did so, Marcon's brow began to furrow, and when Drin reached the end and abruptly stopped, Marcon said: "You've broken the rules."

"I know," said Drin. "I'm sorry."

"And you've made bad enemies. Everyone's afraid of this Nostoc, and of Zeno too. Even the Banjutis are, though they pretend not to be. What I don't get is why you did it. You never even met this girl before. Why spend all your money?"

"It just seemed like the right thing to do," Drin mumbled.

"I shall never understand you. Every time you seem to settle down, you go and do something... out of the ordinary. Finest scout in the army you were, everyone respected you, and then you go and hit that officer..."

Drin was silent. This was turning out even worse than he had feared.

"Then you built up all that money as a trader, and you end up getting carried away in an auction and blowing the lot!"

"No, it wasn't like that. There's something special about this girl, the way she looks at you. I can't explain it, but I had to save her. I couldn't let Nostoc get her."

"Well, you'll have to tell the others," Marcon replied. "They have the right to know what danger they're in, and since you broke the rules, they'll have to decide what to do with you."

There was a silence while Drin took in the idea of telling his story all over again and being judged by his peers.

Marcon spoke more gently: "And we'll have to work out what to do with the girl now she's with us. If I were you, I'd take her over the mountains. She'll be safe in Akond."

"But she might not want to come."

"Then you might have to persuade her, for her own good. Come on, Drin, finish your tea. Everyone feels better after a good cup of Akondian tea."

There were ten of them in all. Marcon sat at one end of the table, and Drin at the other. The others sat on benches on either side. The room was warm and well-lit by candles. Normally it would be full of noise and good humour. These men were not traders like those who sat all day at a stall in the market. They were hardened by the physical challenge of climbing for days up the narrow mountain path with their laden donkeys, of the cold and lack of oxygen in the high pass, and of the dangerous descent on the stony track. If the weather closed in, or if a man or donkey slipped, each man's life would depend on the strength and courage of the others. But none of them ever talked about that; instead they played noisy games with each other or tried out practical jokes.

But there was no joking when they listened to Drin that evening. Normally Drin did not much care what others thought of him, but as he tried for the second time to explain what he had done, he found that he did care how these men judged him.

When he finished, Marcon said: "This Zeno rules a

country called Souvia, a long way inland and north of here. From what I've heard, he killed the king there and put himself on the throne instead, and since then he and the Souvians have conquered one country after another. Nostoc does his dirty work and has spies everywhere, even here in Banjut. Now that Drin's made Nostoc look a fool and insulted Zeno, they'll try to get even. Let's be honest: none of this would have happened, except that Drin broke our rules: he left the walled town on his own; he attended a slave auction; and worst of all, he bought a slave, which is contrary to the law of the gods. So, the question is what should we do? Make him pay a penalty like cleaning out the horses or pay a fine? Or what? I want each of you to think it over and say what you think."

There was silence for a while, and then one of the men spoke up. "It's no good making Drin look after the horses. There's nothing he likes better than looking after those horses. If you ask me, he spends more time talking to those horses than he does to us."

"And there's not much point in trying to make him pay a fine," said another, "when he's just spent all his money."

The others laughed and nodded in agreement.

"No," said an older man on Marcon's right. "Drin may have broken a rule or two, but so what? You say he did the wrong thing because he bought the girl at the slave market. But the only reason he bought her was to set her free. I don't think we should be talking about penalties. What Drin's done is one of the finest things I ever heard of. Who else would have spent every jut he owned in order to save a girl from slavery? We know how many times he's toiled up and down that mountain with the tea one way and the Banjut goods the other. We know, nobody else does, but we know, how rough that mountain can be – and now he hands over the whole lot just to save this girl. And another thing. You say he's put us into danger, but every man here has been helped by Drin up on that mountain. If one of us gets into danger, the others help him out. That's how it's always been. So I vote that we drink Drin's health – he's one of us, and we'll stand by him!"

"Yeah, that's right," said the others, and they banged the table to show their agreement.

Marcon beamed. "To be honest, that's exactly what I think too, but I wanted to be sure everyone felt the same. Jolyon's right. Drin's done a fine thing, and we should stick by him, whatever Nostoc gets up to."

"Now I think about it," said Jolyon, "this evening, as we came back here, there were a couple of fellows hanging around on the corner of the street. I've never seen them before. I thought they might be out to rob us, but maybe they're watching the inn because of Drin and the girl."

"Yes, I saw them too," Marcon said. "Drin, you'd better be careful tomorrow. If I were you, I'd keep the girl inside the inn just in case. Everyone else had better take extra care too. I think we're all right within the walls, but even so nobody should go out on his own, and if anything funny happens, come straight back here."

They all nodded, and Marcon said: "Come on, lads, where are the drinks? Where's the food?"

Drin sat at the end of the table as the normal noisy hubbub resumed around him, and once again he smiled.

The next day he woke early. He stayed behind when the other men went out, and began to take care of the horses. The pass was so steep that only donkeys could cross it, but when they had reached the bottom of the mountain, the traders shifted their goods onto pack horses and left the donkeys behind. Once they arrived in Banjut, the horses could rest for a while until the return journey, but that morning Drin still had to feed them, muck them out, brush them and walk them around for a little exercise.

After a while the girl came out of the inn. She had slept well and eaten a good breakfast, and she was wearing clean clothes in the Banjuti style so that she looked fresher and brighter than during her ordeal of the day before. Her golden hair shone in the morning sun. She greeted him with a smile, and he smiled back. She showed off her new clothes, and he encouraged her to come over and help him brush one of the horses. At first she was nervous of them and seemed unfamiliar with such large animals, but with Drin's gentle encouragement, she gradually overcame her fear; and when the landlady came out to call them for the midday meal, she found the girl riding one of the horses with Drin leading it on a halter.

"Well, I didn't expect to see that," she said. "D'you like it up there on the horse, my dear?" The girl smiled. "She looks a lot happier now. Where's she come from, Drin? She don't speak our language."

"I wish I knew."

"She must've been through a terrible time. Last night, as soon as the two of us got into the kitchen, she started crying and clinging to me, poor thing, and she just didn't stop. She went on sobbing for so long, and all I could do was to hug her and try to comfort her. Then when I put the food in front of her, she ate it up so fast I had to keep refilling her plate. Anyway, I don't know what happened before you took charge, but someone's treated her very badly. You'd better take good care of her from now on, master Drin."

"I shall do my best."

"She was wearing the strangest clothes, more like mats sewn together, and all dirty and breaking up. She looks much better now in a proper clean dress. I can tell she likes things to be clean and neat. Wouldn't go to bed last night before washing herself all over. Back in her home, where she comes from, she must be someone very special. Maybe she's a princess or something like that."

"Perhaps she is. Who knows?"

After they had eaten, Drin and the girl went back to the horses, and he had an idea. "Asterballudrin," he said, pointing at himself. "Drin."

"Drin," she said and gave her bright smile again. Then slowly, pointing at herself, she added: "Alamanda-kamimiko-no-saori."

"Allamma…" he started, but she shook her head.

"Saori," she said.

"Sow-ree," he replied, but she looked troubled.

"Saori," she said again, and he had to keep repeating the name until he obtained her approval.

"Sa-o-ri."

Now they knew each other's names. Even that was a kind of progress, and Drin decided to teach her some Banjuti words. He started with "horse", and they were soon engrossed in a language lesson.

The time went by quickly until the men began to return from the markets with their purchases, and Drin and Saori split up again. She went off with the landlady while Drin joined the other traders for the evening meal. They told him that as they had come back, they had found the same two men hanging around and this time four of the traders had gone up to the men and made them leave the street. They suspected that the men would come back soon enough or others would take their place, but the traders were confident that as long as they were all together, Nostoc's thugs would not dare to attack them.

Dinner was a bright occasion with plenty of jokes, most of them aimed at Drin; but he did not mind. It was pretty much agreed that, as long as she herself wanted to, Saori could go with them across the mountains to the safety of Akond. They were sure that nobody would dare to follow them there.

Chapter 3
An Offer

~

The men were just pushing back their plates at the end of the meal when there was a loud knock on the door. Two armed Banjuti officials burst in and took up position on either side of it.

"Pray rise for President Lazadim and the Lady Katila!" one of them cried.

Drin and his colleagues rose to their feet, more out of surprise than because they understood what was going on. A tall man with a neat grey beard, dressed in the usual Banjuti blue, came in, followed by a woman, whose strong features and fine clothes marked her out as someone important. They went round to the head of the table, and Lazadim said: "Good evening, traders of Akond. May we join you for a little while?"

Even Marcon was taken aback by this sudden entry. He

could not remember any time when someone had burst in on them like this. If it had been anyone else, their natural reaction would have been to kick out the intruders, but they could not do that to this couple: Lazadim was the most powerful man in Banjut, and Katila was his wife. One of the many unusual things about Banjut was that it did not have a king. Instead, the citizens themselves chose a Council of fifteen men, and the Council chose a President to govern the city: Lazadim had been President for twenty years. In theory the citizens had the last word and could overturn the Council's decisions, but no one could remember when that had last happened.

Marcon had two chairs drawn up to the head of the table so that Lazadim and Katila could be seated together. The plates were cleared away, and food and drinks offered to the visitors, but they asked only for Akondian tea. At Katila's bidding, the traders sat down again, squeezing onto the benches five a side.

"It is a great and unexpected honour..." began Marcon, but Lazadim interrupted.

"Which one of you is Asterballudrin?" he asked.

"Me sir," came the reply.

"Is it true that you bought a slave yesterday?"

"Yes, but..."

"A young girl with golden hair?"

"Yes, but..."

"For 960 juts plus charges?"

"Yes, but..."

"And that you set her free?"

"Yes."

"So where is she now?"

"She's with the landlady in the other part of the inn."

Without a word, Katila rose and left the room.

"Marcon," said Lazadim, "do you know about this? What do you make of it? I never heard of one of your men buying a slave before."

"Drin's told us everything that he did, sir, and yes, it's true we have no slaves in Akond, but Drin only bought the girl in order to set her free. Every man here thinks he did the right thing."

"I see," said Lazadim. "But I'm not so sure he did. Do you know that this inn is being watched?"

"Yes, we spotted two men behaving suspiciously outside."

"There were more than two," said Lazadim. He fell silent, sipping his tea.

Drin wondered what was on his mind. Why were Lazadim and Katila so concerned about what he had done in the slave market?

Katila returned to the room and said to Lazadim: "She is sleeping peacefully, and the landlady confirms what we had heard."

"So it is all true," said Lazadim. "You see, Marcon, we found it hard to believe that a man would spend all his money to save someone he did not even know. Admirable perhaps, in one way, but also extremely foolish. Drin has stirred up a hornets' nest and put all of you in far greater danger than you can imagine. Katila and I came here tonight to warn you. The problem is simple: it is not that Drin bought the girl, but that he prevented Zeno from doing so. Do you understand why?"

"Well, everyone seems to be afraid of Zeno," said Marcon. "He's the king of Souvia…"

"Not quite. He doesn't call himself 'king', perhaps because he has no royal blood: we believe he is the son of a washerwoman who lived in the royal palace, and no one has ever been sure who his father was. Zeno's not even his real name: it belonged to the founder of Souvia, Zeno the Great, but when he renamed himself, the new Zeno claimed he was the new founder of the country and would make it great again. I suppose his followers would say he has. When he took power, we didn't bother about it too much. Souvia's a long way away and the Souvians have always been a bit backward – good for fighting, drinking and thieving as my father used to say."

"But no one says that kind of thing now," Katila said.

"No. They don't dare, and when you think of all the people Zeno has murdered, tortured and enslaved, you can't blame them. He started off by killing the king of Souvia, the priests and all the nobles and enslaving their families, and he's carried on from there. Apart from himself, all he cares about is the army. He was the commander of the royal guard when he took power, and he's put everything into building up the army with more men, better weapons and harder training. He even ordered everyone to worship the army's god – Mangra, god of war. Looking back, we should have stopped him then before he became too powerful."

"You did try, before Valosia fell," said Katila.

"Yes. The king, Gandarel, begged me to help him, but for once I couldn't persuade the Council. By then Zeno had already conquered Milesia, Basutia and Coroscania, but everyone was sure that sooner or later he would be defeated or there would be a rebellion against him, and his whole empire would fall apart. Well, they were wrong: he has carried on winning, and with every new country he conquers, his army gets new recruits and more money, and he gets stronger and stronger."

"Now he's not that far from Banjut itself," added Katila.

"Yes, no one doubts any more that this is the most formidable fighting machine which we have ever seen. Zeno aims to conquer the world. He's acquired thousands of new recruits, tens of thousands of slaves, developed new mines, and built factories to make weapons. We have at last put together an alliance of the southern states, and with the help of the gods and a lot of Banjut's money, we will defeat him, but it won't be easy."

Lazadim paused to let his words sink in. None of the traders spoke: they were trying to work out what all this might mean for them.

"And now Zeno wants this girl," said Katila. "We need to find out why. Gadim said that she spoke no language he could recognise. Can you tell us anything more about her?"

"No," said Drin, "except that her name is Saori and she likes horses. Why don't you ask those pirates who sold her?"

"We found one of them this morning," said Katila, "the man called Goollen. His throat had been slit, and his bag was empty. We don't know who killed him. The others have disappeared together with their boat."

"You too are in mortal danger," said Lazadim. "Nostoc will stop at nothing to get the girl. If you want to keep her safe, there is only one option. There is only one safe place left in the world, and that is the citadel. I can guarantee that the Souvians will never be able to enter our walls and that the girl will never fall into their hands if she is with us."

"We want to make you an offer," said Katila. "If you truly care about the welfare of the girl, we suggest you hand her over to us for safe keeping while we work out why Zeno wants her so badly."

"No!" Drin's voice was louder than he had intended, but he would not hand Saori over to anyone, not unless she asked him to. "She'll be safe in Akond with me."

"Think about it, Drin," urged Katila. "She might be safe in Akond, but she has to get there. Reliable sources have told us that Zeno has ordered Nostoc to get hold of her by any method he likes, and he has mobilised a shadowy force of spies and thugs to watch you and the girl and to capture you as soon as you leave the walls. As well as the men posted outside this inn, there are men watching every gate out of Banjut, and we believe there are more watching the main roads outside the city. We have even received reports of Souvian cavalry units operating in the countryside. If you want Saori to be safe, Drin, you must hand her over to us."

"We will refund the money you spent," added Lazadim quietly.

"No!" Drin's voice was even louder than before. "You want me to sell her to you! Well, I won't do it."

"That's not what I meant," said Lazadim, "but I can see that you will not be parted from the girl. Why don't you come to the citadel with her?"

Drin was about to refuse this too, but he hesitated. On the face of it, it was a reasonable offer. He would still be with Saori and able to check that she was treated properly, and the citadel probably was the safest place available. But could he trust Lazadim and Katila? They would put the interests of Banjut above everything else, including Saori's freedom, and he would not be able to stop them. Even more than that, he hated the idea of being cooped up in the citadel: he would much prefer to take his chances in the open country. So he shook his head: "No".

"Marcon, what do you think?" asked Lazadim. "The girl will be safer with us, and you and your men can go home in the normal way."

"Thank you, sir, but it's up to Drin. All of us agreed last night at this table that whatever happened, we'd stand by him. Nothing changes that. If he wants to take Saori to Akond, we'll go with them. All of us have been in the army, and we know how to fight."

"Brave words," said Lazadim, "but believe me, you stand no chance in a fight with the Souvians."

"It'd be best to let us go on our own," said Drin. "Just me and Saori. I'm sorry I got everyone into this mess, and I don't want to put you in more danger. I used to be a pretty good scout once when we were fighting Hatoba. If there's just the two of us, I reckon we can avoid these Souvians."

"No, Drin," said Marcon. "We're all in this together. We'll stand by you."

"You're true friends, but this is my doing, not yours. I can hide in the woods better than anyone. That's our best chance."

"All right," said Marcon after a pause. "We'll let you go on your own. But first you'll have to get out of the town. How are you going to do that without being seen?"

There was silence while Drin thought this through, and in the end he had to admit that it would be hard to leave without being spotted by Nostoc's spies.

Then Marcon spoke to Lazadim and Katila in a quiet voice: "I'm sorry, sir, ma'am: I can only apologise for Drin's behaviour towards you. He spoke too harshly just now when he turned down your offer, but please don't be angry with him. All he cares about is the welfare of this girl, and only you can help them. We men of Akond have never asked for any favours before, but I beg you to help us now."

Lazadim frowned and was silent, but after a moment, Katila replied: "You're making a big mistake, Drin: you should let the girl come with us into the citadel. But since you refuse, and we don't want the girl to fall into Nostoc's hands, we'll have to help you get away. If we do, you must promise that you will both leave Banjut tonight under cover of darkness. We can arrange for you to be smuggled out of the city, but after that you'll have to look after yourselves."

Drin nodded in agreement and thanked her, and Katila continued: "Tell me, which gate do you wish to leave by? I can offer you East, West, North and South. The West is the straight road towards the mountain and will be the most heavily watched. The North leads you straight towards Souvian territory. The South road crosses the bridge over the Banjut river. The Southern Alliance might help you there. Or you could try the Eastern route, by which I mean a boat from Banjut along the coast to a safe port in the South. Personally that's what I would advise, but it's up to you."

"I'm not a sailor. I've never been on the sea in my life, and right now I'd rather stick to what I know. We'll take the South road and try our luck on land."

"In that case, a carriage will come to the inn in the middle of the night. Climb into it and conceal yourselves, and it will take you out of the city." She took a small silver medallion out of a bag hanging at her waist and handed it to Drin. On it was the finely worked design of a sailing ship. "This is my token. Please give it to the girl. She may find it useful some time if ever she needs help from Banjut again."

"Thank you."

"By the way, Drin," said Lazadim, whose frown had vanished, "I have one more question for you. Is it true that you called Zeno a smelly monkey and a fat ox with a stubby horn?"

"Yes, sir, and a big lizard with bad breath."

"I wish I had been there for that," said Lazadim, who looked for a moment as if he was about to sneeze. Then he rose to his feet, said, "Good night to you all, and good luck!", and he and Katila and their guards left the room as suddenly as they had entered.

Chapter 4

Smuggled Out

~

Drin and the landlady waited outside the front door of the inn in the darkness. The town was silent around them. Above shone a half-moon and myriad stars. Drin had packed everything he thought he and Saori would need into two bags, one for himself to carry on his back and a small one with spare clothes for her.

"I wonder what sort of carriage the lady will send," said the landlady quietly. "Maybe you'll get Lazadim's coach with his fancy white horses. That's a lovely sight, that is, when he goes riding through the town."

"No," said Drin. "That'd be too obvious. It's not a parade."

"Poor thing, I'm sure she never hurt a fly. I hate those Souvians…"

"Ssh!" said Drin. "I can hear something coming. What's that smell?"

"It smells like the cart that comes round to empty the toilets. But they did us last week, so it won't come here. The stink when they shovel it out, it's disgusting."

They waited as the sound of the cart drew nearer, and finally came straight through the gates of the inn and stopped in front of them.

"What're you doing here tonight?" she said to the driver. "You can't stop here. We're expecting an important coach to come. What a stink!"

"Don't talk so loud," he said. "The town is full of spies. Are you the two passengers?"

"As I thought," Drin said to the landlady, "we're not getting Lazadim's coach. You'd better go and fetch Saori."

"You can't put her in that", she said. "Not when she likes to be so clean."

"Better go quickly," said Drin, and reluctantly she disappeared into the inn.

Saori was still sleepy when she came out, but she was soon hit by the smell and made a face. "Ooogh!" she said, and when Drin motioned for her to climb in, she drew back. But the landlady hugged her, held her nose and made her laugh, and gently helped her to get up and lie down on the floor of the cart. Drin gave her her bag to act as a pillow and gingerly clambered up beside her with his. Someone had made some effort to wash the floor of the cart, but the air inside was foul and Drin was afraid that their clothes would pick up the stench and stink for evermore. Saori coughed, and Drin patted her shoulder to reassure her, then started to cough himself. The driver shut the doors and climbed to his seat outside.

The horses moved off and turned at a walking pace out

of the courtyard of the inn and into the streets of the old town. Drin lay on the floor, conscious of every bump and turn, trying not to breathe in the dirty air. Saori was stiff and motionless beside him. He wondered what route they were taking. They seemed to be avoiding the main streets, and the sound of the horses and the cart echoed off the houses in narrow lanes. The journey seemed to take an age, but in reality it was not long before they stopped.

"Open the gates!" called the driver.

Drin heard running footsteps and the gentle squeak as the great gates of the walled town were pushed open by the guards. No one asked any questions. The horses moved forward again, this time on a bumpier road. They halted again, and someone joked with the driver about the smell. More gates opened, and Drin could hear the sound of the hooves thudding louder as they crossed a wooden bridge. At the far end they passed through the gates of the fort on the south bank of the river, again without search or question, and now they were out of the city, beyond its protection, with no defence if Nostoc's agents or a Souvian patrol found them. But no one did try to stop the cart, and it carried on trundling southwards, trailing its smell behind it.

Katila's plan had been clever, thought Drin. Even the Souvian spies, who had been posted to watch the exits from the city, would not have seen anything strange when the sewage cart left in the middle of the night. But beyond the first ring of watchers, there were the patrols roving through the countryside. Once he and Saori got down from the cart, he would have to use his cunning to avoid them. He thought back on the days when he had been a scout in the war between Akond and Hatoba. What a long time ago that seemed now. It was strange to say it about a war, but he had quite enjoyed it. The officers had given him orders because they liked to feel that they were in charge of things, but when he had set off on his own into the forest, no one could boss him around, and no one could say what he would encounter. Once, he had spotted an enemy raiding party moving stealthily through the trees and somehow managed to get back to base in time to give his own side a warning and save them from being taken by surprise. Another time, behind enemy lines, he had found a Hatoban messenger riding through the forest, knocked him off his horse and taken his secret messages for King Torquin to read instead of the enemy general. He had made quite a reputation for himself in those days. Since then he had vowed never to go soldiering again, and he never would; but now he needed the old tricks to keep Saori safe.

His thoughts were broken when the driver spoke again: "The sun will be up in another hour or so. Where do you want me to drop you?"

"Can you find somewhere where there aren't any people? The middle of a wood would be best."

"No woods round here," said the driver, but he turned the cart onto a bumpier track to the right, and they rolled on a bit further.

At length the cart stopped. "This is probably as good as anywhere round here. I wish you luck."

Drin climbed down stiffly, helped the girl get down too and took off their bags.

The cart drove away, and they were alone in the darkness. At least the smell had gone, and the air around them was fresh and cool. Drin took some deep breaths to clear his lungs, and though he could not see her face, he heard Saori doing the same and giggling.

Drin's basic plan was to travel during the night and find somewhere to hide and sleep during the day. Before dawn he was hoping to find a hilly, wooded spot where they could shelter among trees and rocks from prying eyes, until night came again and they could walk on, away from Banjut and the Souvians. But Drin did not know this part of the country, and they found themselves in a wide open plain and surrounded by cultivated fields. Although they could not see any villages in the dark, Drin was afraid that the area would be full of people when the sun came up. He and Saori desperately needed to find a hiding place before then. Once the local people had seen them, it would only be a matter of time before a Souvian patrol got hold of the information.

There was nothing to do but continue along the road. They shouldered their packs and began to walk. When they came to a crossroads, Drin turned left to go South again. A pale owl startled them by flying past and screeching as it went. Drin doubted if this was a good omen. He began to wonder if he should have taken Katila's advice and gone by boat. But he quickly dismissed the thought – better to have dry feet planted on the ground than bobbing around on the water.

It was beginning to grow light, and they could see white egrets flying out for a day of feeding in the ditches across the plain. But there was still no hill, no trees, and no hiding place.

Across to their right a lamp was lit. Drin could now see a cluster of houses, and he heard the first sounds of people beginning to wake up and stir about. Off to the left he could just make out a clump of trees. They made their way to it as fast as they could but found only a few pines surrounding a small wooden building, which was raised a couple of feet from the ground with steps at the front. No one was there. There were no bushes or other cover. The only place to hide was inside. They climbed the steps, Drin pushed open one of the double doors, and they went in – and at once Saori gave a little cry and pointed. They were in a small square room, and against the far wall on a low platform stood a shape which for a moment looked human. But as the light grew they could see that it was in fact a wooden statue. The body was a roughly carved tree trunk, and the head was long and pointed, with goggle eyes and strange horns growing out of the forehead. In front of it some dried-up fruit had been placed on a small table. It must be a local god, Drin thought, and hoping that it would shelter them safely, he bowed deeply, got some food out of his bag and put it on the table as his own offering with a muttered prayer. Saori understood what he was doing, bowed too and said something in her own language. They ate some food themselves, and then Drin indicated that Saori should get some sleep while he remained on watch.

But before she could stretch out to rest, they heard horses' hooves outside, and a loud voice:

"Come out of there with your hands on your heads!"

Drin cursed quietly. This was what he had most been fearing. The Souvians had found them. But how had they been so quick? Saori looked at him anxiously, and he knew he had let her down. He had said that he would protect her, but almost at once they had been caught. So much for his proud boasts about how good he would be at hiding from their enemies!

"Come on out! You are surrounded!"

Drin opened the door just enough to look outside. He counted fifteen mounted soldiers in an arc around the temple, and there were likely to be more whom he could not see. Too many to fight. He cursed silently again.

"If you don't come out, we'll burn down the building!"

"No," said Drin, "don't do that. We'll come out."

He could see no other option, even though it meant that he and Saori would be taken prisoner. At least the old god would not be burnt. He opened the door wide and stepped out into the bright sunlight, and Saori followed.

"It's them all right!" said one of the soldiers.

"Silence!" barked the officer. "You and you! Search the man for hidden weapons and tie his wrists together! You! Tie the girl's hands! But remember: no one is to harm the girl."

Soon Drin and Saori were standing with their hands tied in front of the shrine. Drin's knife was still in his boot – no one had ever succeeded in finding that – but it was no use to him now. The officer, a tall man with broad shoulders, got off his horse and walked slowly over. At first sight he had a handsome face, but when he spoke the good looks vanished: his mouth was too wide and he seemed to have too many teeth.

"Tell me your name!" he ordered.

"Tell me yours," said Drin.

The officer slapped him first on the left cheek and then on the right. Drin heard Saori cry out, and that hurt him more than the blows.

"Your name!" repeated the officer.

"Asterballudrin."

"As I thought. So you are the fugitive, and this is the slave girl who belongs to our master. Did you really think you could escape the Souvian army?"

"You know my name. Who are you?"

The officer slapped him again.

"Don't try to be clever with me! I ask the questions, and you answer. Got that?"

Drin stared back at him.

"But I will tell you who I am – General Arichi, Commander of the Cavalry of the Glorious Souvian Army – and you're going to regret you ever met me."

He barked orders, and two of the soldiers pulled Saori back, away from Drin, and held her by the arms. Another handed Arichi a long staff, and two more stood by with heavy clubs. Drin knew that they were going to beat him. They would not kill him. That pleasure was likely to be reserved for Nostoc, but they were going to beat him up and maybe break a bone or two. Drin did not like the thought that Saori would have to watch.

The officer walked slowly round him. He probably hoped that Drin would be scared, and so he was taking his time. He began to whirl the staff around, first slowly and then faster and faster until it became a blur.

"When I was young," he said, "I won the army championships with the quarterstaff, and I'm still pretty good. Answer my questions, or you'll feel the weight of this stick. First, tell me this: who ordered you to buy the girl?"

"No one. No one told me to do anything."

Arichi swung the staff and it struck Drin hard on the back. Saori cried out again.

"Wrong answer. Try again. Who told you to buy the girl?"

"The goddess of mercy."

The staff struck Drin again with a thud.

"I told you not to be clever. If you carry on like this, I'll have to hand you over to Nostoc. Do you know what he'll do to you?"

"He said he'd kill me."

"Yes, he'll kill you, but not quickly. He won't hang you or cut your head off or anything like that. That would be too quick and easy. He'll make sure you die slowly, in the most excruciating pain possible. He's an expert in causing pain. He's studied how to do it. He's conducted experiments. He knows every nerve in the body. When Nostoc gets hold of you, you'll wish you were dead. You'll beg for death. You'll scream to be allowed to die. You'll be desperate to be released from the pain. But he won't let you die, not until he's good and ready. Do you understand what I mean?"

"Yes." Drin understood all too well, but he was glad that Saori could not.

"Lazadim," said Arichi. "You tell me about Lazadim, and just possibly I might persuade our master to let me keep you instead of Nostoc. What do you think of that?"

Drin did not reply.

"All right. So tell me: when did you last meet Lazadim?"

"Last night in our inn in Banjut."

"That's better. Was he alone?"

"No. Katila was with him, and some guards."

"And what did he tell you?"

"He said the girl and I were in danger."

"Anything else?"

"He told us a lot of things about Zeno and how he became so powerful, but he couldn't answer one question: why all this fuss? Why does Zeno care so much about this girl?"

"Didn't Lazadim tell you that?"

"No, he said he didn't know."

"Didn't he tell you who she is?"

"No."

"You're lying. When Lazadim ordered you to buy the girl, he must have told you who she was. Or you're the biggest fool who ever lived."

"I'm telling the truth. I don't know who she is."

Drin could see Arichi tighten his grip on the staff.

"Don't lie to me, Drin, or you'll regret it. Let's go back to the beginning. It was Lazadim, wasn't it? He told you to buy the girl?"

"No, no one told me."

Arichi's face contorted in anger. "I warned you!" he said, and his staff swung round and caught Drin on the back of his legs, then on his shoulders. Drin lost his balance and fell forwards onto the ground. He lay there trying to protect his head with his arms as Arichi rained blows onto his unprotected back. Then, as Arichi raised the staff yet again and started to bring it down and Drin braced himself for the blow, he felt suddenly a warm body lying on top of him. It was Saori, who had broken free from the soldiers and thrown herself on top of Drin to protect him. Arichi tried to check the staff, but he was too far gone with his downswing, and though the blow had little power, it struck Saori's back and made her give a little cry.

Arichi drew back. Soldiers pulled Saori away, and Arichi ordered them to drag her into the little temple to prevent her from doing the same thing again.

"Get up!" he yelled at Drin, and Drin rose slowly and painfully to his feet. As he did so, he looked straight into

Arichi's eyes and said: "Remember: no one is to harm the girl."

Arichi shouted, "Silence!" and punched Drin's face with his gloved fist, and blood began to trickle down the left side.

Arichi stood in front of him, panting slightly, with the circle of soldiers around them in the sun. He spoke slowly, with emphasis on each word: "I give you one last chance. Who told you to buy the girl?"

Drin hesitated. If he said the same as before, he knew that he would be beaten by Arichi and then carted off to Nostoc for more punishment and death. If he had been on his own, Drin would have remained defiant and given the same answer as before. But now he had to think of Saori. She had bravely tried to protect him, but he was the one supposed to be protecting her. How could he do that if he was beaten up and killed?

"Come on. Speak up!"

But still he was silent. They wanted to use him somehow against Lazadim. Perhaps he should go along with it. What did he owe to Lazadim anyway? The only thing that Lazadim had done for him was to smuggle him and Saori out of Banjut, but that might have been as much for Lazadim's own benefit as for theirs. And was it just coincidence that this Souvian general had turned up so quickly to find them? Had they been betrayed by someone in Banjut?

Arichi's pole tapped his shoulder. "I shall count to three."

If Drin gave the answer that Arichi wanted, he and Saori would still be prisoners, but he would be unharmed. Perhaps it made sense to fight another day when the odds were better. What did it matter if he had to tell a few lies?

"One."

Drin looked up to the sky as if he expected to receive some kind of sign from the gods, but there was nothing, just a few fluffy clouds in the blue expanse.

"Two."

He sighed. It was no good. He could not do it. He could not change the way he was made.

"No one," he said. "No one told me to do anything."

Arichi drew back his lips in a cruel smile and raised his staff: "You've made your choice, and now you will pay for it."

Chapter 5
From Temple to Library

~

Before Arichi could swing the pole round, a rider burst into the circle of soldiers at full tilt and brought his horse to a halt in front of him.

"General, sir!" he cried out. "A body of cavalry is heading this way from the South. They're not our men, sir. Probably Southern Alliance."

"Southern Alliance?" said Arichi. "Those amateurs? We'll soon finish them off. Form up for attack!"

"What about the prisoners, sir?"

"Tie this one up properly and put him in the building with the girl. You two! Stay here and don't let them escape! I haven't done with him yet."

Drin found himself bundled back into the shrine with his ankles tied together as well as his wrists. He and Saori were left alone there in the darkness. She was trying to get something out of her bag but finding it difficult with her hands tied.

Drin was able to reach down to his boot and draw out the concealed knife. He whispered to Saori to take it, and she managed with some difficulty to cut through the ropes around his wrists. Then he cut her free and cut the ropes around his own ankles. Saori got a cloth out of her bag and wiped the blood from his face. He told her that he was all right, but still she fussed over him. He remembered how she had tried to protect him and, with gestures, asked if her back hurt from Arichi's blow. She shook her head, and pointed to his, but he would not admit to her, or even himself, that it ached. Inside the shrine, with their hands free, they were beginning to feel more cheerful, and Saori began to smile brightly. But Drin knew that, even though they had escaped the immediate danger, their ordeal was far from over. At any moment the Souvians might return, and then they would face the same threats and violence from Arichi. Two soldiers had been left behind to guard them. He needed to find some way of overcoming them so that he and Saori could make their escape. He found a small hole in the wooden wall where the light came in from outside and tried to see where the soldiers were.

As he did so, riders began to thunder past at a gallop. The dust rose and made it difficult to see, but Drin had no doubt that the first men he saw were wearing the standard brown jerkins and helmets of the Souvian army. He tried to pick out Arichi but could not be sure if he was among the riders. Then there were more horsemen shouting in triumph, and these men wore different colours and had different helmets and shields. These must be the 'amateurs' of the Southern

Alliance, Drin supposed. They outnumbered the Souvians, and that might have accounted for their speedy victory.

A small group of the pursuers slowed their horses as they passed, and one of them shouted: "Look out – there's a Souvian behind that tree." An arrow struck one of the Southerners' shields, and they headed off behind the shrine where Drin could not see them. To his side one of the doors of the shrine creaked. Another Souvian soldier was pushing it open with the idea of hiding inside, but he found that as he did so, a small knife was pressed against his throat. "Don't move!" said Drin quietly. They stood like that for a moment, with the soldier at the open door and Drin hiding behind the other, closed one, until the soldier crumpled to the floor without a sound but with an arrow in his back.

"There might be more of them hiding in there," said one of the Southerners. Drin's heart sank: the Southerners were supposed to be friends, but he had no desire to become their prisoner and to have to answer their questions about Saori.

"Never mind. We don't want to be left behind." And to Drin's relief the whole party rode off in a fresh cloud of dust.

He looked gingerly out from behind the door but could see no one moving. It was hard to believe, but this time they seemed to be truly free. Saori and he hastened to thank the old god for any help he might have given, and then they rounded up the horses of their two dead guards and rode off to the West.

Drin gave up his idea of stopping by day and travelling by night. The best policy was to get away from that spot as fast as they could before any of the soldiers of either side came back. Drin kept looking ahead of them in case there were more soldiers searching the fields, but their luck held, and they saw only the local people gathering in the harvest. Some looked up to see who was riding by, but many just continued their work without a sideways glance. At first Drin led Saori's horse with a long rein, but she soon got the hang of riding and was able to look after herself.

At length the country became more hilly, and instead of the rice and other arable crops which grew on the open plain, they saw flocks of animals grazing in small, grassy fields. Drin climbed the highest hill he could find in order to look at the route ahead, and he and Saori saw the great mountains rising up on the distant horizon – their destination and their hope of safety.

They pressed on with their horses for several days. Once or twice they saw soldiers in the distance and made large detours to avoid them, but Drin was fairly sure that they were Southerners and not Souvians. They had food in their own bags, and they had rummaged through the saddle-bags of the Souvians for more.

When they reached the foothills of the mountains, their route became rougher and steeper, the open fields gave way to dense woodland, and they set the horses free. This country made Drin feel more comfortable. He was used to it, and confident that he could see or hear most other people before they would have any idea he was there. But it was much harder for Saori to climb here on foot than to ride the horse. They went where there were no paths, and much of the way was uphill. Drin was used to the uneven ground and to walking at an angle along the sides of hills, but Saori found it hard going, and she slipped and slithered among the tree roots. They saw a few people far off through the trees, but Drin was confident that no one saw them. Some evenings they heard wolves howling, and Saori became alarmed by the unfamiliar noise, but Drin stayed calm, and that reassured her. He knew that there were also bears and leopards in the hills, but none of these came near. Navigation was difficult: surrounded by trees, they could not get a clear view of the hills around them or of the sky, and even Drin sometimes became confused and headed off in the wrong direction so that they covered more ground than they needed to. But for most of the time the weather was good, and he could navigate by the angle of the sun through the leaves. When they had used up the food they had brought with them, Drin shot a small deer and brought it back to their camp to be skinned and cooked, but to his surprise Saori rejected it. It took him a while to discover why, but eventually he understood that she was upset that he had killed such a gentle creature and refused any idea of eating it. This could have caused a practical problem because they could not live only on the berries and roots they found in the forest, but Saori turned out to be expert at catching fish in the streams and had no objection to eating them.

At length they reached the area where the track led across the mountain to Akond, and from a hidden vantage point they looked down on Gate B. I should explain that both ends of the track were blocked by gates, which could only be opened by an official gatekeeper. The gate on the Banjut side was called Gate B, and the one on the Akond side, Gate A, and next to each of them was a simple lodge for the traders to stay in, surrounded by pastures. This was where the traders shifted their goods from the horses to their donkeys and where the donkeys stayed while the men went to Banjut and back. Marcon had promised to try to leave a donkey in the top pasture for Drin and Saori, but that was empty. Instead, as they looked down on the Gate, they could see a whole herd of donkeys grazing near the lodge, and in front of it was a group of Souvian soldiers, tiny and far off, but menacing just the same.

Drin wondered why the donkeys were still there. By now the traders should be well on the way across the mountain to Akond. Had they been taken prisoner? Or worse – might they even have been executed? Drin was filled with anxiety: he hated the thought that something bad had happened to his friends, and all on his account. Saori understood nothing of this, but the sight of the soldiers aroused her old fears. When Drin saw her worried expression, he realised that, if something had happened to the traders, there was little he could do about it on his own: what he could do was to finish the job of taking her to safety in Akond. They stayed hidden in the woods until dusk, and then Drin led Saori on a long route up steep slopes and through the trees around the Gate so that finally they reached the track well above it without being seen by the Souvian guards. Then they started their ascent.

Along the route up the mountain the Akondians had built refuges so that they could take shelter when there was heavy rain or snow. These were placed off the track so that a stranger passing along it would not notice that they were there, but they were stoutly built and had space for the donkeys as well as the men. There were four refuges on each side of the mountain, and each contained warm clothes, food and plenty of firewood. When they reached the first, Drin was at last able to relax because they found signs that men had stayed there recently: the floor had been swept, a fire had been lit and fresh bedding brought in. So the traders were all right after all. For some reason they had had to leave their donkeys behind, but the men themselves had climbed the track.

The climb was arduous for Saori. It was easier walking along the track than through the pathless woods, but the slope was steeper and beyond the first refuge it climbed steadily. But now that Drin knew that the traders had got away from the Souvians, he felt full of energy, and his enthusiasm helped to push her up the mountain. Even though autumn was now well advanced, they were still fortunate with the weather, and especially so when they reached the pass itself, where no trees grow and the route lies over the bare rock. It had already snowed up here, but the snow was not deep, and they crossed the pass without mishap and made their descent to Akond and safety. When they finally reached Gate A, they found that the Gatekeeper had been told by Marcon to look out for them, and he lent them horses for the journey to Kandalore, which is the old capital of our country and where the mountain traders have their base. On the day after they arrived in the city, Marcon brought them to see me.

I had spent so many hours reading about epic adventures that I could hardly contain my excitement when I heard Drin's story from the man himself, and when he finished, I immediately responded: "That is absolutely brilliant. I will write down exactly what you have told me, and it will be recorded for future generations exactly as I heard it from you, with Marcon as our witness."

I looked eagerly at Marcon and Drin, but was disappointed to find that they did not seem to share my enthusiasm.

Marcon cleared his throat: "Thank you, sir. I'm sure that

will be very valuable, but to be honest, we were hoping that you could help us with something a bit more urgent."

"Oh! What do you mean?"

"I was wondering if you could help us find somewhere for Saori to stay while she's in Akond. I think she'll need a bit of peace and quiet while she gets used to life here. My own house is right in the middle of the town, and the neighbours would never leave her alone; and Drin's place… well, even I wouldn't want to stay there. So I was wondering if you might be able to help, sir – perhaps even let her stay in the palace for a while?"

"Oh!" I said again. So that was why they had come to see me. It took me a while to get my thoughts in order. The palace had been built to be the king's main residence, and ever since my grandfather moved the capital to Nangalay, most of it had been empty.

"Well, why not? There's plenty of space. But I'll need to get my mother's permission."

"Thank you, sir. That's very kind of you."

Just at this point the servants returned with Saori. She looked much better now, in clean clothes, with her hair neatly tied and hanging down her back, and with her radiant smile. But once we had all welcomed her back, I realised that Marcon and Drin were looking expectantly at me.

"Right," I said. "I'll go and ask my mother. You'd better have something to eat while I'm gone."

Chapter 6
A Room for Saori

~

I found my mother, as I expected, in the garden. She was as mad about flowers as I was about books, and the garden had become a great comfort to her. When my father, King Torquin, had died, it had been quite a shock. He had been fit and active with no signs of illness, but he had suddenly collapsed while out riding one day. My brother Hargon succeeded to the throne, and the life of the kingdom carried on peacefully enough, but my mother found it difficult to live in the great palace in the capital. It held too many memories of her life with our father. After some months, she decided to move to Kandalore, and I begged her to take me with her. Hargon was five years older than me, and ever since I could remember, we had been quarrelling. Even now that he was the king, we found it impossible to stop. I knew that his friends made fun of me behind my back, and I hated having to appear in front of everyone at court occasions. It was much better to concentrate on my studies in the peace and quiet of Kandalore.

"Hello, Chaemon," she said. "It's good to see you in the garden and out of that fusty library of yours. What do you think is wrong with this loquat tree? It wasn't happy over there by the wall, so I moved it into the sun, but it doesn't seem to like it here either."

"Maybe it needs more water," I said. "Actually I came to ask you something."

"Water? This is the first dry day we've had for a week. It can't be that."

"Two of the mountain traders have told me an amazing story, and they've brought with them a girl they freed from the slave market and she looks quite unlike anyone I've ever seen."

"Chaemon, I sometimes think you live in another world. You read too many stories. That's the trouble."

"But it's true," I said. "The traders were there and saw it and did it themselves, and the girl is real and she's in the palace right now. Let me tell you what happened." And I repeated Drin's story to my mother. I kept it short, but even so I was not sure how much she was listening. She carried on walking round the garden as I talked, cutting off dead flower heads and tying up loose shoots.

"Well," she said when I had finished, "that was all very interesting. Shall we go inside and have a cup of tea now? I think I'm ready to sit down for a bit."

"Yes, and I can bring along the traders and the girl to meet you."

"But do I have to meet them just now? Couldn't they come along later?"

"No, not really. The whole point is that she has nowhere to stay. She needs somewhere peaceful to settle into life here in Akond, and we're all hoping you'll agree that she can stay in the palace, at least for a while. We've got plenty of room."

"Stay in the palace? We have to be careful about that, Chaemon. Your father never invited anyone to stay unless he was sure that they were trustworthy. You do not even know where this mysterious girl comes from."

"Well, I think she might be a princess from the East."

"Might be?" said my mother. "I can tell you from long experience that many girls might be princesses, but very few actually are. Your brother used to bring the most unsuitable girls to the palace at one time, but I did not expect to have the same problem with you."

"No, no," I said. "This is completely different. Please, Mother, couldn't you at least meet them? Marcon knew my father, and Drin was a scout in the army, and you may think differently about Saori if you meet her."

"Oh, all right. I will meet Marcon first. There's something I want to ask him."

A few minutes later Marcon and I were waiting in my mother's reception room, and when she came in, she said: "Do you recognise this swallow brooch?"

"Yes, ma'am," said Marcon. "I bought that in Banjut about five years ago for His Majesty the late King. But, begging your pardon, ma'am, the bird it represents is not a swallow. It's called a 'tern' in Banjuti. It has a forked tail like a swallow, but it lives over water and dives in to catch small fish. You can see that the beak is longer than a swallow's."

"That explains it," said my mother. "I have always loved

this brooch and always been puzzled that it wasn't quite right for a swallow. A 'tern'. It's so beautifully made. Thank you for buying it."

"It was an honour to serve the king."

"My son has been telling me a long tale about the adventures of your man, Drin, with slave girls and wicked kings. It sounds as if it all came out of one of his books."

"Yes, ma'am, but I can assure you that it's true. Drin's made many mistakes in his life and he goes his own way, but he's never learnt how to lie."

"Then tell me your part of it. How did you and your men come back to Akond? My son missed that bit out." So she had been paying attention after all, I thought.

"Well, there's not much to tell really. When Drin and Saori had left Banjut, we finished our business in the town and set off in the normal way and reached our regular camping site for our first night on the road. The next morning at dawn the Souvians turned up, about fifty of them, and when their commander demanded that we tell him where Drin and Saori were, I told him we had no idea. They searched everywhere, but of course they found nothing. Then they began to knock us around a bit, but we did what we'd agreed beforehand, and none of us fought back, even though it was hard not to, and in the end, their officer called his men off, and they rode away."

"Well done," said my mother quietly.

"We picked ourselves up and went on our way again, but we knew they were watching us all the time. If Drin and Saori had come anywhere near us, they'd have been caught for sure. When we eventually arrived at Gate B, we found a different gang of Souvians occupying our quarters in the lodge, and they wouldn't let us go through the Gate. We had to unload the horses and put all our goods in a store, and they kept us there, camping outside. On the fifth day some Souvian waggons arrived, and our goods were loaded onto them and driven away. It was pure robbery! That was when I realised they'd never let us cross the mountain; the only reason we hadn't already been killed was because they were using us as bait to help them catch Drin and Saori."

"How awful!"

"So we decided to escape. The Souvians always set guards during the night to raise the alarm if we tried to get away. So we had to do as we learnt in the war: we crept silently up on the guards and dealt with them, and then we raced as fast as we could up the track. I don't know if they followed us, but we never saw them. Even so, to be honest, we were glad when we arrived back here in Akond – and even happier when Drin and Saori came too."

"You did well," said my mother. "My husband would have been proud of you – true Akondians! I should like to meet Drin and Saori now. Would you mind asking them to join us?"

Drin came in first and bowed, and my mother said that she had heard all about him and said many nice things, and he looked embarrassed and took a seat next to Marcon.

Then it was Saori's turn, but instead of bowing in the doorway as is the Akondian custom, she went straight up to my mother, knelt in front of her and raised my mother's hand to her own forehead. My mother lifted Saori's head and looked into her eyes, and something passed between them because at once my mother said:

"Chaemon, bring your chair over here so that Saori can sit next to me. No, closer than that. Look at her beautiful hair. She is someone special. You have only to look at her for a moment to know that."

"Well, I did say she might be a princess."

"We must make sure that she is properly looked after. She has had such a dreadful time. Has she had a hot bath?"

"Yes, Mother."

"And been anointed with fragrant oils and lotions?"

"Yes."

"And I can see that her hair has been washed and she has been given fresh clothes, but surely she could have been given something a bit better than this old green thing. Faziah," she said to her maid, "bring me that loose coat with the pattern of red cherries, the one I got last year for the crane festival. Chaemon, have you had her room prepared yet?"

"Well, no... which room do you think she should have?"

"The one next to mine is nice. Let's put her in there."

"But that's the king's room," I said. "If he comes to Kandalore, that's where he'll expect to stay."

"Yes, I suppose you're right, although he doesn't seem to come very often, does he? Why don't we put her in the next room, beyond Hargon's?"

"But that's my room."

"Yes, but it won't take you long to move your things out. There's a nice room you can have in the East wing. Saori is a special guest, and we must make her feel welcome."

I remember wondering afterwards how I had managed to let Hargon keep his room and at the same time lose my own. Compared with the three large bedrooms on the upper floor of the main palace building, my new room was small and dark, but I could not complain.

"Come on, my dear, I will show you my garden. Perhaps

you will know what to do with loquat trees." And with that my mother led Saori out of the room.

After they had left, Marcon and Drin said what a wonderful lady they thought my mother was – which is the reaction of most people who meet her.

"We need to teach Saori to speak Akondian," I said.

"Akondian?" said Drin. "Are you sure?"

"Yes. We all speak Akondian, don't we?"

Drin looked thoroughly uncomfortable.

"What's the matter, Drin?" asked Marcon. "Come on. Out with it."

"I've taught her how to say some things already," said Drin. "Except that it wasn't Akondian. I taught her to speak in Banjuti because we were on that side of the mountains. It might confuse her if we start teaching her a different language now."

"You may be right," said Marcon. "I've been thinking: she might not want to stay here. She might prefer to go home, and in that case she'd have to cross the mountain again, and then she'd need Banjuti more than Akondian, to be honest."

"But she may prefer to stay here," I said, "and even if she doesn't, she'll have to stay in Akond for the next few months, because the pass is closed."

"Akondian or Banjuti?" said Marcon. "None of us knows what she wants to do, and until we have a common language with her, we can't find out."

There was no easy answer to this puzzle, and we sat in silence for a while.

At length, I said: "I wish I could speak Banjuti. I've been thinking about it for quite some time. I can read it a bit, but I've never learnt it properly. So I've been wondering, Marcon, it's a big thing to ask, but would you be my teacher? Everyone says you're completely fluent."

Marcon was not very keen on this and said that he had a lot of other things to do; but his opposition made me persist all the more, and in the end he reluctantly agreed.

"Then that settles it," said Drin.

"Settles what?" I asked.

"If you're having lessons in Banjuti, Saori can join you."

Chapter 7

Language Lessons

~

At first Saori found it hard to settle down in the palace. She had learnt to trust Drin and firmly believed that the goddess who protected her island home had sent him to protect her in the strange and violent new world in which she now found herself. He had brought her to a place of safety where the people were kind to her and lived in peace with each other, and she found it natural that my mother should be in charge of the palace since it was the women who ruled in the islands. But our everyday customs were often difficult for her to understand.

Ever since she could remember, she had slept on the soft sandy ground in the same room as the unmarried girls of her clan. But on her first day with us, when evening came, Faziah took her into a big, upstairs room and after showing her all the furniture and the view out onto the garden, left her on her own to sleep. Saori immediately felt lonely and afraid, and she went out and looked around until she found my mother's room and tried to move in with her. But my mother guided her gently back into her own room and showed her the bed. Saori now understood that she had to stay there, and seeking the safest place to sleep, curled up on the hard wooden floor in the corner furthest from the door; but this could not help her from remembering the demons who had brought her to Banjut and thinking of other terrors in the dark of the night. Faziah found her like this in the morning, tired and anxious, and tried to show her how to sleep in the bed. But this gave Saori another idea: if only Faziah would sleep in the bed, they would be in the same room, and she would feel safe. But however hard she tried to explain this in sign language, Faziah kept shaking her head, and in the end Saori had to accept that her message was not getting through. What Faziah did understand was that for some reason Saori had chosen to sleep in the corner, and so she had the bed moved over there, away from the middle of the room. Thus it was that Saori slept every night in the bed in the corner of the room, but only after she had prayed to her goddess and checked carefully under the bed with a light to make sure that no demons were hiding there.

Because of this and a whole series of other misunderstandings, about food and table manners, washing, and even going to the toilet, Saori was soon keen to learn our language and delighted when she and I became Marcon's pupils and began to study Banjuti every morning. To start with, she found it quite easy to learn the names of everyday objects and even to form simple sentences, and she was thrilled that at last she could communicate with Drin, Marcon and me in words instead of signs. But fresh problems arose when she tried to use this new knowledge to talk to my mother, Faziah and other people around the palace since they did not understand Banjuti. Saori thought they must be pretending not to understand on purpose, but she could not imagine why. We tried to explain to her the dilemma of the two languages, but that was still too complicated for her to grasp. In the end my mother found a solution by teaching her simple phrases in Akondian every evening.

In the afternoons Saori accompanied us on visits outside the palace. She went first with my mother and me to the Temple of the Cranes, which is Kandalore's biggest shrine, and was happy to worship the gods with us and be blessed by the chief priest. But while she was there, word spread in the town of her appearance, and the big crowd which gathered around the temple made Saori nervous. We took her up to the upper floor of the temple tower so that as many people as possible could see her, and encouraged her to wave and smile at them, and my mother spoke to the people to reassure them. Saori could feel the crowd become more friendly and was sure that it was because they trusted the queen and believed what she had said.

After that, her outings aroused much less excitement, and she was able to learn about our country and our way of life. The only city Saori had ever seen before was Banjut, and that was not a happy memory, but over time, as she was taken to buy things in the market, to see the castle and other principal buildings and to walk along the streets, she became used to the bustle and noise of Kandalore, and her smile and natural good nature made her many friends among the people.

We took her out into the countryside too. On her islands people grew vegetables and corn in little fields, but she had never seen anything like the terraced fields on our hillsides, and was impressed by the hard work which had gone into making and maintaining them. Our most precious crop, tea, was also new to her, and at first she found it bitter and shocked everyone by spitting it out, but after we took her to see the women plucking the tips of the leaves from the bushes, she tried again to appreciate the taste. Nothing, however, could persuade her to eat meat or to accept that we kept animals for food, and her disapproving stare made us feel awkward whenever we had beef or pork for dinner.

Saori desperately missed the sea. All her life she had been surrounded by it. She had learnt to swim almost before she could walk, and to handle a boat not long after that. There were five main islands, and the calm shallow water around each of them teemed with fish and other life. The best we could offer in Akond was Lake Kandalore, which seemed to us a wide expanse of water, but was more like a pond to Saori. She was shocked by how cold the water was and decided not to swim in it, but she soon made friends with the local fishermen and learnt how to sail their boats and to catch fish with their nets and lines. There was one thing she could do which amazed everyone, and that was spearing fish under water. On her island everyone learnt to do it when they were small and thought it nothing special, but things look at a different angle when they are in water, and no one in Akond had believed it possible to be accurate every time like Saori. People would line up on the bank to watch as if it was some kind of public show, and the fishermen claimed her as one of their own and became proud of what she could do.

It was autumn when Saori arrived in Kandalore and already getting cold and wet. She did not like that at all. In her home it was warm all year round, and apart from the season of storms most days were sunny with a blue sky above the pure blue sea. The Akondian winter was hard on her. She learnt how to wrap up well in our thick woollen clothes, and with my mother's encouragement she built up quite a wardrobe of different colours and styles. The palace was kept warm by fires, and water was heated every evening for her to bathe in, but even so she caught colds a couple of times, and once she went down with a fever. This frightened her: how could she be burning hot when everywhere was so cold? My mother fussed over her as if she were a small child, and summoned doctors and priests from all over Akond, but I am not sure that their potions and prayers made much difference. In the end Saori recovered, and all was well.

Meanwhile, she was making good progress in learning Banjuti. It helped that the language itself is fairly simple and does not have complicated grammar. This is because it is used on the other side of the mountains as a common language. Most of the countries have their own languages like Souvian and Valosian, but over many years they have found it convenient for everyone to use a simplified form of Banjuti to speak to each other. Although there is an older, classical form of the language, that is only used by the Banjutis among themselves.

If, like me, Saori had had only to learn new words, she would have learnt Banjuti very quickly, but she was slowed down because she often found it hard to understand the ideas behind them. When Marcon introduced the word for 'king', for example, she found it difficult to understand that in our countries the rulers were men, not women, and when we went on to explain that in most cases the crown was passed on to the eldest son, she was even more confused. It took a long time before she could accept that it was my brother and not my mother who ruled Akond – and I probably did not help much when I said that Hargon was a complete idiot. We even had trouble trying to work out how old she was, because in her home everyone was one year old when they were born and became a year older on the longest day of the year. Saori said she was nineteen, but she was at least one year younger and possibly two by our way of counting.

But this was nothing compared with the difficulty which Marcon caused when he introduced the word 'slave'. Saori could see that her clothes, for example, belonged to her, and, though she did not much like it, she understood that an animal could have an owner and be bought and sold, but she was repulsed by the idea of buying and selling people. And then, as we tried clumsily to explain the concept, the truth suddenly hit her. She herself had been a slave. She herself had been sold in that tent in Banjut. Events which had been horrible but mysterious at the time, now became clear – the stage, the little auctioneer with the loud voice, the two men bidding, the payment of all those coins. Suddenly it all made sense, and it led her to a most appalling conclusion: she had been bought by Drin as a slave. Her mind raced ahead: was she still a slave? Was she being kept here in the palace as a slave? My mother, me, Marcon, even Drin: did we all see her as our possession? Like a horse, or a dog, or one of the poor animals which we ate in front of her? She screamed. She had to get away from us, to break free: and so she ran into her room, slammed the door and moved all the furniture to block it and stop any of us from entering.

One by one we tried to speak to her through the door, but

this only made her even more determined not to speak to us. She would not even listen to my mother, who was beside herself with worry and blamed us for making Saori so upset. Inside her room, the same thoughts went round and round in Saori's head. She longed to be home, away from this strange, cold place where everyone betrayed her and even people could be bought and sold. In this state of mind she passed the night, and when dawn broke, she lay still in her bed, exhausted and miserable. Far off she could hear the voice of Faziah speaking Banjuti – was this a dream? Faziah was repeating what we had taught her to say, that there were no slaves in Akond, over and over again. In spite of herself, Saori listened, and through the door she began to ask questions, which we were happy to answer, until at last she agreed to open it. Later, when she understood what Drin had actually done, she was filled with remorse and apologised to him, and they were once again firm friends, but none of us forgot how hurt she had been.

As the lessons went on, Saori learnt enough to begin to answer our questions about where she came from, and one day, with help from Marcon for some of the more difficult expressions and sometimes with tears welling in her eyes, she told us how she had arrived in Banjut.

Her people believed that there were gods all around them. Every hill and river had a divine spirit, and the islands were full of little shrines, but the holiest place was an island out in the sea to the West. This was sacred to the Goddess of the Peaceful Sea, and no one was allowed to set foot on it except five girls, one from each island, who were chosen each year as priestesses. Saori said that it was from this island that she had been seized and carried away.

Every year the islanders endured a season of great storms when the rain came down like bowls of water being upturned and the wind smashed solid objects to pieces. They built their houses partly underground and made the roofs heavy with stones, and when the storm season was approaching, they pulled their boats high onto the shore and piled sand up around them, and they did everything else they could to save their belongings from the violent winds and lashing rain. But every year some things were broken or carried away in the storms. Because they could not go out fishing, they lived mainly off food which they had stored in advance, and on some days they did not even dare to go out of their houses for fear of being blown away. It was a terrible and frightening time.

They believed that the reason that this happened was that the goddess, who normally protected them, left her island and visited her father in the moon, and while she was away the storm-god escaped from his cave under the sea and turned everything upside down. But when she returned, she captured him and shut him away again: and then the sea became calm, the rain stopped, the winds fell away, and life returned to normal. That was when the moon shone particularly brightly, and on the night of the full moon, a ceremony took place on the holy island to thank the goddess for restoring peace and to seek her blessing for the coming year. The five priestesses took offerings to her shrine, and on the beach they danced a special dance and sang a special song to celebrate her victory over the storm-god.

Saori had been immensely proud when she had been selected as the priestess for her island. Her mother had made a great fuss over the preparations, and both had worked hard to ensure that on the day every detail was perfect. They had made special clothes of mats sewn together which covered her from head to toe and made it hard to move quickly, and in the middle of her chest they had attached the big round disc of the full moon to show that she was a holy messenger. Her body had been massaged with precious oils, her long hair was held together by bright, crescent-shaped pins, and on her head was placed a wreath of flowers. All the people of her island came to see her off as she rode in the ceremonial outrigger boat, and many of them followed in their own boats across the calm sea, men and women paddling together.

She remembered the meeting point in mid-ocean when they were joined by the boats from the other islands, and there was singing and laughing among the crews. Then the boats carrying the priestesses led the way to the sacred island. It had two conical hills, in the North and the South, covered by rich green forest and joined together by a narrow neck of land where the shrine stood. By the time they arrived the sun had set, and it was in the light of the full moon that the five girls landed on the small sandy beach on the eastern side of the island in front of the shrine, and the boats pulled back into the bay. The girls turned to look out to sea, and as the discs on their chests reflected the moonlight, the watchers in the boats began to sing an old song praising the goddess and praying for her protection. The girls' hearts were filled with reverence. They could feel the presence of those past generations, who had performed the same ritual in the same place year after year. Slowly they climbed the steps of the little wooden shrine and stood on the threshold. It was a moment of perfect happiness and perfect peace, just as it had always been for so many generations before.

But then, suddenly, without warning, four devils jumped out from inside. The girls screamed and ran back towards the sea. The boat crews began to paddle with a shout towards the beach. Saori, who had been the first to climb the steps, tripped as she ran down the steps. She landed heavily on the sand. Strong arms lifted her up. She wriggled and fought against them but was not strong enough. She screamed, but a dirty cloth was tied across her mouth. The devils carried her behind the shrine to the western shore of the island and into the shallows and threw her into the bottom of a boat. She tried to climb out of it, but someone was sitting on her and tying her feet together, then her hands. Two of them were straining at long paddles, and the boat was beginning to move. A sail was up, and a slight offshore breeze began to fill it. She crawled up to look over the side of the boat, and saw that they were already drawing away from the island. Who were these devils? What were they doing in the goddess's shrine? Had Saori done something to anger the goddess? Her head was spinning with fear and shock.

Once they were out to sea, one of the devils came over. Half his teeth were missing, and his breath smelt. He held her chin and said something in a language she did not understand, and laughed. But one of the others pulled him back and they started shouting at each other. Saori thought that they were going to fight, but the first demon eventually snarled and gave way. They untied the cloth covering her mouth and gave her some water, and left her alone. Sometimes at home in the dark evenings around the fire her grandmother had told stories of an evil world peopled with devils and witches, and the children had shivered with make-believe terror, but now Saori felt she was in that world, and the terror was for real.

The breeze stayed steady from the East, and they sailed on for hours, perhaps for days. Saori remembered little of the voyage because she fell ill with a fever and had pains in her joints and was unconscious for long periods. She thought that she was going to die and reached a stage of fear and misery when she did not much care whether she died or not. But in the end she came through the sickness and was beginning to regain her strength when the devils sighted land and shouted out in jubilation. They angled the sail, and the boat changed course so that the wind came from the port side, and they were heading south along the coast. The boat was deeper than those she was used to, and unlike the outriggers which had two hulls linked together by cross-poles, this boat had only one hull with benches across it inside.

Saori remembered seeing the high cliff on which the citadel of Banjut stood with its stone buildings and the gold statues which flashed in the sunlight, and she marvelled because she had never seen such a place before. She began to hope that her fate might improve when they steered into the harbour and she saw the bustle of the boats and the faces of ordinary people going about their business. But there followed a miserable few days locked up in a tiny, dirty room with only scraps to eat, and then the ordeal of the slave market.

"At first," she said, "I thought Drin was another demon – so big and wild, with long hair and beard, and looking so angry – and when he brought out the knife, I was very afraid. But he was sent to save me."

She looked more serious. "I must go home. I like this place, because you all help me, and your mother is so kind, but I must go home as fast as I can. I think my parents worry about me, and my sister and brother too, and I must show I am alive and well. Also, I must tell our people what happened to me. They must be very afraid when this terrible thing happened in the holy ceremony, and they do not know why. Perhaps they say the goddess is angry with me, or my family. Who knows what they will think? So I must go home."

"To be honest, that's what I thought you'd say," said Marcon. "As soon as the winter is over and we can cross the pass, we'll make a start on your journey."

Chapter 8
The Prisoner

~

About a week later Marcon had to go away on business to the capital, but Saori and I were continuing our Banjuti practice with Drin one morning when a servant brought news of a great commotion in the main square of the city. The Governor, who administered the province of Kandalore on behalf of the king, had ridden in with a prisoner, whom he intended to lock up in the castle. But on the way he had decided to show him off to the people of the city and to announce that he had come from across the mountains. No one except the traders had ever seen anyone from the other side of the mountains before, and soon almost the whole population of Kandalore was crowding into the square, and the Governor and his men were stuck in the middle, unable to go forwards or back.

Although my brother thought the Governor was

wonderful, I thought that he was rather creepy and found it quite funny that he had got himself stuck in the crowd. But Saori and Drin were interested in the prisoner, not the Governor. Who was he? How had he got here? Above all, why had he come? So Drin suggested that the three of us visit the castle and see what we could find out.

When we arrived, we were shown into the Governor's private apartments, and he latched onto me in his usual fawning manner.

"What an honour, Your Highness, for you to come and see us in our humble home and to bring your noble guests! Of course since I brought in the prisoner today, almost all the better class of people in Kandalore have been keen to visit the castle and see him for themselves, but to have Your Highness come is an unexpected and delightful pleasure."

"Would you like to partake of some refreshment, sir?" added his wife. "Although I am afraid that what we can offer will be far below what you are used to in the palace."

"Thank you, but we're fine," I said. Everyone seemed to expect me to say something else, so I introduced Saori and Drin, and added: "Where's the prisoner?"

"Safe in the dungeon, Your Highness. Let me tell you and your friends the whole story. As you know, I have always been a loyal and humble servant of your illustrious family, and I have already sent a report about this momentous event to His Majesty, your brother. Never before in the history of our country has a governor of Kandalore had to face such a crisis: a foreigner from over the mountains has illegally and without warning invaded our country. But I have arrested him, and the nation is safe."

"Well, that's great."

"Thank you, sir. Yesterday, just after breakfast, I was sitting here in the castle studying important documents when a messenger arrived with an urgent request from Gatekeeper A for me to go to the Gate with a party of cavalry. I immediately stopped what I had been doing and rode up there with some of my men. It is a steep and difficult path, but we thought nothing of that in our haste to serve our country. As soon as we arrived, the Gatekeeper showed us the prisoner and told us that he had been found a few days before, high up on the mountain."

"Did he tell you exactly how he was found?" asked Drin.

"Yes indeed, sir, and I shall tell you exactly what he said. One of his duties is to check that the refuges on the Akond side... I presume that you know about the refuges, Your Highness?"

"Yes, of course," I replied.

"Well, the Gatekeeper had to check that the refuges were in good condition after the winter storms and, if not, to organise the necessary repairs. So he and his assistant climbed the track and checked the three lower refuges; and since the weather appeared stable, they decided to push on towards the highest one to have a look at that too. They found, however, that there had been a great snowstorm on the higher slopes, and they were about to turn round and go back down when their two dogs suddenly rushed off barking into the trees. The Gatekeeper says he called them, but they didn't come back; and so the two men ended up following their tracks across the snow. Fortunately the dogs had not gone far, and when the Gatekeeper and his assistant caught up with them, they discovered that the reason for the dogs' strange behaviour was that they had found the body of a man."

The Governor paused. "Well, sir, I am sure that you understand the significance of this moment – because that man is now my prisoner in this very castle!"

I did not know what to say to this, so I nodded, and he carried on.

"At first they thought he must be dead, but then they detected faint signs of life and gave first aid before carrying him down through the snow and back to the track. Here they lit a fire to warm him up and gave him a hot drink, and then they managed with some difficulty to move him down to the third refuge where they nursed him. To start with, he slept most of the time; sometimes he had wild dreams and they heard him call out. But he is strong and after a day or so he regained his senses, and they were able to bring him down to the Gate. Of course, their first thought then was to call for me. After all, who else would they call for at such a moment?

"When I arrived, I immediately took charge of the situation. I established that the man was well enough to travel on to Kandalore. I also established that he did not speak our language, but I employed the Gatekeeper as my interpreter. By this means I apprehended that the prisoner was called Minondas and that he had crossed the mountains. I therefore arrested him, charged him with an illegal invasion of our territory and brought him here for imprisonment until we can organise a trial – a trial, need I say, which will attract the attention of the whole nation.

"That, sir, is the true story of how I have handled the crisis up to this point in time. I have never been one to hog the limelight, as your illustrious father was aware, but I cannot help feeling that the eyes of history are upon me at this moment!"

He beamed at each of us in turn, as if expecting applause. Definitely creepy, I decided.

"What was he wearing when they found him?" asked Drin.

The Governor was taken aback by the directness of the question, but agreed to let us examine the prisoner's clothes and sent a servant to fetch them. In the interval, I explained to Saori in Banjuti what the Governor had told us in Akondian. "Do you think he came here because of me?" she asked; but none of us was ready to answer.

As soon as he saw the clothes, Drin said that, without doubt, the man was a Souvian soldier. The brown leather helmet, jerkin and tunic were all standard issue. But we noticed one other thing, which neither Drin nor Saori could remember on the Souvian soldiers with Arichi: just below the neck on the front of the jerkin was an image of a double axe picked out in gold.

"I wonder if he's a member of a special unit, like Zeno's Guards," Drin said. "That might be their insignia."

"Do you think he was alone?" I asked.

"The basic unit of the Souvian army is five men, which they call a 'Hand'," Drin said. "So Zeno is unlikely to have sent fewer than five."

"Which means that there are at least four more," I said.

"Yes. If they survived the storm, they could've come down to the Gate by now, or even the city."

"What?!" the Governor broke in. He appeared extremely agitated. "Are you saying that there are four more of them here in Kandalore? Four more enemy soldiers? This is terrible.

Our country is being invaded. We shall need reinforcements. This is a national emergency."

"If I were you," said Drin, "I'd strengthen the guard on the castle. They might try to rescue their comrade."

This threw the Governor into even more of a state. "They might attack this castle? But that's awful. My dear wife and I live here. It's our home. What are we to do if enemy soldiers attack us? What a situation! We've always lived in peace here in Kandalore, and now we have this invasion. Why are these men coming across? At least five of them, you say? There could be hundreds! What am I to do? The whole situation was under control with this man in prison, and now we could all be murdered in our beds. What am I to do?"

He paused, with anguish written across his face, and we were all silent for a moment. I took advantage of this to brief Saori and did not notice that the Governor's expression had changed until, with his eyes narrowed, he said:

"How do you know that he was not alone? Do you have any proof? If there were more of them, why haven't we found them? Perhaps the others all perished in the storm. Perhaps there were no others in the first place. Where is the proof? If I tell the people that there are more Souvians roaming around, I could easily cause a panic; and if I report to the king that enemy soldiers are at large, he will mobilise all the forces of the kingdom to combat them. But how could I justify raising so much alarm without any proof? 'Where is the evidence?' the king would ask. I am sorry, Your Highness, but all we know is that one man crossed the mountain. Everything else is guesswork, and we can't make policy on guesswork, can we?"

"There is a difference between guesswork and logic,"

Drin said. "But the only person who knows is the prisoner. Is it all right if we talk to him and see what we can find out?"

The Governor went on arguing about evidence a bit longer, but in the end he took us down to the cells, and we met the prisoner for the first time. He was of average height, but he looked muscular and full of energy, almost like a bull held in a pen at the market, which made you wonder if the bars would be strong enough to hold him.

Being a prince, I thought I should speak to him first: "I am Chaemon, Prince of Akond..."

But I stopped when I realised that Minondas was not paying me any attention. Instead, his eyes were riveted on Saori, and he had a look of happy amazement on his face.

"It is you," he mumbled. "You're the one. I found you. The Great Leader was right. The girl with the golden hair."

"You were sent here to look for me?" asked Saori.

"Yes, of course. The Great Leader told us himself. 'Cross the mountains and you will find her,' he said, and here you are. The Great Leader is never mistaken."

"But why? Why did he send you?"

"He wants to meet you. The Great Leader sent us to find you and bring you back. I shall take you to him."

"But what if I don't want to go?"

"Now you are testing me, but there is no need to fear. I serve the Great Leader, and you can trust me to carry out his orders."

"But I don't want to meet him. Why can't he leave me alone?"

"You are saying strange things, but have no doubt. I may be a prisoner now, but I promise you: without fail I shall take you to meet the Great Leader. His order must be obeyed."

Saori sighed. Every question led back to the same answer.

She tried again: "Do you know why he wants to meet me?"

"Because you are special. You are the girl with the golden hair."

"So he's curious about my hair? Is that it?"

"I cannot say. The Great Leader has his own reasons. All we can do is obey his orders."

Saori sighed again. Drin whispered to her: "Is he alone?" but Minondas heard him and suddenly pointed to Drin, me and the Governor and asked: "Who are these men? Are these the ones who stole you and brought you here?" It was as if he had only just noticed that we were in the room.

"No," replied Saori. "Nobody stole me."

"You were stolen. The Great Leader told us, and he is never mistaken."

"But I've just told you: I was not stolen by anyone."

"You are saying strange things. I thought at first that you were testing me, but perhaps, perhaps you have been bewitched. It makes no difference. I belong to the Souvian Guard, and even if you have been bewitched, I will take you to meet the Great Leader."

"Because his orders must be obeyed?"

"Exactly!"

"Did he send only one soldier on this mission?"

"One Hand was sent. The Great Leader chose us himself! The five best men in the whole army!"

"Then where are the other four?"

"I cannot tell. We were separated on the mountain. Everything was white, all around us. Even the wind was white. I lost sight of the others. It was a test sent by demons, but do not be afraid: Lord Mangra will prevail. Even on my own I shall rescue you and take you back."

"Rescue me? From what?"

"From your enemies, who stole you."

"But everything you say is wrong."

"Nothing is wrong. Tell me – where are they keeping you? Here, in this castle?"

"No, I live in the palace. But why do you say I must be rescued? I'm free now. I don't need you to rescue me."

"You have been bewitched. Otherwise you would not say such things."

"How many times must I tell you? I don't want to go back with you."

"The Great Leader's orders must be obeyed."

"But I don't want to meet him."

"You will meet him. It is the will of Lord Mangra."

"Why don't you listen to me?" Saori shook her head in frustration and said to us: "It's no good. Let's go now."

Back in the Governor's apartment we explained to him in Akondian that Minondas had had four companions and had been separated from them in a snowstorm. We urged him again to beef up his guards on the castle, but he was in no mind to listen. So we went home and reported everything to my mother, who hugged Saori and told her not to be afraid.

"So now we know that Zeno has sent his guards to look for Saori," I said. "But we still don't know why."

"I don't care why!" Saori said. "I just wish he would leave me alone. I felt so safe here, and now…"

There was a look on Saori's face which was hard to describe. At the same time, she looked so angry that her brows were drawn up into something like Drin's habitual scowl, and so upset that her lips were drawn tight together and I thought that at any minute she might burst into tears.

"Chaemon, go away and read something," my mother said. "You too, Drin. Saori and I need time to talk to each other alone."

After that, we did our best to tighten the security of the palace, and Drin moved from his own house into an empty room on the ground floor so as to be nearer to Saori if there was an emergency. But we received no help from the Governor, who still refused to admit that some of the other Souvians could have survived. Only the king could overrule him, but I had little hope that Hargon would grasp the situation. Some weeks before, I had sent him a full account of Saori's arrival based on what Drin had told me, but I had never received any reply.

I was surprised, therefore, when one evening, when I was reading in my library, my brother suddenly strode in.

"Hargon, what are you doing here?"

"Hello, Chaemon. Now look here, I want you to tell me what you've been up to."

"Yes, of course."

"So who is this girl who has the magic powers? And why has she lured soldiers from across the mountains to enter Akond?"

"Wait a minute," I said. "What are you talking about?"

"Don't try to dodge out of answering me. Just tell me the truth. You're not a kid any more. I want to know exactly what's going on."

"And I'm happy to tell you, except your questions don't make any sense."

"Look! Tell me about this girl."

"What girl?"

"The girl you've brought to live in the palace."

"Oh, you mean Saori," I said. "She was rescued from the

slave market by one of our mountain traders, who brought her to see me…"

"Yes, that's what I heard. First she bewitched a mountain trader, and then she bewitched you."

"Bewitched?" I said. "Where'd you get that from?"

"Chaemon, have you any idea how much danger you are exposing our mother to?"

"There's no danger from Saori."

"No danger? What about the enemy soldier who's crossed the mountains?"

"But that's not her fault."

"Then why did he come?"

"Well, she didn't invite him here, if that's what you think. Who's been telling you such a load of nonsense?"

"It's not nonsense."

"I bet it was the Governor."

"The Governor is a loyal servant of the kingdom. He's right to be alarmed."

"So you take his word against mine."

"What if I do?"

"… Anyway, Saori is not a witch!"

"That's what you say."

"And it's the truth."

"But you would say that, wouldn't you? If you were bewitched."

Even by his own annoying standards my brother was being very annoying indeed. "Didn't you read my report? I sent you a full report of Saori's arrival several weeks ago."

"What report?"

"I wrote everything down and sent it to you… but you didn't even bother to read it, did you?"

"I don't have time, Chaemon. I'm the king. I can't sit around in a library, reading manuscripts all day. I have to be out and about meeting the people and solving their problems."

"Well, if you'd read it, you wouldn't be making these ridiculous accusations."

"There's nothing ridiculous about it. Because of this sorceress, our country is in danger."

"Saori is not a sorceress. She's the one we have to protect."

"That proves it!"

"Proves what?"

"That she's a witch of course."

"But I just said she wasn't."

"Exactly!"

A bell tinkled near the door of the room, and we both looked round. Faziah, who had known us since we were born, was standing there. "Her Majesty is ready to receive you now," she said with the same tone of voice that she had used when we were little boys. Slightly embarrassed, we followed her to our mother's room.

After Hargon and our mother had embraced each other, he began: "I have been hearing some alarming reports and I've come to make sure that you're safe, Mother. We've never before had a foreign soldier enter our territory from over the mountains."

"Well, fortunately he is locked up in Kandalore Castle," she replied.

"Which is more than can be said for the mysterious girl that Chaemon has brought into this palace."

"Mysterious girl? Chaemon, have you been bringing mysterious girls here?"

"He means Saori," I said.

"I am reliably informed that she is in fact a powerful sorceress," said Hargon. "She placed a spell on one of the mountain traders, and then on Chaemon, and now she's begun to bring over our enemies so that with their help she can take control of the kingdom."

"But that's all nonsense," said our mother. "Someone has been spreading false rumours again."

Hargon opened his mouth and closed it. It had been a long time since our mother had last told him he was talking nonsense.

"But," he said at last, "if she's not a witch, why has this foreign soldier come here?"

"Didn't Chaemon explain that to you?"

"I did try," I said, "but he wouldn't listen."

"Well, in that case, you had better try again."

So I told Hargon the whole story, about Zeno and the slave market and Saori's escape from Banjut with Drin and the unit of Souvians who had been sent to Akond to look for her. My mother nodded in approval when I had finished.

"So you see," she said. "Saori is the one we should protect."

"I see. Perhaps I was a little hasty about the girl," Hargon said after a pause. "Things are not quite as I had thought."

I almost doubted my ears, but he had definitely said it. My brother had admitted making a mistake!

"Would you like to meet her? Chaemon, go and find Saori and ask her to join us."

"No, thank you, Mother," said Hargon. "Not tonight. It's getting late, and I'd better see the Governor and make plans for tomorrow. In the morning I shall need to interrogate the prisoner, and we may need to send out search parties in case there are any more of these Souvians about."

"It's so good that you're here, Hargon," said our mother. "Now I am sure that all of us will be safe and sound."

Which sounded comforting at the time, but in fact, just for once, my mother was completely wrong.

Chapter 9
The Battle

~

I t was the shouting and screaming which woke me up. At first I wondered if one of my dreams had somehow spilled over into consciousness so that even when I was half-awake I was still in the realm of nightmares; but I pinched my arm to check that I was awake, and I heard the shouting again even louder than before. At this point my brain finally started to think properly, and I realised that some kind of battle was going on nearby. It had to be the Souvians. Drin and I must have been right when we had said that they had survived, and now they were attacking the palace. It was still dark in my room, but I jumped out of bed and felt my way to the door and flung it open. There was a hideous scream from outside somewhere, and then more shouting and doors banging. I felt a twinge of fear – I would be no match for a trained soldier like Minondas if I met him in a dark corridor

– but I was determined not to be a coward. I lit a lamp and took my sword out of its scabbard, and, still in my nightshirt, I headed along the corridor towards the stairs.

I was surprised to find that there was no one around. I went down the stairs and through the dark corridors to the foot of the grand staircase in the main building, and there I was even more surprised to find Drin. He was making some great gesture towards the door and saying something which I could not catch. As he wheeled round, he saw me and said: "Chaemon, they won't listen to me. I need help to protect Saori, but they just rush off."

"Who won't?"

"The king's men."

"Why not?"

"Because he's ordered them all to go with him to the front gate. There's a big fire there, and someone's shooting arrows, but any fool can see that's just a diversion. It's Saori who needs protecting, not the gate."

I was fully awake now and I could see that Drin was right. It would be senseless for the Souvians to launch a direct attack on the well-defended front gate when their real objective was to take away Saori. But how could we persuade some of the king's bodyguards to ignore his orders and go upstairs to protect her? They would not listen to me any more than they had listened to Drin. They took their orders only from the king, and there was no sign of him.

Then I had an idea. We went outside and found four soldiers coming out of the West wing, where some of them had been billeted. "Come quickly!" I shouted at them. "The enemy are upstairs trying to kidnap my mother, the queen."

"But we were told…"

"Never mind what you were told. We must save the queen!"

It worked. They followed me, and in the dark the six of us charged up the broad wooden stairs. But as we reached the landing, without any warning, the first man toppled back on top of us. An arrow was sticking out of his neck, and he was dead.

Later, when the whole incident was over, we pieced together what must have happened. The four Souvians had survived the storm. Either they had taken shelter together, or they had managed to find each other when the storm had passed. They probably took some time to search for their missing comrade, but they had no luck because he had already been found by Gatekeeper A. At length they headed down the track until they reached a point where they could see the Gate without being seen themselves. Here they observed the Governor and his men leaving the lodge, and with them was Minondas. They set out to follow the riders and see where they took him. Since they had no horses themselves, this would ordinarily have been difficult, but the Governor proceeded at a walking pace, and they were easily able to keep up.

They were initially nervous of following the Governor and his party into the city, but when they saw the great press of the crowd which filled the streets, they saw their opportunity. They took off their weapons and helmets and hid them by the road, and then they joined the throng. Everyone around them was desperate to catch a glimpse of the prisoner, and no one paid any attention to the four young Souvians in their matching brown clothes. So they were able to watch as the Governor and his men pushed their way through the crowd and entered the castle with their prisoner.

The Souvians decided that their first priority should be to rescue Minondas. Somehow they managed to steal some horses and Akondian clothes. Both thefts were unusual in our province, but no one connected them to each other, still less to the Souvians. Then, dressed as Akondians, they returned to the city and studied the defences of the castle and the general layout of the streets. Again no one paid any particular attention to them at the time, and they made their plans undisturbed.

At one point in the castle wall some of the stones had collapsed and left a partial gap. Strangely enough, the Governor's financial accounts showed that a large sum of money had been spent on repairs, but there was no sign that any repairs had actually been carried out. On that fateful night, the four Souvians, now dressed for battle, scaled the broken wall, crept up behind the sentry on guard there and slit his throat with a knife. Further on, another sentry met the same fate. They had carried out this kind of night attack before in their many wars of conquest: it was an efficient and deadly routine. They made their way to the Governor's apartments, despatching another guard on the way, and broke in through an unlocked kitchen window. They found the Governor and his wife asleep in bed. She was gagged, tied up and left on the floor. He was forced at sword-point to go down to the dungeon to unlock Minondas's cell. We do not know exactly what passed between him and the Souvians because no one alive could tell us, but we do know that the Souvians killed the Governor and left his flabby body sprawled out on the cold flagstones in a pool of blood.

Once freed, Minondas told the others about his meeting with Saori, and they must have been extremely excited to hear his news, for now they knew not only that she was in Kandalore but also where she was living. They had observed in their earlier reconnaissance that there was a large walled compound with a fine set of buildings about a mile outside the city walls, and they decided that that must be the palace. Here was their chance to fulfil their mission. They had already entered the castle and freed Minondas; now they just had to do the same thing again in the palace to free Saori. Then they would take her back with them across the mountain, in obedience to the Great Leader's orders and the will of Mangra, and they would become heroes of the Souvian nation.

Unlike the castle, the palace wall was in good repair all round, but it was easy to climb over. My great-grandfather had built the palace in a time of peace when he had found the castle too cramped for his large family, and it had never been designed for defence. But the Souvians were surprised to find how many guards were patrolling the walls – far more than they had encountered at the castle. They assumed that this was in order to protect Saori, although in fact it was to protect the king. They decided that they would have to distract the guards: two of the Souvians would pretend to attack the main gate while the other three would climb over the back wall into the garden and make their way into the main building in the centre of the compound, where they expected that Saori was being held.

About an hour before dawn they launched their attack.

As soon as she first heard the shouting, Saori was sure that it was the Souvians coming to get her. She had a moment of panic, but that soon passed. She told herself that she was well defended by all the soldiers who had come with the king – surely four or even five men could not break through the defences which had been put in place that night? They would soon be captured or killed, and this whole nightmare of Minondas and his companions would be ended.

As the shouting continued, however, she began to become anxious again. Why was it taking so long? What if the Souvians did manage to break through? Minondas had looked tough and strong, and she knew from what he had said to her that he was fanatical in his devotion to Zeno. If the others were like him, they might be too much for the Akondians to handle. After all, Akond was a land of peace, but the Souvians had been engaged in warfare for many years. Would the young King Hargon know how to defeat them? She was sure that Drin would know; she thought of going to look for him, but felt nervous about leaving her own room in the dark.

Saori decided that she should be prepared in case the Souvians did get to her room and try to drag her off. When she had been kidnapped the first time from the holy island, she had ended up struggling vainly as the devils carried her to the boat. She was determined not to let that happen again. She lit the lamps in the room and got dressed, and still the shouting continued outside. She opened the door a crack, but it was dark on the landing, and she could see nothing. She went back inside and moved a chest across the door to block it, although she knew that that would not delay the Souvians for long.

She picked up the spear she used to catch fish in the lake and stood holding it in the middle of the room. She was ready to throw it at Minondas or any other attacker who came through the door. She felt the balance of it in her hand, and it gave her confidence. She knew that her aim was good and the spear-point was sharp, and she was ready to defend herself, whatever might happen.

Her mind drifted back to that afternoon when she and the other girls had landed on the holy island, and she began for the umpteenth time to wonder why it had all gone so wrong and how she had ended up so far from home and all the people dearest to her. She had been so happy that day, in her new clothes, surrounded by all the people of her island, so proud to be their chosen priestess, with the moon shining and all the world at peace; and now here she was: standing alone in someone else's house far from home, fearing that at any moment she would be dragged away by the soldiers of an evil ruler. Was this some kind of divine punishment, and if so, for what? Or was this what the goddess wished? Was this part of a plan which only the goddess could comprehend?

Saori thought of her mother and wondered if she would be able to make sense of what was happening. So many times her mother had taught her that the foolishness of men was to think that problems could be solved by violence and that was why it was so important that their islands were ruled by women, who solved problems by talking together and praying to the goddess. Saori had not understood this very well at the time, but now she did. She dropped the spear. Even if she managed to kill one of the attackers, what would that solve? The survivors would still be able to overpower her, and their hearts would be filled with bitterness towards her for killing their comrade. Her mother had been right: violence was not the answer. Saori decided to put her trust in the goddess, and she began to pray.

She was still praying when someone tried to come in through the door. Was it Drin? She called out, but there was no reply, and she watched as the heavy chest was pushed back and the door opened. Saori's heart sank. It was not Drin who came in, but Minondas and another Souvian. So this was it. They had managed to get past the guards and to reach her room, and now they would try to take her away. She was determined not to let them, and as she stood there, with her back straight and her head held high, she felt a surge of power flooding through her body. Her heart was beating as quickly as if she were running in a race, but she was quite motionless. It was the emotion which drove her, and all the fears and stubbornness and fury within her. Did this come from the goddess? Was this the answer to her prayers? She felt a cold tingle down her spine. Whatever it was, this time she would not let her mother down. She directed her look towards Minondas and caught his eyes and engaged them with an invisible force.

"What are you doing here? In my room?" She spoke slowly and felt strangely calm.

"We have come to rescue you," he replied. "Come, quickly, we do not have much time."

"But I told you already that I do not want to go. You must listen to me."

"There… there is a spell on you."

"Yes, there is a spell. It is my spell, and you can feel it. You cannot resist me. I have too much power and you will do as I say: I tell you to go. Go away now."

"No, you must come. The Great Leader's orders…"

"No, you must do what I say. You must obey me. I have the power now, and I command you to leave. You must go now."

The other soldier said something to Minondas, probably in Souvian, since Saori could not understand the words, but he sounded impatient. She ignored him and kept her gaze fixed on Minondas.

"Do you know who I am?" she asked.

"You are the one we seek, the girl with the golden hair."

"Do you know how much power I have?"

Minondas did not reply.

"I have the power of the Goddess of the Peaceful Sea, the daughter of the moon. No one can resist her power. You must hear what I say, and you must do what I say."

Still he was silent. He lent forward as if he was straining to hear something.

"You cannot imagine what powers the goddess has given to me. I command you to go. You should not be in this place. Through her power, I command you to leave."

Minondas tried to turn his eyes away from Saori's, but the intensity of her regard prevented it. Her heart was beating faster than ever, and the power within her growing stronger.

"Minondas! We must obey our orders," said the other Souvian, this time in Banjuti.

Saori turned her gaze on him. "Stand back! The power from the goddess is within me. Turn round and go!"

"But Lord Mangra is with us," mumbled the Souvian, as her eyes caught his. He made no move towards her.

"We must take you with us," said Minondas as if he was trying to recall something he had learnt long ago. Saori could feel their resistance beginning to crumble.

"No. I will not go with you, and you cannot force me. You must go. Go now. Leave this place. Leave now while you still can."

Again there was silence. She felt the force strong within her. She was about to speak again because she had to keep on pressing them and using this strange power inside her to conquer their spirits.

But just as she opened her mouth, there was a yell from someone outside and a loud crash as something heavy struck the door, and the Souvians looked round in surprise – and in that instant the spell was broken. When they turned back towards Saori, they were no longer numbed by her gaze: they were alert and ready for action. They came forwards with their arms stretched out to grab her, one on the left and one on the right. But Saori spotted a gap between them, ducked down and did a forward roll to escape them, and then another, and ended up facing the door – just as Drin came through it. She threw herself into his arms. Now, at last, she must be safe.

Chapter 10
Murder and Mayhem

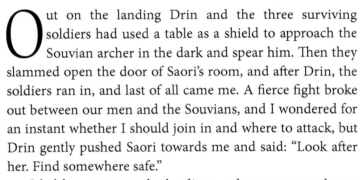

O ut on the landing Drin and the three surviving soldiers had used a table as a shield to approach the Souvian archer in the dark and spear him. Then they slammed open the door of Saori's room, and after Drin, the soldiers ran in, and last of all came me. A fierce fight broke out between our men and the Souvians, and I wondered for an instant whether I should join in and where to attack, but Drin gently pushed Saori towards me and said: "Look after her. Find somewhere safe."

I led her out onto the landing, and as we stepped over the body of the Souvian archer, Saori said: "What about the queen? Is she all right?"

We went to my mother's room and knocked on the door. When she let us in, she looked as neat as ever, with her hair pinned together and wearing a beautiful blue robe, but for once she was agitated and let it show.

"Chaemon, Saori, thank the gods that you're both safe. But what's going on? And where's Hargon?"

We blocked the door as best we could with a heavy wooden wardrobe, and made my mother sit down, and we talked quietly to her until Drin knocked on the door and said that all was clear. The battle in Saori's room had been fast and furious. Drin said he had never met men who fought so well as the two Souvians. They managed to kill another of our men and injure Drin and the two others, but in the end they were overcome by superior numbers.

While we were attending to their wounds, Hargon turned up. Someone had told him there was fighting in the main building, and he had run across from the front gate with a party of soldiers. None of us told him that he was too late, but he must have understood. I remember him glaring at Saori as if she were to blame for what had happened.

The next morning, when we investigated the night's events, the scale of the casualties became clear. All the Souvians had been killed. The two who had created the diversion at the gate had nearly escaped on their stolen horses, but our cavalry under the command of an officer called Radlon had hunted them down. On our side the losses had been heavy: seventeen men dead, and many more injured.

After so many years of peace, there was great commotion in the city when people heard about the fighting. All kinds of rumours and falsehoods were spread around. Hargon decided that the only way to calm things down was to display the bodies of the Souvians in the main square so that everyone could see them with their own eyes. With me and our mother by his side, he told the crowd that all the men who had crossed the mountain to attack Akond had been killed, and he praised our martyrs, including the Governor, who had died heroic deaths resisting the invaders, and promised they would all be given full ceremonial funerals. He said that the enemy had been defeated and Akond was safe, and when they heard this, the people cheered their king. They always cheered my brother – "Just like his father," they liked to say.

I myself was not at all impressed by what Hargon had done, but I remember also feeling rather uncomfortable about my own role in the night's events. This was the first time in my life that I had been involved in an attack on Akond by enemies of the kingdom, but instead of a proper battle, there had been a series of confusing episodes in the dark when I had not been sure what was going on. Drin told me that I had been a great help in saving Saori, but somehow I still felt that as a prince of Akond, I should have done something more heroic.

That evening Hargon called us together. As well as me and my mother, there were Saori, Drin, Marcon, who had been at home in the city the night before and had missed all the excitement, Radlon and a couple of other officers. I sat next to Saori and translated what was being said into Banjuti for her.

Hargon began by asking Marcon what Zeno would do next, and he replied that when Zeno's men did not return, he would probably send more, and not five men next time, but five Hands.

"That's just what I think," said Hargon. "And if five men can cause this much murder and mayhem, just think what twenty-five will do. We must protect Akond from any more of this."

It turned out that his main aim was to make Saori leave

Akond, and since she herself wanted to leave as soon as the pass was open, that was soon agreed.

But what if the Souvians came anyway? Radlon had the answer: "Perhaps, sir, we could set an ambush for them on the mountain. That way we could stop them from getting to Kandalore."

"Excellent!" said Hargon. "That's a capital plan."

Marcon agreed: "I know just the place between the first and second refuges where an ambush could succeed. If the Souvians were surrounded by our men, I might be able to go and tell them Saori had left and persuade them to go home quietly and leave us alone."

"If anyone is to tell them to leave, I rather think it should be me," said Hargon. "But in any case, Radlon, you and Marcon should work out a plan."

"Yes, sir," said Marcon. "But may I also make a request? Given what's been happening, we can't carry on our trade to Banjut, and my men will lose their livelihoods. Would you let us join the army instead? All of us were soldiers once."

"Request granted!" said Hargon.

"There is one other thing," said my mother. "I'm worried about sending Saori into Souvian territory on her own. Zeno's men will be looking for her everywhere, and she'll be in great danger."

This time it was Drin's turn to reply: "She won't be on her own. I'll go with her and keep her safe, as best I can."

"Thank you so much, Drin," said my mother. "I was hoping you would say that."

And then I said: "And I shall go too!"

The words just popped out, without any conscious thought, and even I was a bit surprised I had said it.

After a short pause, everyone seemed to speak at once.

"You, Chaemon? Are you sure that's wise?" asked my mother.

"Don't be stupid, Chaemon. What use will you be against Zeno and his men?" said my brother.

"Perhaps I should go instead of you, sir?" offered Marcon.

Drin just looked at the floor.

I must admit that I was disappointed by these reactions. When Drin had said he would go and protect Saori, everyone had seemed so pleased, and I thought that they might be pleased that I was going to go too.

The day was saved by Saori, who took a minute or two to understand what we had been saying, but who then gave her brilliant smile and said: "That's wonderful. Chaemon is so clever. Now I shall have two powerful protectors on the other side – Drin and Chaemon!" Her words settled the issue. Everyone else shook their heads or shrugged their shoulders, but none of them continued to object. Only my mother was still unhappy, and she said: "Chaemon, let's talk it over later."

I still have no idea why I decided to go. Of course I wanted to help Saori, but there was something more. Later on, when we were alone and she tried to persuade me to stay at home, I tried to explain it to my mother, but what I said confused even me. I was, however, absolutely sure that I wanted to go, whatever dangers and difficulties might lie ahead.

When he thought that everything was arranged in Kandalore, Hargon returned to the capital, and Drin, Saori and I began to make preparations for our journey.

Almost every day we discussed with Marcon what route we should take. Our mission was to return Saori to her island in the middle of the sea. To do that, we had to cross the mountains and then the plains to the coast without being captured by the Souvians. Then we would have to get a boat. None of us except Saori knew anything much about the sea, and she was worried by one thing: she did not know what direction to take in order to go from the coast back to her island. Once you were in a boat, she said, and went some miles out from the shore, you lost sight of land, and all around you was water, which all looked much the same. There were no landmarks or roads, you were driven by the waves and wind, and you could only navigate by the sun and stars.

This sounded impossible to me, and I could not see how anyone could find anywhere in the middle of the sea except by pure chance. But Marcon quizzed Saori on whether anyone from outside had ever visited the islands, and she remembered that once a year two large outrigger boats arrived there. The captains and crew spoke Saori's language with a strange accent, and they came from another island far away. Their skins were burnt deep brown by the sun and salt wind. In return for the ornaments which Saori's people made, they handed over metal and other rare items. They called themselves "navigators", and they were welcomed with ceremonies and feasting. The key point for us was that they must know how to find Saori's island across the open sea.

The next question was how to find the navigators. Try as we might, the only thing we could think of was to seek the help of Lazadim and Katila again. Since the navigators were traders and Banjut was the centre of trade, they probably went there after visiting the islands.

But how could we get safely to Banjut? We considered trying to skirt round the Souvian territory by heading South into the countries which Zeno had not yet conquered and then making for the coast and getting a boat. But Marcon was worried that we would be captured by the Southern Alliance and they might keep Saori prisoner for their own reasons in their war with Zeno.

At this point I remembered a clever idea from one of the adventures I had read about: "We could disguise ourselves as travelling priests. The Souvians are looking for two people – a big man with long hair and a full beard, and a girl with long, flowing, golden hair. So we should change ourselves into a group of three priests – a grown man, a young man and a boy."

"But I'm not a young man," said Saori. "I'm a girl."

"That's the point," I said. "I'm the young man, and we'll change you into a boy. All we have to do is to shave off our hair and put on priestly robes."

"Shave off our hair?" said Drin. "I suppose I could do that, but what about my beard?"

"Your beard would have to go as well, I'm afraid. That's the easiest way of telling who you are."

"All right," said Drin. "I'll shave it off."

"And I'll shave off my hair too."

"But I will not!" Saori was most emphatic. Drin and I had been so busy settling the question of his beard that we were caught by surprise.

"But as soon as they see your hair, everyone will know who you are."

"I don't care. I will not shave my hair."

"All right. We don't have to shave it all off. We could just cut it short, as long as you look like a boy," I said, rather desperately.

"I will not shave my hair, and I will not cut my hair. I will not do it, and that's all!" Saori's face had gone red, and I was afraid she was going to hit me.

"I don't think that you should cut Saori's hair," said Marcon. "Not if she doesn't like it. The idea of a disguise is a good one, but she can wear a hood to hide her head. The problem is that, even with a disguise, there's a good chance you'll be recognised on the road to Banjut. Zeno is bound to have offered a handsome reward, and there will be soldiers everywhere."

This made us think again about how to reach Banjut, and we spent a long time trying to find a solution.

In the end it was Saori who came up with the best idea: "Why go by road?" she asked. "Why not go by water? We could get a boat and go by river to Banjut."

Marcon and Drin agreed that if the Souvians did not know we were in a boat, we might be able to slip past them on the river.

"But where are we going to get a boat?" I asked.

"We can buy one in a village in the hills," said Drin.

"Or hire a boatman who knows the river," suggested Marcon.

Looking back now, our plan seems much too vague and optimistic, but we were so determined to succeed that we did not devote much time to imagining what could go wrong. We thought we would just have to cope with any problems as they arose – and that, I suppose, is pretty much what we ended up doing.

We spent the next couple of weeks getting together all the things we thought we would need – clothes, money, food, weapons and so on – and packing them in waterproof bags which we could load on the donkeys for the first leg of our journey and later carry on our own backs. Meanwhile Marcon and Radlon with a party of soldiers set off up the track to keep a lookout for any more Souvians who might emerge from the pass.

After a couple of weeks, the word came from the Gatekeeper that the snow was melting and we too should set off. We kept our farewells simple. My mother and Saori hugged and wept. I hugged my mother too, and though I did not cry, I had a big lump in my throat. Quite a crowd turned out to wave as the three of us set off on our horses down the familiar street.

Chapter 11

Over the Mountain

~

Later that day we reached Gate A and had supper with the Gatekeeper, who asked what we would do if, as we headed east over the mountain, we met a party of Souvians coming the other way – there would be nowhere to hide, and we could be captured before our journey had really begun. But Drin was unconcerned: he knew every step of the path and was sure that, if he kept his eyes and ears open, he would detect any Souvians first and keep us out of their way.

We had a good night's sleep and a hearty breakfast, and then loaded our bags onto the backs of three solid donkeys and began to climb on foot. The earth was beginning to warm up in the springtime sun, and the trees had swelling buds. Here and there patches of yellow or blue flowers covered the ground. The birds were singing on all sides, and because the leaves had not yet emerged to give them cover, we could see the bright yellows, greens and blues of the different flycatchers and warblers as they perched on the branches and announced who they were. The path was quite steep and sometimes went down as well as up since we were still in the foothills, but we made good progress. Sometimes it rained, but anyone who lives in Akond gets used to rain, and we carried on regardless. Each of us had reason to be cheerful – Saori because these were the first steps of her return home, me because they were the start of our adventure, and Drin because he loved being out in the woods and this was the best of seasons.

We camped that night beneath the stars, and I slept like a log. It was only when I woke up the next morning that I realised that all was not well. My leg muscles were an agony of pain, and my feet felt sore all over. At first I could barely stand. I tried not to groan too loudly when I stepped forward or reached down, but Saori soon realised that I was in pain. She herself seemed untroubled by any stiffness, and so I did my best to pretend that I was not so bad either and waved away her gentle efforts to help me. After we had had breakfast and I had moved around a bit, it did start to get a little better, and we set off again up the path. But this time I could only go at a snail's pace. The path seemed twice as steep as the day before, and I constantly lagged behind. The others were patient, and they stopped frequently to allow me to catch up, but I felt that I was being a nuisance. My pride would have accepted that I could not climb as fast as Drin the mountain trader; but it was hard to be outpaced also by Saori, who seemed to glide up the slope without effort.

And so it went on the next day, and day after day after that. I felt as if the climb would go on without end, walking up the path, trying to overcome the exhaustion of my body and the agony of my legs, just thinking about the next step and the one after, conscious all the time of the others, who could have pushed on faster but always had to wait for me. At one point we came across Radlon and some of our soldiers planning the details of the proposed ambush, and Drin talked to them about positions and angles, while I sat down, grateful to have a short break. But all too soon we moved off again, and again all I could think about was forcing my legs to lift the rest of me up the path, step by painful step.

Later, as we advanced above the second refuge, I was dimly aware that the trees in the forest around us were changing from our familiar broadleaf oaks and limes to firs and other conifers. It became colder too, and the air seemed to have less body, and even Drin began to pause occasionally for breath. Normally these changes would have aroused my curiosity, and I would have made notes of what we experienced, but I had no spare energy for that. It was all I could do to keep going forward and up, step after step, hour after hour, one foot after the other.

At last, after what seemed like an eternity, we approached the fourth refuge. Around us now the mountain was white with a thin covering of snow, and the wind was bitterly cold. The trees, which were not much taller than bushes, stood out black by contrast, and the path zigzagged up the steep slopes between them. Much of it passed over bare rocks, and we had to take care over where we stepped to avoid slipping or tripping up. There seemed to be much less air to breathe, and we were all panting as we moved. We were wearing all the thick clothes which the donkeys had been carrying for us, and for the first time I had put on one of the red woollen coats which had become like a uniform for our traders. Drin said that the bright colour was to make it easier to find a man who became detached from the group, in a snowstorm for example. We all wore fur hats to keep our heads warm, but mine seemed to be pressing inwards all the time and making my head feel dizzy. Even when I took it off, the effect continued.

As we climbed up the last stage to the refuge, which was cleverly concealed in a hollow, the sky began to darken and the clouds grew thicker. The wind was even stronger and seemed to be pushing against us. Far off among the peaks I thought I heard the rumble of thunder. All of us feared that a storm was about to begin, and it was a relief when we finally reached shelter.

As we stumbled into the refuge, we were pleased to find Marcon inside with four soldiers. They said that they had been on the slopes higher up for several days, keeping watch on the spot where any Souvians would come out of the pass onto our side of the mountain, but because of the threatening weather, they had decided to spend the night in the safety of the refuge. Marcon thought that as they were leaving their observation post he had caught sight of a group of men emerging from the pass, but nobody else had been able to see them, and they had decided not to wait but to search again in the morning. If it was the Souvians and they were out on the open slopes, they would have a hard time of it during the storm.

Marcon said that he and his companions had been expecting us to arrive sooner and had worried that we might have had an accident on the way, and I had to admit that I was the cause of the delay and felt thoroughly embarrassed.

But everyone was in good spirits, and we were happy to enjoy the company of friends after so many days on our own on the track. That night as I drifted off into another exhausted sleep, I could hear the men teaching Saori an old Akondian song.

Next morning the storm had passed. I woke late and found that Drin had joined Marcon and the soldiers and headed off to their observation post. Saori and I waited in the refuge and looked after the animals. She said that the storm had been noisy and violent, but I had slept so soundly that I had not noticed anything. After a while Drin returned and told us that Marcon had been right: they had seen the Souvians high up near the exit of the pass. As expected, there were about two dozen of them, and they were beginning to descend the path. Three of our soldiers were going down ahead of them, as fast as they could, to warn our own forces and set up the ambush. Marcon and the other one were still at the observation post. Drin said we should stay in the refuge until the Souvians had gone past and were well down the track, and so we waited in silence. We did not dare to light a fire in case the smoke could be seen. As time passed by, I found myself becoming restless and worrying that something might have gone wrong. Why was it taking so long? Had the Souvians spotted someone and stopped their descent?

"How will we know when it's safe to move?" I whispered in the end.

"Marcon will send a messenger to tell us," said Drin, and at that moment the messenger arrived and said that the Souvians had just passed the level of the refuge and were heading fast down the track. Then he raced off to rejoin Marcon so that they could follow them down and check what they did.

We got the donkeys ready, and then set off in the opposite direction, up the slope to the mouth of the pass. This was the hardest climb we had undertaken so far: the path was the steepest, the cold the most intense, the air the feeblest, and the snow so bright as to be almost blinding. But now that we knew that the Souvians had passed us, we were in a hurry to cross the mountain, and somehow we scrambled up.

In my library I had imagined that the pass would be a simple V-shaped valley between two great peaks, with a straight path running through it, but it was more complicated than that. There was a valley, but it curved a winding route through lower ridges, which rose up on either side and obscured the view of the high peaks. In the warmest part of the summer the valley bottom must have been in some places wide and marshy and in others a bubbling mountain stream, but at this time of year all the water was frozen solid. Fresh snow covered the slopes, and though Drin claimed to be taking us along the path, I could see little trace of it. Sometimes he led us across a steep slope, sometimes round great boulders, and sometimes along the valley floor, but at every step the ice and snow made the route treacherous. At one point or another each of us slipped and fell over, and we were lucky not to break a leg or twist an ankle. Even our sure-footed donkeys became alarmed at times and brayed loudly. The sound made us all jump amid the stillness of the high mountains, and for a moment I imagined that the Souvians would hear it and come back for us, but in fact they were well out of earshot. The air up here was thin and dry, and all of us had to stop from time to time to catch our breath. My head still felt as if it was being constantly squeezed by my hat, and Saori too complained of a headache and of feeling sick.

I could not imagine how the traders managed to cross this pass again and again with a long train of donkeys carrying their precious goods.

After we had spent the afternoon struggling along, Drin announced that we had come to a good place to make camp, although I could see no obvious reason to distinguish that spot from any other. We were still deep in the valley, and all around the snow stretched its white carpet over the slopes. Nevertheless, we followed Drin as he climbed up the northern slope and showed us a shallow cave hidden by a large rock, almost invisible from below, which would provide some protection from a storm. Here we bedded down with the donkeys for one of the coldest nights I have ever experienced. We huddled close to each other and piled on top of us everything which might help to keep us warm, but it made little difference. I slept from time to time out of sheer exhaustion, but whenever I awoke I started to shiver, and it felt as if my feet had turned to ice.

The next morning the sky was still gloomy, and Drin feared another storm, and so we pressed on as fast as we could. The path now zigzagged along the slope above a broad sheet of ice which filled the bottom of the valley. My thick red coat felt as if it was made of thin linen, and I could no longer move my fingers, even inside my gloves. Only the exertion of scrambling along the path gave us some warmth, and I remember thinking that if a man died up there, his body might be frozen solid as if he had been carved into an ice statue. After another long trek Drin said that we had reached the halfway point through the pass and that from there on we should be going downhill, and that gave us some encouragement. Although there was no immediate change in the path, we began to feel that we were going down towards warmth and proper air and trees and all the things which we had taken for granted before but which now seemed like elements of paradise.

We kept on going, and after a while the path did start to descend, and finally, late in the day, the valley began to broaden out and we could see open sky ahead of us. Drin said nothing but made us scramble up to the top of a small peak at the side of the path, and when we got there and looked out at the view, Saori and I both stood open-mouthed in amazement. Spread out before us were the foothills of the mountain chain, and beyond them, far off, we could see a green plain. We strained to see the sea beyond that, but Drin said that it was so far off that we could see it only in our imaginations. A few small white clouds sailed across the sky below us, but otherwise all was bathed in sunshine. Here it was at last – the other side – the world of Banjut and Souvia and all the other kingdoms which I had read about with so much fascination. Now they were in plain view before us. All of us were smiling. We had crossed the pass.

Chapter 12

The Dangoys

~

The way down was easier than the way up had been. Drin kept warning us against damaging our knees or twisting our ankles by rushing down too fast and taking a careless step, but even with this prudent advice, we made good progress. After the first phase of our descent the path became less steep and threaded its way through an area of high hills and narrow valleys. We were soon back down among the broadleaved trees, and here too it was spring. The first leaves were appearing and covering the forest in a dusting of fresh, light green. As in Akond, the birds were singing loudly all around us and whirring to and fro as they chased each other and carried beakfuls of moss and feathers to build their nests. The forest itself was similar to our Akondian forests, but more open, and I began to notice other small differences: some of the flowering trees and bushes were unfamiliar, and

117

so were the songs of some of the birds. When I remarked on these things and wished that I had time to make notes, Saori smiled and said that she was glad I was back to normal – and she was right. This was the first time that I had been able to take an intelligent interest in my surroundings since our first night on the mountain.

After a few more days we reached the lowest refuge on the B side, and then our time as carefree travellers came to an end, and the tension returned. There had been reminders of the Souvians on the way down as we had found the remains of their overnight camps, but since we knew that the men who had made them were now far away, they had aroused little anxiety. But now that we were within a day's walk of Gate B, our old fears returned. Drin went ahead to spy out the lie of the land, and when he came back, he confirmed that the Gate was swarming with enemy soldiers.

That evening we hid our warm clothes near the refuge, together with everything else which we would not need from now on, went down the path as close to the Gate as we dared, and waited for nightfall. Then in the gloaming we shouldered our bags ourselves and let the donkeys go. They wandered off towards the green pastures at the Gate, and Drin led us off above it through the black woods towards the south. I do not know how he found his way through the forest that night. I was constantly bumping into branches and tripping over roots in the darkness and had no idea how far we had gone or in what direction. We were working our way across the foothills, always going up or down or along a slope, and that made it even more confusing. When I asked him later, Drin said something mysterious about the stars, but I could not get him to explain what he meant in a way that I could understand. Saori had been through all this once before, but she too stumbled in the dark and once tumbled all the way down a steep slope until she could catch onto a tree to stop herself.

After a long march Drin let us stop and get some sleep, but he woke us before dawn, and we set off again through the pathless woods, still heading south according to Drin's navigation. When it grew light, we could see that we were deep in the forest without any sign that people had ever passed that way before. It was a long time since I had been in such a wild wood, and it inspired a strange mixture of fear and contentment. The beauty of the forest was always a source of interest and joy, but as dusk came again we heard wolves howling, and there were other, unexplained noises. I told myself that there were no demons lurking around us, but once or twice the hair on the back of my neck stood up when we heard a strange cry in the middle of the night.

"Drin, how far is it now from the river?" asked Saori on our third evening in the forest.

"It can't be far away," he replied. "There are many streams here cutting through the hills, and further down they join to make the Banjut river."

"So tomorrow we might meet some local people?" I asked.

"Yes, this is where things become more dangerous. Anyone we meet could betray us to the Souvians, but if we're going to get a boat, we have to get it from someone."

"We'd better adopt our disguises," I said.

"Chaemon, I will not…" began Saori.

"I know. I just meant Drin and me."

And so with much fuss and several small cuts, Drin and I shaved off all the hair from our heads.

"You look strange," said Saori afterwards. "Not at all like yourselves. Weird, scary."

The next morning Saori went off, as she usually did, to wash in the nearest stream, and Drin and I were tidying up our campsite so as to leave no sign of our presence when we suddenly heard a scream. Drin was off and racing through the trees before I could think what had happened. I ran after him as fast as I could, and we found Saori on the edge of the stream looking grimly across at four men, who stood on the other bank with bows and arrows ready to shoot at her. When we appeared they shifted their aim to us.

"Who are you? What do you want?" asked Drin.

"These woods belong to us. Who are you?" replied one of the men, and his companions made a strange, unfriendly humming noise.

They were relatively short and muscular, with long faces and wispy beards. Their hair was not straight like ours but curling, and two of them wore brightly coloured feathers in it. They were dressed in neatly sewn animal furs, and their leader had a necklace made of the claws of a bear. I had read about these people. They were called Dangoy, and they lived in their villages in the upper reaches of the rivers. They were expert at fishing and hunting, and they obtained the metal and other items they wanted from a few traders whom they trusted, by exchanging them for furs. It was said that in the past they had raided villages in the plains at dead of night and stolen what they wanted, but when the plains people sent an army into the forest to punish them, they could never find the Dangoys, however hard they looked. Now the Dangoys had given up their raids, but they remained deeply suspicious of strangers.

"We will do you no harm," said Drin. "We are travellers, passing through."

"Travellers? Why do you have no hair?" said one of the Dangoys.

"Because we're priests," I said.

"No priests can come here," he said. "We worship the gods of our fathers and mothers from long before, not your gods."

The other men frowned and made more threatening sounds. So much for my priestly disguise, I thought. Better leave this to Drin.

"As I said, we're passing through," he said. "We want to go to Banjut by the river."

"You cannot. This is our land. You cannot pass. If you cross this stream, we kill you."

"But we will do you no harm."

"We will kill you."

"All right," said Drin. "Have it your own way. We will leave your land."

Saori came up the bank and joined us, and we began to walk slowly away from the Dangoys. I could sense the tension in them and perhaps an element of fear. I felt a little bit afraid myself.

Drin turned and said quietly: "Are those the best arrows you've got?"

"Our arrows can kill you."

"Yes, you can kill us, but if you had to shoot a soldier, you'd do better with the arrows I've got in our camp. I could give some to you if you help us. I could give you other things too – but we're leaving, as you told us."

"Wait," said the Dangoy leader. "We need your weapons. What else do you have?"

"Spear-heads. Axe-heads. Even bronze and silver pins and brooches. All you have to do is help us get a boat down the river."

"You cannot go on the river," said the Dangoy. "But take us to your camp and give us these things."

We went back to the camp with the four Dangoys following us, still with their bows drawn. When we got there, Drin picked four new arrows out of his bag and laid them on the ground, one in front of each of the men. One by one they put their own arrows in their quivers and fitted Drin's arrows to their bows, which they still pointed at us.

"Anyone who saw us now would call me a fool," said Drin.

"Why?"

"They would laugh and laugh."

"Why?"

"I gave you new arrows, and now you point them at us. People will say: 'What a fool! He was shot with his own arrows. He gave the Dangoys new arrows, and they used them to shoot him.'"

The Dangoys looked at each other and at Drin, and suddenly they started to laugh and lowered their bows. Everyone began to relax a little.

"Maybe we will not shoot you if you do what we say," said the leader. "First tell us who you are. You do not act like a priest."

"I've been a trader and a soldier and many things besides, but right now my job is to protect this lady," said Drin.

"And who is she?"

"I am a priestess," said Saori. "I come from an island far away, and my goddess calls me to go home. So we must go down the river and then across the sea."

"You cannot."

"Why? Because I'm a priestess?"

"No."

"Then why do you say it's impossible?"

"Because we cannot use boats at this season. Too much water comes down from the mountains. The river flows too fast. Nobody can go on the river."

"Then we'll have to walk," said Drin. "If we go downstream far enough, perhaps we can find a place where it slows down and then we can get a boat."

"Maybe," said the Dangoy, "but not in our land. Our river is too fast." He made a sweeping motion with his arm to show how fast the water went by.

"Then show us where it slows down. Can you help us get a boat down there?"

"Men say that in this season they use boats below the fort, but that is outside our land. We never go there."

"Why not? Don't you like the soldiers?"

"We hate the soldiers," said the Dangoy with a sudden fury. "They come to our village. They tell us to do what they say or they will punish us. They burn our houses, they steal our food, and they catch our men, three men, and beat them." One of the other Dangoys spoke angrily in his own language, and the leader added: "Yes, they take away our women. They take away his mother." He pointed at a third man: "Also his wife." The Dangoys were humming again with anger.

"That's terrible," said Saori. "Why did they do that?"

"These are new soldiers. They are called Souvian – much worse than the soldiers before. But we are warriors. We must fight them as our fathers did long before."

"Why don't you?" asked Drin. "Are they too strong?"

"No. We don't fight because our chief is afraid. There are

many soldiers, and they have sharp arrows like yours and strong swords, and the old men are afraid."

"Maybe we could help you. I've fought soldiers like this before."

"How can you help?"

"I can teach you how to beat the Souvians. You know the woods. You can creep up on a deer, and you can shoot an arrow into its heart. You can do the same to the Souvians, and then you can take their weapons."

The four Dangoys fell silent as they thought about this, and they began to mutter in their own language.

Drin added: "I have more arrow-heads in my bag."

"Show us," said the Dangoy leader. "Show us what is inside."

Drin reached inside his bag and pulled out some arrow- and spear-heads and a knife. The Dangoys looked at them intently. "Show us the river," Drin said, "and you can share these gifts with your people." He reached under his coat and this time pulled out a silver ring and held it up for everyone to see.

"If we can set your mother free, this would make a fine present for her."

That did it. The Dangoys relaxed again and their leader said: "Follow us. We will take you to our village."

Their earlier hostility had vanished now, and they were almost too friendly: one of them touched Saori's hair and held it up in a shaft of sunlight, and Drin had to intervene gently to stop him. But that did not stop another man from rubbing the top of my bald head with the palm of his hand, and I had to pretend that this was a great joke. Drin and the leader were chatting away like long-lost friends. Saori put on her outer coat with its hood to avoid any more unwelcome attentions. It was unnerving how quickly the men's mood had changed. We had to be careful, I thought, or else it could change back again just as fast.

We picked up our bags and followed the Dangoys through the forest, and after a while one of them cupped his hands and gave a whistle which sounded like a bird call. A similar call came in reply. There was a proper path now, and soon we could see the roofs of houses. Our guides took us right into the centre of their village and stopped.

Chapter 13

The Mysterious Stranger

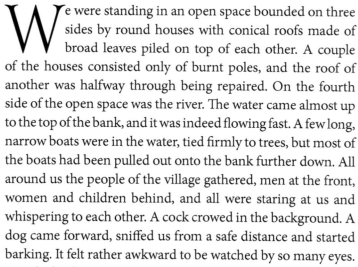

We were standing in an open space bounded on three sides by round houses with conical roofs made of broad leaves piled on top of each other. A couple of the houses consisted only of burnt poles, and the roof of another was halfway through being repaired. On the fourth side of the open space was the river. The water came almost up to the top of the bank, and it was indeed flowing fast. A few long, narrow boats were in the water, tied firmly to trees, but most of the boats had been pulled out onto the bank further down. All around us the people of the village gathered, men at the front, women and children behind, and all were staring at us and whispering to each other. A cock crowed in the background. A dog came forward, sniffed us from a safe distance and started barking. It felt rather awkward to be watched by so many eyes.

The leader of our new friends began to speak to the crowd

in his own language. I supposed that he was explaining how they had found us and why they had brought us into the village. He pointed repeatedly at Drin and showed off his new arrow, and the people listened intently. But he was interrupted in mid-flow as a horn was blown from the back of the crowd, and the villagers moved aside to make a path through to where we were standing. A little group of older men came forward, together with the trumpeter and a taller man, who was dressed as they were but was clearly not a Dangoy by origin. He stood very upright, and he had straight, grey hair. I guessed he was of middle age, and I liked his fine, intelligent face. I hoped that we would get a chance to talk to him and hear his story. It could be worth including in the record of our travels which I planned to write if I ever returned home.

Our young Dangoy friend began to have a blazing row with one of the old men, whom I took to be the village chief. They were shouting at each other and waving their arms in a very excited fashion. Occasionally another of the old men would join in on the side of the chief, but everyone else was silent. I guessed that the subject of the argument must be us. The young man had told us of his anger at their treatment by the Souvians and the caution of the elders, but would our arrival alter the balance of the argument? Would the chief be persuaded to launch an attack with Drin's help? Or would caution still prevail? Either way, we could be in trouble. Our fate might depend on the outcome of an argument we could not understand among people we had never seen before.

It was hard to sense the mood of the people, but some of them were starting to make the low humming sound, which seemed to indicate anger. I looked to Drin to see if he would intervene, but he made no move, and it was Saori who suddenly took action. She told us afterwards that she could not bear to listen any longer to the two men shouting at each other. So she walked straight past them and joined the women at the back of the crowd. She picked out two of them – by instinct, as she had no idea who was who – took their hands and turned round to face us. Her action was so unexpected that the two men paused in their argument, and for a moment silence reigned. Then the tall stranger spoke. His voice was quiet, but everyone listened respectfully. When he finished, the chief appeared to agree with him, and so did the crowd. Only the younger man and his companions looked troubled and angry, and with a violent gesture he led them rapidly away through the people and the houses and back into the forest.

The stranger spoke to us in Banjuti: "I'm awfully sorry. Please don't get the wrong impression, but we don't get many visitors in this neck of the woods, and your arrival has stirred up a bit of a ruckus as you might have noticed. I do apologise, we've been very rude and we haven't even introduced ourselves. So, first, let me tell you that you've come to the village of the great and glorious Chief Xargolyt, whose name will live forever among the whispering beeches." The chief looked very pleased by this introduction. "Second, the young man whom you encountered in the woods and who has just departed was his son, Ptarmoxal; it's such a pity that he and his father do not always see eye to eye. This gentleman is the Chief's Adviser of the Right Side, and… well, actually I don't expect you'll remember all the names and I haven't the time to introduce everyone… but if you don't mind, perhaps I should just introduce myself. I am Elkan, and you may be surprised to learn that I am the Adviser of the Left." Elkan bowed his head to us and smiled in a nervous sort of way.

"Actually, the thing is, I have to give you a message from the chief. As you may have gathered, we weren't quite sure, to start with, how to respond to your unexpected arrival, but everything is settled now, and it is my humble duty to convey to you the decision of our wise leader. It goes as follows: Chief Xargolyt says that he has heard that you are travellers passing through, and that you have offered to help us. He thanks you for that kind proposal, but, he says, we are the Dangoys, and we live within our own lands. If we have troubles, we solve them in our own way, and we have no need of help from strangers. This is what we have learnt from our fathers and mothers from the time long before. We do not allow strangers to enter our lands, and any who do come must leave as soon as possible. Chief Xargolyt therefore commands me to tell you that you must leave his territory this very day. However, since you were brought to this village by his own son, he feels that he owes you some hospitality. Before you leave, he wishes you to enjoy food and drink, and he has commanded me to invite you to my house – a very humble abode indeed, I'm afraid – where I shall be happy to entertain you. This is the decision of Chief Xargolyt."

Saori and I smiled with relief when we heard this, but I could not detect any change in Drin's expression, and I wondered what he was thinking.

"Thank you very much for your invitation," said Saori. "We are happy to visit your house, and then we will leave the village and hope everyone can live in peace."

Elkan spoke rapidly in the Dangoy language, and the villagers relaxed and began to crowd round touching us, just as the four hunters had done in the woods. One or two of the men tried to open our bags and take things out, but we clasped them closely to our bodies. For a short while we were overwhelmed by the press of people, and we were glad when the trumpet sounded again and Elkan led us out along the bank of the surging river.

He stopped at the edge of the village where his own house stood. It was made in the same way as the others, but it was smaller and neater, and instead of a simple opening to go in and out, he had fitted a door, which was tied shut with knotted rope. He undid the knots and invited us to go in. Some of the people gathered outside and chatted to each other as they waited for us to come out again. In a country which strangers were forbidden to enter, any who did get in were the subject of great curiosity.

It was dark inside, but our eyes slowly adjusted to the gloom. Elkan removed a large wooden shutter from an opening in the wall to let more light in, but it was soon filled with children's faces, and he had to shoo them away. He bustled around, fanning the fire and setting cooking pots. "I'm afraid you'll have to take pot luck as we used to call it. Had I known you were coming, I could have laid on something better, but of course none of us knew that you were on the way. I'm so sorry, I don't know your name, sir, but would you mind awfully if I asked you to reach up and pass over the smoked venison above your head?"

This was directed to Drin, who did as he was asked, and Elkan began to expertly cut slices off the joint of meat and put them into a pot of boiling water with herbs and vegetables to make a kind of stew. We sat round the fire and waited. The fire was in the middle of the earthen floor and the smoke rose up into the rafters. I could see other foodstuffs hanging from the beams of the roof, presumably to keep them safe from mice. On the far side was a pile of furs on a slightly raised platform, which must have been Elkan's bed. Clothes hung from a rope, which stretched across from one beam to another. On the opposite wall from the window was a large flat stone, and on top of that was a wooden box, and on top of that stood small statues of three gods – a larger female figure and two smaller ones.

Who was this man? I could not bear it any longer. I had to ask: "Thank you for inviting us like this, but you don't look like a Dangoy. Why do you live here with them?"

"There's no need to thank me," said Elkan. He seemed to be speaking louder than before. "I don't often have guests in this little house, and I'm happy to welcome you. As for where I come from… Well, perhaps someday I shall have the occasion to tell you, but not now, I'm afraid. It's a long story, and not a terribly happy one."

I was tempted to ask again, but Elkan was still talking.

"You must be hungry," he said. "I'm afraid it will take a little longer before the hotpot is ready, but while you wait I'd like to offer you some of this baked fish. It's one of the Dangoys' favourite dishes, and I think you'll find it tastes rather good. The fish have been cooked slowly for a long time, and you can eat all of them, even the bones."

He was right: the fish was delicious. But as we ate, a change came over him. Instead of playing the jovial host, he began to look anxiously at the window and door. Then, cautiously, he leant forward and said in a whisper so quiet that we could barely hear: "They are outside, and some of them understand Banjuti, so be careful."

"Why?" Drin asked. "What's the big secret?"

"Haven't you guessed? This is a trap. They mean to hand you over to the soldiers. Please speak quietly, or they'll know that I have betrayed them."

I realised then that I had been naïve to take Xargolyt's words at face value. We could not trust the Dangoys or anyone else. Wherever we went, anyone we met could betray us at any time. Saori looked almost as downcast as I felt.

Only Drin seemed untroubled. "Why are you telling us this?" he asked.

"Because I know who you are," said Elkan, "and this young lady is the best hope we have."

"What do you mean by that?"

"Only the Alamanda can save us now."

"How do you know my name?" asked Saori.

"Please forgive me," said Elkan. "I'm terribly sorry, but I have no time to explain that now."

"Do you know who I am?" asked Drin.

"Yes, you are the trader from over the mountain who insulted Zeno and will meet a painful death, or at least that's what the Souvians told us. But they did not inform us about this young man."

"Chaemon," I said, "scholar from Akond."

"Scholar? That is splendid. I am happy to meet a scholar."

"Are you a scholar yourself?" I asked, but Elkan only smiled and gave no reply.

"What happens next?" asked Drin. "What are they planning to do?"

"While I keep you here eating this meal, a party of them is running to the fort. They will tell the soldiers about you and lead them to a small clearing on the edge of their territory. I am supposed to take you to the same place, where you will be surrounded and arrested."

"So they lied to us," Drin said.

"I suppose in a way you could say that, but I hope you

will not judge them too harshly. You see, they are terrified of the soldiers. A company of Souvians came here a little time ago, burnt down some houses, beat up some of the men and took some of the women as hostages. It was very nasty, and the poor old Dangoys don't know what to do next. The young men want to fight, but the chief thinks that would lead to the tribe's destruction. He thinks that if they hand you over, the hostages might be released."

"How can we escape?" asked Drin. "Can you guide us through the forest to avoid the ambush?"

"Oh no, that would never work," said Elkan. "The Dangoys know everything which moves in the forest. Last autumn when you passed through, I bet you didn't see them, but they saw you. No, even I could not throw them off the trail."

"So what can we do?" asked Saori.

"How was the fish?" asked Elkan, speaking loudly again, and I had the strange feeling that he was enjoying this.

"Very good!" she said.

"The stew is ready now. Please allow me to serve you." Elkan lowered his head as he held out a bowl of stew in both hands to each of us in turn. When Saori said she did not eat meat, he was full of apologies and pressed her to eat more fish. In everything he said and did, he was strangely polite for a man who lived in a small round hut in the middle of the forest.

"Listen," said Drin after we had eaten. "All we want to do is leave peacefully. I don't want to fight these people if we can avoid it."

"There is no need for that," said Elkan. "Not if we follow your original idea and go by the river."

"But the Dangoy hunters told us that was impossible," Saori said.

"It's risky but not impossible," said Elkan. "I think I have acquired enough skill to take a boat down the river even when it's like this."

"So you will come with us?"

"Yes."

"And you choose to help us rather than them?"

"Because of you, Alamanda, because of you. Was it pure chance that you came to this village and found me? No, of course not. It was a signal from the gods, a signal that we will be saved."

As he said this, Elkan seemed filled with a strange kind of excitement, but Drin brought him down to earth.

"Tell us your plan," he said.

"First we go back to the riverbank. I'll tell them that before you leave, the young lady wishes to pray beside the river."

"Then what?"

"As it happens my own boat is already in the water. When I give the signal I want everyone to throw their bags into it. We must get on board as fast as possible – first you go and sit in the middle" (he pointed at Drin), "then you in the bow" (me), "then you in the stern" (Saori), "and finally me. Once the rope is undone, the boat will fly down the river. I shall steer it with as much skill as I possess, but I must request you to do exactly what I tell you. Is all that clear?"

We nodded in silent assent. It sounded risky, but none of us had a better plan, and Elkan seemed very sure of himself. Who was he? And why had such a cultured man been living so long in the woods?

Chapter 14

Down the River

~

We watched as Elkan put the shutter across the window again and went over to his bed. He cut a large hole in the earthen wall behind it, and a sack fell onto the floor. When he opened it, we could see that it was full of clothes, not the furs worn by the Dangoy but the woven clothes of farming people. He wrapped some of them around the three statues on his wooden box, and put them into the sack. Then he threw the furs off his bed, lifted a flat piece of wood from the earth platform beneath it and brought out a long, narrow cylinder of the type which would normally hold a tightly rolled scroll. He wrapped this up in a shirt and pushed it down carefully inside the sack. I longed to ask if there was indeed a scroll inside, but I had the sense to hold back.

"That's all I shall need," Elkan said, "but perhaps it would be wise to take some food as well." So each of us put into our bags as much as we could of the food hanging down from the beams.

"I think we are now ready to go."

Elkan led us out, shut the door and re-tied the knots, as if he was planning to return later. We formed a little procession to the riverbank and stopped next to where the boats were tied up. The Dangoys followed us, chatting cheerfully to each other. Elkan made a short announcement and tried to get them to move back to give us space, but they were reluctant to do so until Saori removed her hood and for the first time they saw her golden hair tumbling out. Then everyone gasped, a small child began to scream, and they scrambled back to where Elkan had told them to go. Once all was ready, he told Saori to go ahead, and she began to sing in her own language. Her voice was clear and strong, and the tune was slow and rhythmic.

It felt strange, standing there listening to Saori's song while the river rushed and roared behind us. Along the bank a few gnarled trees clung onto the bank with their roots exposed, and leant out over the water. All around us the Dangoys stood in a big semicircle, no longer with the men in front and women behind but all mixed together. Small children clung onto their mothers' hands, and their mouths were pursed together as they joined in humming Saori's tune. Even the village dogs stopped and stared. Beyond the people stood their round houses, and beyond them the forest trees with the fresh, green leaves of spring.

Saori's hair shone in the sunlight as her pure voice rose up into the sky, like a line of curling smoke from a campfire on a still day, and gradually her song began to affect me strangely. The scene in front of us began to seem unreal, like a picture painted by an old artist, not the actual view that we could see now but something recorded in fading colours. Stealthily the song was filling my heart with a deep feeling of peace. I was being carried away to a new place, a wide spread of blue with dots of white. There was something fresh and soothing in the breeze, and I could feel a regular rocking movement, as when a mother gently moves the cradle to and fro where her baby is asleep. The scene on the riverbank had faded away now, and my mind was emptied of all thoughts except the expanse of blue and the glittering sunlight playing and flashing on it, and still that steady, regular rocking rhythm. Saori's gentle voice sang on, unrolling its enchantment and then returning to begin the same simple tune again.

I was in this dream state when I was roughly shaken. I looked round. Drin had gone. He was getting into the boat, and I remembered where we were. The Dangoys remained motionless: they were still in the dream where I had been. I hurried to follow Drin and clambered over him to the bow of the boat. Saori had stopped singing now, and one or two of the Dangoys were looking at us. They shouted, but we were all in the boat, and Elkan was struggling to undo the rope which tied it to a tree. A few arrows whistled past our heads. "Cut the rope!" Drin yelled. We crouched down. Some of the men were running forward, only a few paces from the bank. In a moment they would be able to grab the boat, and we should be lost. But just in time it swung free, and we were being carried off at breakneck speed down the river. Elkan steered us into the middle where the fastest current flowed, and we soon left the Dangoys far behind. They could do nothing but watch us racing away downstream and shout in anger at having been tricked.

I took a deep breath as the danger passed, and in the

same instant a wave of river water splashed over me. I did not mind. It was exhilarating to feel the speed of the boat and to see the trees on the banks rushing by. But very soon a fresh danger appeared: we were racing towards rocks, and the river foamed into white waves as it passed over them. Elkan shouted for us to hold on tight and at once the rapids were upon us. At any moment I thought that we would crash into one of the rocks, the boat would be smashed in and we would all be thrown into the roaring water. But somehow Elkan managed to keep the boat heading along the fastest course where the water flowed most strongly and carried us over the obstacles. Waves of cold water broke over me in the bow, one after another, and the noise of the rushing river drowned out all other sound. All I could do was to cling on. Again and again a mighty rock approached the bow right under my eyes, and then at the last minute the boat twisted away and narrowly slid past it. And then we were past the rocks and back in open water racing past the banks as we had done at the beginning, and fear once more gave way to excitement.

After a while we could hear a far-off roar, and Elkan warned that there was a waterfall ahead and steered us over to the bank. With all four of us lifting and pulling we managed to haul the boat up out of the water and onto the bank, and Elkan showed us the best way to manhandle it without damage down the rocky slope beside the waterfall and launch it again into the quiet pool below. A kingfisher watched our panting efforts and flew off like a shining blue arrow fired low over the water.

As the sun was beginning to set, we came to an island. The main channel was to its right, and on that side the water raced on down, but Elkan steered the boat into the shallower channel to the left, where the current was slower, and beached it on the shore of the island. Here we made camp and ate a cold meal. We did not dare to make a fire. Over the roar of the river we heard an owl giving a three-note call from one of the trees.

"What's the plan for tomorrow?" asked Drin. "The Souvians will come looking for us as soon as it gets light."

"At least we have a boat," I said. "All we have to do is to keep racing downriver."

"I am sorry to have to tell you, but it will not be that easy," said Elkan. "According to the traders who came to our village, the Souvians control both banks of the river and have built forts along it. They would be bound to see us if we tried to go past by boat."

"Then perhaps we should travel by night," I said. "They won't see us in the dark."

"I suppose we could get past the nearest fort, which is beside one of the tributaries which flow into the Banjut, but..."

"But what?" asked Drin.

"But beyond that we should have to go past the garrison at Kundulbatin, where they have thrown a barrier across the river so that they can check any passing boats. I believe that there are also more rapids further downstream, and I should not dare to take the boat over them in the dark."

"So you're saying you don't have a plan?" said Drin. "A fair old mess you've got us into!"

"With great respect, I must point out that you got yourselves into the mess when you arrived unannounced at the Dangoy village. It was I who saved you from immediate arrest."

"So you say," replied Drin. "But we've only got your word for it."

"Are you calling me a liar?"

"Please," Saori intervened. "Both of you, stop. This is no time to argue. Why do men always argue?"

"I'm sorry, Saori," said Drin. "He's right. I got us into this mess."

"I have no wish to argue with anyone," said Elkan.

"Anyway, we need a new plan," I said. "We'll have to leave the river and travel overland."

"That too will not be easy," said Elkan. "After crushing the Southern Alliance the Souvians control all the country from here to the southern desert. Only Banjut is still holding out, and Zeno has begun a siege of the city with a huge army."

"Zeno has defeated the Southern Alliance?" I asked.

"Yes. They were destroyed at the battle of Katano last summer."

"And Banjut is surrounded by Souvians?"

"Yes."

"Aiyah!" said Saori. "What can we do now? How can we get to Banjut?"

"I don't suppose we could go back to my idea of disguising ourselves as priests?" I said.

"That would not be advisable," said Elkan. "The traders complained that the Souvians had set up checkpoints on all the roads, and everyone who passed had to prove who they were. Any priest is liable to be arrested unless he worships Zeno's god, Mangra. The only people who move freely around the country are the soldiers, and everyone else is so scared of them that they keep out of their way."

"Then perhaps we should become soldiers?" I said. I had

meant it as a joke but immediately regretted saying it. "No, I didn't mean that. I don't really want to be like a Souvian."

We were all silent for a moment. The owl called again. We could barely see each other's shapes in the gloom.

"What will happen to the Dangoys?" asked Saori. "Will they be all right?"

"I have to confess that I have been worrying about that," said Elkan. "I'm very much afraid that the soldiers will think that the Dangoys tricked them, by persuading them to wait in the woods while we escaped down the river. They are most unlikely to believe the truth, that the Dangoys themselves were tricked. I'm awfully worried that they will go to the village and mete out punishment, and the Dangoys will suffer all over again. I really wish I could think of some way of helping them."

"In the old days," I said, "they used to hide in the forest until their enemies gave up and went away."

"How do you know that?" asked Elkan.

"I'm a scholar. I read it."

"Well, they did do that in the past, and it's probably the best they can do now, but it still leaves the problem of the hostages."

We fell silent again.

"It may look difficult at present," said Elkan suddenly, "but I am sure that all will turn out for the best. The gods are on our side. I was sure of that as soon as I saw you, Alamanda. Only you can save our people from the monster, Zeno."

"You said that before," said Saori, "but I don't understand why. Here I am, my clothes all dirty with mud, sitting on the riverbank. How can I save people from Zeno?"

"No, no, there is no need to pretend with me. Did you

not charm the Dangoys on the riverbank with your magic song? Even Chaemon was in a trance. Why would Zeno be so desperate to capture you if you were not special? The dirt on your clothes is of no importance. It is who you are that matters."

"How do you know my name?"

"Because everything about Alamanda is described in the poem. Surely as a scholar, Chaemon, you must know that."

"I'm sorry," I said, "but I never read about Alamanda in any poem."

"Do you mean that you have not read the greatest poem ever written – the Epic of Tenjin?"

"I'm embarrassed to admit it, but I haven't. I've heard of it, of course, and even seen a couple of short passages translated into Banjuti, but that's all I could get hold of in Akond."

"Then a great delight awaits you. Without doubt, it is best in the original Valosian, but even if you read it in a Banjuti translation, you will find that it more than repays the effort."

"What does it say about Alamanda?"

"You really should read the poem, but I will try to explain as briefly as I can. Tenjin, the hero, meets Alamanda towards the end of his travels. She is very beautiful and has long golden hair, just like this lady, and she lives on an island in the middle of the blue ocean. The shallow sea around it is full of fish of many colours, the forests which grow up the sides of its mountains echo to the songs of birds, the trees produce sweet, juicy fruit, and everyone lives peacefully until a ripe old age. They worship a goddess who protects their island from storms and all misfortune, as long as they perform the rituals handed down from their ancestors, and the heart of those rituals is the sacred dance performed by their ruler and chief priestess, the Alamanda. Tenjin is washed up onto the island after his boat sinks in a terrific storm, and the islanders find him and are kind to him. When he tells them the story of his adventures, Alamanda thinks him so brave and handsome that she falls in love with him, and at first he too is filled with the desire to marry her and to live on the island with her for ever and ever."

"But something goes wrong?"

"The god Falco, who sent him on his quest, appears to him in a dream and reminds him that he must return home to Hoxxkorn, for otherwise he cannot fulfil his destiny and lead his people out of darkness. Tenjin resists, but Falco appears again and again whenever he falls asleep, and in the end Tenjin accepts that he must do his duty. He begs Alamanda to come with him, but she cannot leave her home without angering the goddess and destroying the peaceful lives of her own people, and so Tenjin must leave on his own. This passage contains some of the finest poetry ever written. I have seen the hardest warriors burst into tears when it is recited."

"It does sound like Saori's island," I said, "but why would all this interest Zeno? He doesn't sound like the sort of man who'd be interested in a love story."

"I cannot tell you the answer to that. It puzzles me too, but whatever his motives, he is desperate to get hold of you, Alamanda, and that is why you are the one person who can destroy him. Ever since I first heard that they were searching for you, I have pictured this scene many times. When you meet him, he will take you into his palace, and at the time for dinner he will seat you next to him at his table, and that will be your chance. Here, I have a gift for you. The Dangoys make this poison from a small scarlet frog, and it can kill a man in a few minutes. All you have to do is to scratch this onto his skin, and I and all my people will have our revenge."

"Poison him?" said Saori. "Oh no, I could never do that. That would be murder."

"Murder? No, surely not. How can it be murder to kill such a man? Think of the thousands of people, tens of thousands, who have been killed, tortured and enslaved by him. Think of the children who have been torn away from their mothers and fathers, the wives who have lost their husbands, the parents who have seen their children killed in front of their eyes. Think of the even more terrible crimes he will commit if he goes on living. How can it be murder to save the world from such a man?"

"I see... I understand what you mean... but I still could not kill him. And anyway, I don't want to meet Zeno. Eating with him would be horrible."

"Then please forgive me for talking like this. Dear Alamanda, I have upset you, and that is the last thing I wanted to do. I was wrong to push my own ideas upon you, but I am sure that it is your destiny to save us from Zeno. There must be another way. As the poet said, it is always the least expected road which the gods prepare. But I have spoken too much. I hope that you will accept my apologies."

I have set down Elkan's words as accurately as I can remember them. They tumbled out with great passion as if he had been reflecting upon these things for many long hours and this was his chance to pour out his thoughts.

"That's the answer!" said Drin suddenly.

"What? Poison Zeno?!" asked Saori.

"No, no," said Drin. "What I mean is the unexpected

road. There's one place they'll never expect us to go. Elkan, are the hostages in the fort?"

"I assume so, unless they have been sent to Kundulbatin."

"How many soldiers are stationed there?"

"Normally one company. That's ten Hands, enough to keep watch on the Dangoys and the forest."

"Do they have horses?"

"They have some, but I'm afraid I don't know how many."

"How long would it take them to get more men from Kundulbatin?"

"I would guess that if a messenger set off at dawn on horseback and the soldiers from Kundulbatin were ready at once to march to the fort, they could be there by midday. But why do you ask so many questions?"

"If the garrison go out looking for us, there's a chance they'll only leave a few men behind to guard the fort. If we could get in there, we might be able to release the hostages and get some horses."

"That is an excellent plan," said Elkan. "I wish I had thought of it. If we can enter the fort, we can also take up Chaemon's brilliant idea."

"My idea? What idea?" I burbled.

"You suggested that we should become Souvian soldiers. If the three of us wore soldiers' uniforms, we could pretend that Saori was our prisoner, and the Souvians would let us through their checkpoints."

"I'm not sure about that," said Drin. "I don't like the idea of dressing up as an enemy soldier."

"Do you have a better one?" asked Elkan.

But Drin did not, and so that became our plan, and it was all because of my brilliant idea.

Chapter 15
Elkan Makes a Tally

~

The next morning we were up well before dawn and back in the boat. Elkan steered us a short way down the river, and we landed on the southern bank just beyond the point where it was joined by another smaller stream. We took out our bags and cast the boat adrift. It vanished quickly into the dark, and we paused for a moment to watch it go.

Elkan led us along the bank of the smaller river until we could see houses and small fields. There Drin made us hide behind a dense thicket and went on alone. We sat in silence, as slowly the eastern sky turned to red. Two riders clattered by, heading off in a hurry along the side of the river, and we heard the sounds of the village waking up, people talking in low voices and cockerels crowing. It was almost daylight by the time Drin reappeared.

"It looks good," he said. "Two riders have left the fort,

heading, I suppose, for Kundulbatin. But the main group of soldiers – about 40 of them – crossed the stream and headed off into the forest, towards the Dangoys. The question is how many of them are left in the fort, and there's only one way to find that out."

He outlined his plan.

Then he and Elkan went off around the village using what cover they could find to avoid detection. Saori and I counted to 100, and walked straight into the village along its dusty main street.

"Princess of the East!" I yelled as loudly as I could. "The Princess of the East has come to pray in the temple. Make way for the Princess of the East!"

People came out of their houses and stared. Children began to run beside us, calling out "Princess of the East". Stray dogs joined the excitement, and chickens scattered in front of us. Saori ignored all of them and walked on in silence at a steady pace. An older man came out and stood in our way as if to stop us, but he backed off when Saori looked straight at him and kept on walking.

"Call the soldiers!" I cried. "Call the soldiers for the Princess of the East!"

We came to an open space, where there stood a large statue, made of painted wood – a god in human form, standing with his legs together and his arms raised. Underneath his feet was the figure of a small crouching man whose body was tied up with ropes – to represent an enemy prisoner, I supposed. The god wore a short kilt around his waist, but his chest, legs and arms were unclothed and painted yellow, and the sculptor had taken care to show his bulging muscles. In one hand he held a sword, which had a red blade as if it was covered in blood, and in the other what looked like shrunken human heads held aloft by their hair. But it was his own head which caught my attention – the black beard jutting out, the high, narrow nose like a fish eagle's beak, the small, deep-set eyes and the lines of a frown on his sloping forehead. Instead of hair, burning flames came straight out of the top of his head. I said quietly to Saori that this must be Mangra, and she made a face of disapproval.

On the far side of the square stood two huge ginkgo trees and an old wooden building which was raised off the ground on pillars. We walked over to it, and the people gathered round. Mynah birds called in the trees like flute players warming up.

"Now the Princess of the East will pray to the gods," I declared, and Saori began to sing her slow and magical song just as she had in the Dangoy village. At first the people listened in silence, and then they began to hum the tune quietly and enter the dream, but this time I made sure that I kept my wits about me.

It was a little while before the soldiers came, but when they did, it was at a gallop. There were only three, on horseback, and the crowd ran away as soon as they saw them.

"You!" one of them shouted at Saori. "What are you doing here?"

"This is the Princess of the East," I said, "and she has come to pray to the gods."

The soldiers looked at each other for a moment, as if not sure how to proceed. Then one of them said: "You're coming with us to the fort. You can wait there until the commander gets back and decides what to do with you. Come on! March!"

The two of us walked along the track with the three

mounted soldiers close behind us. The fort was on a slight rise, protected by a ditch and a wooden palisade, and we went round to the main gate. The soldiers shouted, and the gate opened, although we could not see anyone inside. We went in, and found ourselves in a courtyard with buildings on three sides attached to the fort's outer walls – stables for the horses to the left, kitchens and washrooms to the right, and a two-storey building straight ahead, which seemed to be the living quarters for the men.

"Stop right there!" Drin said from behind us. "You are surrounded."

We all turned round and saw him standing beside the gate with a bow and arrow pointed at the leading soldier.

"Dismount!" Elkan came out from the main building, also with a bow and arrow. "Get off your horses!"

Saori and I moved to stand next to Drin.

Slowly the soldiers dismounted and stood in a line in front of us.

"Take off your sword-belts!"

They dropped their sword-belts in the dirt, and I went over and gathered them up.

"Now your helmets and jerkins."

I gathered these up too.

"Over to you, Elkan. You're the expert with knots," Drin said.

Elkan gave his bow and arrow to me, while he tied the men's wrists together and searched for any hidden weapons.

"They only left one Hand in the fort," said Drin. "So when three of them went out to look for you, only two stayed behind. We've tied them up inside. Now we need to find the hostages and the spare uniforms, and let's hope there's one more horse."

"I've been thinking," said Elkan. "We shall need one other thing – a tally. Nothing moves in the Souvian army without a tally."

Drin glared. "What's a tally?"

"It's made of two flat sheets of wood tied together," said Elkan. "On the inside the officer writes who is being sent where. The proper name for it is a movement order. Without one of those we will be stopped and arrested at the first checkpoint."

"Why didn't you say this before?"

"I'm awfully sorry but I've only just remembered it."

Drin looked at the three soldiers standing in line before us, bare-headed with their hands tied behind their backs.

"Right. Listen to this. You will show me, first, where the Dangoy hostages are, and, second, where the commander's room is. Come on. We're going inside."

He turned to Saori and me. "See if you can find horses and uniforms while Elkan and I work out this tally business."

Saori and I piled up the helmets and jerkins belonging to the Souvians we had captured, and then went inside and looked around until we found an armoury where the Souvians kept spare weapons and uniforms. We picked out the biggest helmet, tunic and jerkin we could find for Drin, as well as uniforms for me and Elkan, took them outside and added them to the pile. Then we looked in the stables and found two horses, but when we led them out it was obvious that one of them was lame. We saddled up the good horse and lined it up with the three mounts of the Souvians who had escorted us from the village. Then we gave all five horses food and water.

It seemed like an age before Drin and Elkan came out of the building. With them were four Dangoy women, still dressed in their furs. Elkan was talking rapidly to them in their own language, but they seemed to be arguing with him. At last he said to us: "I'm afraid that they refuse to leave. They're convinced that if they do, their whole village will be destroyed by the soldiers. I have done my best to explain the situation, but to no avail."

Drin had a look like thunder, but it was not the stubbornness of the Dangoy women which was bothering him. "Never mind them. Show this tally thing to Chaemon."

"Yes, of course. Chaemon, do please have a look at this. Do you think it will pass muster?"

I took from Elkan the wooden tally and looked at the writing inside. It said that three soldiers were being sent urgently with a prisoner to Commissioner Nostoc in the General Headquarters outside Banjut and they should be given all assistance.

"I based it on some old ones which we found in the commander's room, and Drin made the soldier show us where they kept his seal. I inserted Nostoc's name because everyone is frightened of him. Quite a nice piece of handiwork, don't you think?" Elkan was obviously pleased with himself.

"I've never seen a tally before," I said, "but this looks official. Where did you get these names from? Banseltas, Marjomon and Gandash. Which of us is which?"

"Those are the names of real soldiers. I chose to be Gandash, and Drin is Banseltas, so you have to be Marjomon."

"And who is Saori?"

"The name of the prisoner is a state secret. She will have to keep her hood on so that nobody can see who she is."

"All this stuff's too small," said Drin. "Is this all you could find? And one of the horses is lame."

I hastened to explain to Drin what we had found, and he struggled into the largest helmet and jerkin. It was probably a good thing that he had shaved off his hair and beard because otherwise the helmet might not have fitted.

"I wish we didn't have to put on this stuff," he said. "And I hate this nonsense about tallies. I don't know why Elkan loves it so much – orders on bits of wood and pretending to be someone I'm not."

Elkan sighed and shook his head.

"Where did you find the hostages?" I asked.

"They were stuffed into a small jail cell. We've put the soldiers in there instead. Serves them right. But where have the hostages gone? And where's Saori?"

We all looked round and saw the Dangoy women standing by the gate and smiling as each of them embraced Saori in turn.

Elkan talked with them and then said to us: "I don't know what magic Saori has used, but they all seem quite happy now and they want to go home to their families. They're sure the Souvians will never find them in the woods."

So we bade them farewell and sent them on their way.

Before we ourselves set off, Elkan annoyed Drin even more by checking that he and I were wearing our Souvian uniforms properly, and even Saori protested when he brought out a large pin and fixed it across her hood so that there was only a small hole left for her to look out of. When he was satisfied, we mounted our horses and rode out on a track leading away from the village and the river.

I felt rather elated. Drin's plan had worked perfectly. We

had taken the fort, freed the hostages and acquired Souvian uniforms and horses. Perhaps Elkan was right and the gods were on our side. I knew that when the real Souvians returned to the fort and found what we had done, they would be furious and determined to get their revenge – but they would have to catch us first.

We passed through small valleys nestling among low, forested hills with scattered farms, and we made good progress. The first time that we had to halt was when our track met a larger road where a few bored soldiers were manning a checkpoint. Elkan showed them our tally, and they waved us through without reading it. "We passed our first test," he said with an air of triumph.

Much the same happened at a second checkpoint, and it was nearing midday when we came to a more open area where the land was flatter and cultivated in small fields. The road led straight to a walled town perched on top of a small rise. We could see men hard at work ploughing the fields with oxen under the warm sun. But the road itself was empty. Whenever anyone coming along it saw us, he or she immediately turned off into the fields and watched us from a safe distance. Such was the fear which Souvian soldiers inspired. I hated it. I wanted to call out to the people not to be afraid. But we had to stick with our disguise, and so we rode on as if it was normal for people to run away at the very sight of us.

"It's risky going into the town," Drin said. "If your tally doesn't work…"

"Don't worry," said Elkan. "Nothing will go wrong. If there is a garrison here, we can ask for fresh horses. Leave it all to me."

A small contingent of soldiers greeted us at the gate of

the town, and Elkan said: "We are on an urgent mission. Where can we get fresh horses?"

"Hold on a minute," one of them said. "First, we need to check your movement order, and then we might get onto the question of horses."

"As you can see," said Elkan, handing it over, "we have orders to escort this prisoner to Commissioner Nostoc with the utmost speed."

The soldier, who seemed to be the officer in charge, looked at the tally. "All the way from Dangoy-land to Commissioner Nostoc at GHQ. That's interesting. Now, which one of you is Banseltas?"

There was a silence. Drin must have forgotten his new name, I thought; now what do we do? But just as I was beginning to panic, he thundered out: "I am Banseltas."

"And Marjomon?"

"That's me," I said.

"So you must be Gandash."

Elkan nodded.

"It's funny: I'm sure I've met you before somewhere, but I can't quite think where."

"No, we have never met," said Elkan rather stiffly.

"But I'm sure we have. There's something about your voice that's familiar. I expect it'll come back to me in a moment or two. Anyway, what's the name of the prisoner?"

"I am not authorised to reveal that," Elkan said.

"Then pull back his hood so as I can see his face."

"That too is not authorised."

"Top secret. Very mysterious. But you can't stop us being curious, can you? Have you found that girl Nostoc's been looking for? There is a big reward out for her."

"As our orders make clear, we are in a hurry. May we now proceed?"

"That's it. You're from Valosia, aren't you? I can hear it in your voice. That's where we must have met. I'm from Valosia myself, born and bred. Finest little country in the world, it was."

"You are right," said Elkan. "Valosia was a fine country."

"Everything's different now of course. We serve the Great Leader now. But it's funny you're called Gandash. Belpano, that's me; you only have to hear my name to know where I come from. But Gandash – that's not a Valosian name, is it? How'd you get a name like that?"

Elkan did not respond, and I became anxious again. We had to find an explanation and find one quickly. And then it came to me: "His parents moved to Valosia when he was little."

"That's right," said Elkan. "I was a baby at the time."

The officer said something in a language I did not understand.

"Now that we are in the army," said Elkan, "we should use the common language."

"I suppose you're right. Then tell me: what did your father do, in the old days in Valosia?"

"He was in the service of the king," said Elkan.

"Up in the palace? Very grand. But wait a minute. Talking of the king, maybe that's it. It's funny, but your voice sounds like his. It's hard to tell with the helmet on, but you look a bit like him too."

"Nonsense. I am nothing like the king. Nothing at all."

"I wonder what became of him after he ran away."

"Who knows?"

"Good riddance! That's what I say!" said the officer. "Well, we mustn't delay the important work of Commissioner Nostoc, must we? When you get to the garrison at the end of the street on the left, give them this, and you'll get your horses."

With that we rode on down the main street of the town, and everyone moved quickly out of our way. About halfway along we came to a large statue which looked like the one in the village by the river, but bigger and carved with more skill.

"We had better dismount," said Elkan. "This is Mangra whom the Souvian army worship. If we want to keep up our disguise, we shall have to pretend to pray to him."

"What kind of god is he supposed to be?" I asked. "The god of murder?"

"Keep your voice down! We must bow twice and clap our hands three times."

"Not me," said Saori. "I will not bow to that."

"Then you can be excused," said Elkan, "as a prisoner, but the rest of us must honour the god."

So Elkan, Drin and I bowed and clapped. Then we rode to the garrison building, where after further delay we were at last given fresh horses.

"Let's get out of here," said Drin, "before we meet any more of Elkan's old friends."

We all agreed with that and headed out to the eastern gate. But when we got there, it was closed, and a ring of soldiers was waiting. Belpano was standing next to an older, thick-set officer, who shouted: "Stop! You will not leave this town until you've answered some questions."

"Yes," added Belpano. "We have reason to believe that you are not who you say you are. This man is not called Gandash, and the rest of you are also using false names. The penalty for impersonating soldiers of the Souvian army is death. You are all under arrest, and after interrogation, you will be executed."

Chapter 16

Souvian Escort

~

D rin was silently cursing himself. He had let Elkan lead us into a trap, and he could see no escape. Right from the beginning he had distrusted Elkan: everything about him was fake. He made speeches about wanting to help "Alamanda", but they were all lies, and this was the proof. Drin felt his sword-hilt, but he knew that we could not fight our way out. He wished that we had left Elkan locked up with the Souvian soldiers in the fort, but now it was too late. The worst thing was that he had let Saori down and put her in danger again, and all because Elkan had seemed to know all the answers.

Certainly he seemed full of confidence now. "What nonsense is this?" he said. "How dare you make such absurd allegations? We are on an urgent mission to Commissioner Nostoc. Let us through."

"Remove your helmets," said the commander. "And get off your horses!"

"What right have you to give such orders?" said Elkan. "If you think we have done something wrong, show us your evidence."

"All right. I will. You say your name is Gandash. Is that correct?"

"Yes, of course."

The commander turned to one of his men. "Soldier, tell him what you told me."

"Yes, sir," said the soldier. "My name is Stambush, sir, and Gandash and I grew up together, in Coroscania, sir. The last I heard, sir, he'd been posted to Kundulbatin."

"And is this man here Gandash?"

"No, sir. He's older and thinner, and he talks different, sir."

"So, my friend," the commander was addressing Elkan again, "who are you? And why are you pretending to be somebody else?"

"I am Gandash. Do you think there is only one soldier called Gandash in the whole of the Souvian army?"

"Enough of your lies! I ordered you to get off your horses. Dismount! Or I'll order my men to shoot."

Elkan looked round in a rather nervous way and swung off his horse onto the ground. The rest of us did the same.

"Remove your helmets!"

We did as we were told.

"Drop your weapons!"

As he obeyed, Drin remembered giving these same orders to the soldiers in the fort. He expected that the next order would be to remove the prisoner's hood. But then Elkan spoke to the commander in a new, quieter tone: "General, is there somewhere private where you and I could talk to each other, just the two of us? The truth is that I am engaged in a rather sensitive mission, and you have left me no choice but to explain certain things to you."

"If you have something to say, say it here."

"I am afraid that that would not be possible. My orders are very precise, and I am only authorised to reveal this information to a senior officer in strictest confidence when there is no possible alternative."

"Search him!" said the commander. "Make sure he has no concealed weapons."

Elkan was made to remove his jerkin and boots, and then he was carefully checked all over.

"Follow me."

The commander led Elkan over to the gatehouse, and they disappeared inside with Belpano.

"I don't trust him," Drin said quietly. "He's up to some trick with the Souvians."

"He's a clever man," I replied. "Maybe he's got a plan to trick them."

Drin shook his head. He was even more sure now that Elkan was betraying us. Why else would he ask for a secret meeting? But with armed Souvians all around us, there was nothing we could do except wait. He began to wonder who Elkan really was. A Valosian for sure, but was he the king who had run away? Or was that yet another false trail in this web of deceit? Either way, Drin thought, the sooner we can get away from him, the better.

At last the commander and Elkan emerged from the gatehouse with Belpano.

"What happened?" I asked Elkan when he came over to join us. "Will they let us go?"

"I have persuaded the commander to let us leave the town and continue on our way," he replied.

"So we're free. That's brilliant."

"Well, not quite. The commander has added one condition. From here until we reach our destination, we shall be accompanied for our own safety by Captain Belpano and two Hands of cavalry."

Drin's anger boiled over. Elkan had arranged an armed guard to deliver us all to Nostoc! So that was his game! Drin clenched his fist: he was going to punch Elkan's lying face!

But somehow Saori had sensed what was going through his mind and gently touched his arm. Drin's spasm of fury passed, and his body relaxed; but he was still angry at Elkan, who said quietly: "Be careful, Banseltas. Remember where we are."

"What did you tell them in there?" asked Drin.

"I'm very sorry, but that must remain a secret."

Drin silently cursed again.

As we resumed our journey, now with our Souvian escort, we made even better progress than we had before. Their new movement order convinced every guard post to let us through without question. At every station on the road we obtained fresh horses without difficulty and could even enjoy freshly cooked meals. Each night we stayed in a military rest-house, and Elkan insisted that Saori be given her own room so that she could eat, sleep and wash on her own and nobody would learn her identity.

Yet Drin, Saori and I hated being with the Souvians. To

start with, they picked on me and pushed me around, and when Drin threatened to punch one of them if the bullying did not stop, they dared him to go ahead because he could be executed for striking a fellow soldier. It was only when Elkan told Belpano to keep his men in order that they backed off, and after that we kept an uneasy silence with them. Meanwhile Elkan and Belpano appeared to become best friends: they talked together in their own Valosian language and sometimes burst into laughter at some joke which no one else could understand. I could see that this was making Drin even more angry with Elkan, though I myself thought that maybe he was trying to lull the Souvians into a false sense of security. I wished we could talk about how to escape from them, but we were never left alone.

On the second day we joined a major road, which ran northwards back towards the river, and on the third day we came to a large town with a bridge and crossed to the northern bank. We were now on the same East-West road which the Akondian traders had used to travel with their pack horses from Gate B to Banjut. Belpano spoke proudly of the Souvian road system, which enabled them to send messengers and even whole units of the army rapidly from one end of their empire to the other. Everything was governed by the tally system, and by listening to what he said, I deduced that there were four speeds. The slowest was called "routine" and was used for supply carts and waggons. Next was "priority" for regular troop movements. Our tally was graded "immediate", which allowed us to overtake everyone on the road. The fastest was "flash", and when as a joke Elkan said he wished we had one of those, Belpano became serious and told us that a flash message could only be addressed to Zeno himself and must be of exceptional importance and urgency. If Zeno judged the message not to merit the flash status, the officer who sent it would be executed. Flash messengers were always sent in pairs so that if one had an accident the other could still go on. Along their journey they had to be provided with the fastest horses and given food and water immediately, and they even had the right to take someone else's horse if they needed it. Their sole mission was to get their message to Zeno as fast as humanly possible.

One evening, when we were eating in a rest-house, Elkan started to talk to an officer journeying in the opposite direction from us and asked about the situation in Banjut. The officer gave what, for us, was bad news. He said the city was completely encircled by Souvian forces on the landward side, and nothing was allowed in or out. They did not control the seaward side, but they did control all the ports along the coast and were preventing any boats from leaving harbour. He was sure that Banjut was running out of food and would soon be captured, and the blue-coats punished in the name of Mangra.

As we went on, we passed work-parties of slaves who were widening the road or building new checkpoints. Most of them were women and children with a few old men, and all looked exhausted and half-starving; but their Souvian overseers were fat and well-fed. They kept shouting at the slaves to work harder and beating them with sticks if they flagged. There were bodies too, lying unburied, of slaves who had been executed by the overseers or simply died from exhaustion and starvation. Once or twice I had a strong urge to seize one of the whips and use it on the Souvian who was thrashing a poor slave, but I knew that we could not afford to do that, or our own true identity would be exposed. I was sure that Saori would not be able to bear the sight of such cruelty, but fortunately her hood prevented her from seeing anything to the sides, and she rode on in silence.

One day we were having our midday meal when Drin asked: "We must be getting close to the main army now. How much longer till we reach HQ?"

"At this pace," said Belpano, "we should have the pleasure of Commissioner Nostoc's company before nightfall tomorrow. Gandash, what do you think he'll say when we deliver our prisoner to him safe and sound?"

"I am sure that he will give us a generous reward," said Elkan, and Belpano gave a greedy laugh.

After that it was clearer than ever that we were hastening to our doom. If we did not find some way to escape, Belpano and his men would hand us over to Nostoc.

That afternoon we were going along a straight stretch of road when Saori's horse went lame. Belpano examined its leg and said that there was nothing wrong with it, but when Saori mounted her horse again, it began again to limp. Drin went over, checked the leg, talked to the horse and walked it up and down, but it was no good. Saori and I had to double up on another horse, but we could not go as fast, and as the sun began to set, we were still well short of the official rest-house where the Souvians had been planning to spend the night.

We ended up in an ordinary inn, which was next to a bridge over a broad stream, a tributary of the Banjut river. It was a big old wooden building with rooms on three storeys. On the side near the river there were stables around a courtyard. Drin and Saori spent a few minutes together there examining her horse before she was taken off to her room for the night, and he stayed in the stables for some time after that before coming in and joining the rest of us for the evening meal. In the rest-houses we had all slept in one big dormitory, but in the inn the rooms were smaller, and we were split up; somehow Drin and I managed to get the room closest to the ladder which led downstairs.

"Wait until they've all gone to sleep," he whispered to me in Akondian as we lay down that night, and I waited in the pitch-dark listening to the sounds of the Souvians snoring in the other rooms until Drin lightly touched my shoulder. We crept out onto the landing, but as we turned to climb down the ladder, the floor creaked under my foot, and my heart jumped, but the snoring continued as before. We felt our way down, scarcely daring to breathe. In the room below, where we had eaten, a few embers were still glowing red in the hearth. Drin stirred the fire and lit a wooden torch from it, and by its light we headed out into the courtyard.

To my surprise, the horses in the first three stables were already saddled and ready to go. Drin brought them out and gave me the reins. He slung his bag onto one of them and said: "Take them round to the other side of the inn. Saori'll be waiting for you there."

Then he thrust his torch into the straw and ran along, opening the doors of the stalls one by one, letting out the startled horses and setting fire to their stables. From the inn came a shout: "Fire! Fire!", and Drin yelled: "Save the horses!", but as he did so, a dark figure ran out and hurled itself on top of him, and I could see the two of them fighting by the light of the blazing fire. Drin would have to look after himself, I thought; I had better do what he had told me.

I pulled the three saddled horses and ran out of the courtyard and round the building. Behind me I could hear more shouting and hear and smell the burning straw and wood. "Fire! Save the horses!" Flames were rising up into the sky. Loose horses came galloping out and ran across the bridge into the night. It was all I could do to keep my horses from joining them, but somehow I made them follow me round the corner, away from the fire and commotion. We hurried round to the far side of the inn, where it was still quiet and dark.

"Saori!" I called as loudly as I dared. "Saori!"

"Chaemon!" came the reply, but I could not see her anywhere. "I'm up here, at the window. They locked my door. I cannot come out."

I looked up and saw against the sky the silhouette of a head poking out of a second-floor window. Now what should I do?

There were lights inside the inn, and men shouting. Horses whinnied in fear and their hooves clattered along the road. A woman screamed and doors banged. The fire had woken everyone up: any minute now I and my horses were sure to be found.

As I tried to think what to do, Drin came round the corner, out of breath.

"Where's Saori?" he asked.

"Up there," I said. "She's locked in her room. Hold the horses and I'll go in and get her out."

"No time for that. Saori, throw down your robe, the one the queen gave you."

A moment later the dress, Saori's most treasured possession, dropped to the ground in a ball beside us. My mother had had it made specially for her out of the finest woollen cloth.

"Chaemon, you take one side, and I'll take the other. Saori, climb out of the window and jump. Brace yourself, Chaemon."

I wrapped my side of the dress round my arms to get as strong a grip as I could. I hoped it would be strong enough to break Saori's fall, and I would be strong enough to hold it firmly. I braced myself with my weight leaning outwards.

"There you are!" said a familiar voice. It was Elkan, who had suddenly appeared round the corner. "I thought I might find you here."

"Grab a corner of this," said Drin. "We've got to catch Saori. Pull hard."

Elkan did as he was told. We saw a dark shape emerge from the window and hang down from the sill.

"I jump now," she cried.

We saw her body for a second before her weight struck the dress. The cloth held, but I was pulled forwards and nearly fell on top of her on the ground.

"Are you all right?" Drin asked Saori.

"Yes, I think so."

We got up and stood together in the pale light of the quarter moon.

"Then let's go!"

"But there are only three horses," said Elkan.

Drin said nothing but punched him hard on the side of the head, and Elkan crumpled and fell to the ground.

"Drin!" cried Saori. "You hit him!"

"We're better off without him. Let's go!"

Saori hesitated for a moment, but Drin repeated: "Let's go!" with even more urgency, and she mounted her horse, and we rode out onto the road. There were horses everywhere, and it was hard at first to thread our way through them, but we headed away from the bridge towards the west. Someone shouted behind us, but we paid no attention. We just galloped off down the road as fast as we could.

Chapter 17

The Moor

~

After we had left the inn well behind, Drin led us off the main road onto a track leading north. We had to slow down here because it was hard to see where we were going, but Drin seemed to have eyes which could see in the dark, and we followed him. All I could work out was that we were going through an area of pastures where cattle and sheep were kept, and that the track was steadily leading us uphill. As we went on, it narrowed until it was more like an animal's trail than a human path, and soon we had to dismount and lead the horses in single file. But we pressed doggedly on, tripping over stones and roots as we went. It grew colder, and I began to feel tired and hungry.

At length Drin called a halt and said we had better get some sleep until dawn. He and I no longer had our Souvian helmets or jerkins, and we put on our own clothes to keep warm. We could not see anywhere to seek shelter, but I could feel that the ground was covered by feathery plants, as high as our knees and spreading out all around us.

Suddenly Saori said: "I'm so happy. We've left the Souvians behind. No more hood. No more Belpano. No more being a prisoner. Drin, you've saved us again! But... Well... I can't help worrying about Elkan..."

"I'm sorry," said Drin. "I'm sorry if that's upset you, but it was the only way to get rid of him quickly. We can't trust him. We don't even know who he really is."

"I bet he's the king who ran away," I said.

"I don't think he's the sort of man who runs away," said Saori.

"Anyway," said Drin, "we're better off without him. What worries me is the horses. I tried to let them all escape, but Belpano jumped me, and I ran out of time."

"How did you get away from him?" I asked.

"Stuck my knife in his leg," said Drin.

"There were lots of horses running around," said Saori. "I'm sure it was all right."

"Let's hope so," said Drin. "Better get some sleep now."

When Drin woke me, I still felt tired and hungry, but the darkness had been replaced by a grey, misty light. Gently he woke Saori too, and we looked around. It was a barren scene. We were in a broad, shallow bowl of land, which was covered all over by the brown, straggly plants on which we had slept. Around the edges of it and above our heads we could see only thick grey cloud. There was no sign of anything made by man, no track, no wall or gate, no sign even of an animal.

"Has anyone got any food?" I asked. "I'm starving."

We looked in our bags but found only a few small flat loaves and some fruit, which we shared. The next thing should have been water for ourselves and the horses, but there was no sign of a stream or pool. None of us talked much. It felt eerie to be surrounded by the mist, as if at any moment, an enemy army might emerge silently from the grey mirk and catch us unawares. Almost anything might be out there, invisible eyes watching us greedily while we were blinded by the fog.

At last Drin decided that he could just make out the direction of the sun, and we headed off towards what he judged to be the north-east, away from the road but still in the direction of the sea. We urged the horses forward through the plants but quickly found that their hooves were sinking into an area of soft black mud. We led them round the bog onto drier land, but again and again, just as we thought we had found a straight, dry route, we would stumble into another mire and have to make another detour to get round it; and all around us the same expanse of plants stretched out, featureless, to the same wall of cloud. Twice, a round bird startled us by flying off with a loud call which sounded like "Go back! Go back!". But we could not go back now: there was no way to be sure which way we had come. I began to worry that we were not heading in a consistent direction but going round and round in circles, and we would never find our way out of the bogs and mist.

At length Drin stopped and said it was probably about midday. We sat and rested but had nothing to eat or drink. Even Saori had lost her bright smile.

"What is this place?" I complained. "No sun. No water. Just grey sky, scratchy plants, filthy mud."

"This is the moor," said Drin. He was talking quietly as if someone might overhear. "Some of the traders in Banjut used to talk about it. They came from the north, and they used to claim that the moor made their road out of Banjut even harder than ours over the mountain, not that any of them had ever been anywhere near the mountain, of course. They said the moor was covered with a plant – I think they called it 'heather' or something like that – which the horses couldn't eat, and full of bogs where a man might sink in and not be able to get out. They said it was always covered in mist so that even a man who'd been there many times could still get lost and never be seen again. We thought they were making it up, just to show off as people do."

"The moor," I said. "I remember reading about that."

"Did you read about the way to get out of it?" asked Saori.

"No. I'm afraid not. The thing I read was about a priest from Hoxxkorn called Quafteq. He was a most unusual man. Shall I tell you his story?"

No one replied, and I liked the story, so I continued.

"Quafteq was a very holy man, who lived hundreds of years ago, and one day he decided to come to the moor to purify himself. He spent 40 days here without eating, and he drank only rain water and dew, and while he meditated and prayed to the gods, for 40 days the mist surrounded him, and he couldn't see the sun. He grew thinner and thinner, and weaker and weaker, and his spirit became more and more pure as his bodily strength faded away. At last, when he was on the verge of death, the gods took pity on him and came down to talk to him in the mist. When they first appeared before his eyes, he feared that he would be punished for daring to look at them, but they told him not to worry, and they revealed all kinds of wisdom about the universe, life after death and the future of mankind.

"On the 40th day the mist cleared, and the sun shone brightly, and Quafteq understood that it was time to go back to Hoxxkorn and record the extraordinary things which the gods had told him. He wrote them down on copper sheets, which are now the most treasured possessions of the Hoxxkorn priests. Only four of them are allowed to read them, two men and two women. Whenever one of them dies, the other three choose his or her successor very carefully, and the newcomer's training includes a spell out here on the moor. Who knows? Perhaps if we stayed here long enough, and our souls became as clear as running water, we might meet the gods too."

"It's a nice story," said Saori, and at last she was smiling, "but I don't want to stay in this place for 40 days."

So we set off again, and carried on tramping across the moor all afternoon. The same brown plants, wet bogs and grey mist continued, but now it began to drizzle and gradually became colder and wetter; and as night fell, we were still out in the open with no shelter and forced again to sleep on the heather. The next morning we were tired, hungry, thirsty, cold and damp, but there was no choice but to push on. We began to worry about the horses, who were thirsty and hungry too, and I kept returning to the thought that, in spite of Drin's confidence in his navigation, we were actually going round in circles. But eventually we had proof that we were making some kind of progress when we saw in front of us a slightly steeper valley which we had certainly not been to before.

"Stop!" said Saori. "I can hear water." She was right: there was a tiny rivulet of yellowish water trickling down the slope to our left. We drank, and the horses drank, and we followed the water downhill where the flow was a little greater, and all of us drank again. Perhaps, just perhaps, we thought, the little brook would lead us down off the moor to somewhere with green fields and houses – but our hopes were soon dashed. It flowed into the largest bog we had yet encountered, and we struggled to find a way round it.

That night as we lay down to sleep, I felt unusually tired, my joints ached and my head was heavy. The damp seemed not only to have soaked through my clothes but into my bones as well. I fell quickly into a sound sleep, but even in the morning I did not feel my usual self. Even so, I was determined not to be the weak link this time and battled on without a word to the others.

I had been cold when I awoke, but by midday I was boiling with an unnatural heat, and I began to take off my coat and other warm clothes as we walked along. I felt even more tired now, and I began to stumble and sway. Somehow we agreed that I would ride one of the horses, which Drin would lead, and that was easier for a while, but at last I must have fainted and fallen off the horse onto the heather, because I found myself looking up into Drin and Saori's worried faces.

I felt a hand on my forehead. "He feels as if he's on fire," said Saori.

They began to talk about me as if I was not there, and I did not have the strength to interrupt. It was a jumble of phrases: "… get him something to drink… go on ahead… get him off the moor… just have to rest here…" I lay back on the heather and I must have slept.

When I next awoke, it was dark all around, and everything

was still. My head was clear, but I could not move my limbs, and I knew exactly what was going to happen: I was going to die. Out here on the moor my spirit would be freed from my body and travel to a new place, free from the pain and temptations of this world. I was glad I had come on this journey with Drin and Saori, but in the end I had to accept that I was more suited for the library than for adventure. I lay back in the cold heather, looked up at the dark cloud and waited for the end.

As I did so, I spotted a faint light far above my head – a star, I thought, and then remembered that the stars were blotted out by the mist. It grew brighter and larger and came down towards me, and I had no fear of it. As it came closer, I began to see that it was shaped like the flame of a candle and within the flame was the figure of a woman. She was not young, but not old either, and she had long curling hair billowing out around her. She was dressed in a long cloak, which seemed to be in motion, like a fountain of water which was flowing down from her shoulders to her feet in a series of waves. I tried to make out her face, but however close she came and however hard I looked, her features escaped me. At one moment I thought she was a little like my mother, until a second later she looked more like Saori, but then again she looked older. Was this how Saori would look in the future? But then I lost it again, and the face changed, and I could not make it out.

"Who are you?" I asked.

But there was no reply.

"Please tell me who you are."

But she remained silent, and I realised my mistake in asking the question.

"I'm sorry. I meant no harm."

But to this too there was no reply.

"Have you come to take me to another world? Is this what death is like?"

And now at last she spoke, though whether I heard what she said or simply absorbed it in some way in my mind, I am still not sure.

"You are the one I chose."

This frightened me, just for a moment, and my spine tingled: then I tried to understand what she meant.

"You chose me? But why? I'm not much use. I'm going to die."

There was no reply, and I foolishly persisted: "I'm not a fighter like my father. I'm not strong like Drin. I can't even shoot straight like Hargon. Why me?"

"Yet you are the one I chose."

"It's something to do with Saori, isn't it? I promise I'll do my best to help her."

But there was only silence, as the lady and the light around her began to rise up into the sky, until once again she was no more than a tiny dot of light, and I strained to see her, and then she disappeared altogether, and everything was dark again.

Chapter 18

The Sea

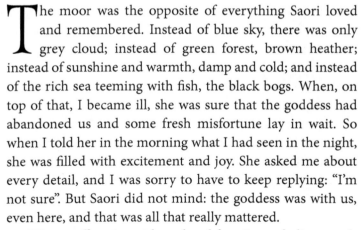

The moor was the opposite of everything Saori loved and remembered. Instead of blue sky, there was only grey cloud; instead of green forest, brown heather; instead of sunshine and warmth, damp and cold; and instead of the rich sea teeming with fish, the black bogs. When, on top of that, I became ill, she was sure that the goddess had abandoned us and some fresh misfortune lay in wait. So when I told her in the morning what I had seen in the night, she was filled with excitement and joy. She asked me about every detail, and I was sorry to have to keep replying: "I'm not sure". But Saori did not mind: the goddess was with us, even here, and that was all that really mattered.

We set off again, without breakfast. I was feeling much better than the day before and insisted on walking, but after a while Drin said I should rest and once again he put me on a horse and led it forward. It was about midday when suddenly he brought us to a halt. Far off in the silence of the mist we could hear men's voices and the rattle of waggons. "At last!" Drin said. "It's the road. We've finally reached the road from Banjut to the north."

He went forward to have a look while Saori and I waited with the horses, but when he came back, he looked even more grim-faced than usual.

"It is the road, all right, and it's full of soldiers, waggons and horses. They keep on coming without a break, in both directions. We'll have to wait for nightfall if we're to cross it safely."

We sat on the heather, and Drin told us his plan. When the men made their camps for the night, we would look out for a gap and run across without being seen. Since we could not do that with the horses, and since anyway it was unfair to keep the horses on the moor any longer without food, we would have to set them free. Drin was sure that someone on the road would look after them. He would take them further up the road and let them go so as not to give our position away. Saori and I were happy with this, and we all rested until it grew dark.

Then Drin took the horses off, and Saori and I moved closer to the road without being seen and looked for a gap between the camps. I felt more tired again and hungry, but filled with courage by the thought of the goddess. An owl called, but we knew that it was Drin, and when I returned the call, he found us at the spot we had chosen for the crossing. Everything was quiet. There were no human voices or any other sound. The world was asleep, or so it seemed.

I sneezed.

"Shh!" said Saori. We listened anxiously in case anyone had heard me, but everything was still silent.

I sneezed again.

"Here, use this," she said quietly and gave me a handkerchief made of some fine material.

"Thank you. I'm sorry. I couldn't help it."

I wiped my nose and stuffed the handkerchief into my pocket.

All remained silent, and as far as we could judge, the road was clear. When Drin whispered "Go!", we all ran down the slope as fast as we could. The road at the bottom was raised up higher than the land on either side, and as we reached it, I tripped on the bank and fell to the ground. A dog began to bark in the distance. I got to my feet. A man's voice yelled: "What's the matter?" I found Drin's big hand grabbing my arm, and we began to run again. We ran for our lives – as if a leopard was pawing at our heels – and we carried on running up the slope on the other side and over the heather until I could run no more. I was drawing in great gulps of air, and even Drin was panting.

"What happened?" asked Saori.

"I'm sorry, I tripped," I said and sneezed again. I felt in my pocket for the handkerchief, but it was not there.

"I dropped the handkerchief," I said. "I'm really sorry. It might be on the road. It might give away who we are. I'm very sorry. I'm completely useless."

"No, you're not useless," said Saori. "You are chosen – remember?"

"The main thing is we got across the road," said Drin. "But we'd better keep going, just in case."

We started off again through the heather. The ground was

more broken on this side of the road with steeper slopes and higher ridges, and we found more streams running down the shallow valleys so that we were able to drink as much as we wanted. After a while Drin said that even he was not sure of the right direction, and so we rested until daybreak and then set off again. We went eastwards now since we were sure that we were well north of Banjut, and we stopped from time to time to listen for any sound of men pursuing us, but we never saw or heard anyone at all.

Sometime after midday we noticed that the ground was gradually sloping downwards in front of us, and the mist was slightly less dense. The heather became patchier and was mixed with areas of grass. We began to move faster, and that was nearly our undoing, because suddenly in the mist we came to the edge of a cliff and had to stop sharply before we went over. A pair of black birds flew off and startled us with their calls of "Chaow!". Carefully we peered over the edge, but all we could see was a steep drop and then the mist below. It felt almost as if we had reached the end of the world, and I shivered with an imaginary dread.

Drin pulled us back to reality.

"Left or right?" he asked. "North or south?"

"Banjut is south," said Saori.

"But so's Zeno," I said.

"Then we go north," she decided.

We moved back from the edge and walked parallel to it on the short grass, still surrounded by the walls of damp mist. We kept looking for a way to go down, but there was no sign that even a goat had tried to descend, until at last we came to a spot where the edge had slipped in a landslide and the earth was tumbled in piles of soil and rocks beneath us.

Gingerly we climbed down. It was not easy to find a route because the earth had fallen in a series of giant steps rather than an even slope and we risked breaking a leg or twisting an ankle whenever we had to jump from one level to another.

"Look!" said Saori suddenly, and I turned my eyes up from my feet and looked out at the view. We had descended below the level of the mist, which remained as a white ceiling above us, and for the first time in five days we could see a long way off. The cliffs formed a broad semicircle, and between them was a grey, flat, heaving mass with flecks of white, which stretched far off into the distance.

"The sea!" Saori could hardly contain her excitement. It was not the clean blue water of home, but it was still unmistakeably the sea. After so many months crossing plains, mountains, hills and finally the moor, she had arrived back at the sea, and nothing now lay between her and home but water.

"Come on!" she cried. "Let's go down."

Immediately below us was a flat area of sand in the shape of a semicircle. It met the sea in a straight line of white foam, and all around it the cliffs rose up steeply without a break.

"Look! There's a boat." Saori was pointing to the water's edge where a keeled boat with a small cabin was leaning on the sand. It was so far below us that it looked like a toy. "That could be just what we need."

She was jumping down the cliff now at great speed. "Be careful!" Drin called after her, but she paid no attention, and he and I followed her as fast as we dared. As soon as she reached the bottom, Saori ran out across the beach and into the water splashing and jumping and calling out: "The sea! Come on! It's the sea!"

Drin and I looked round cautiously. There was a shack

under the cliff, which looked as if it had been made of old boat-timbers for none of its planks was straight and the roof was shaped like a boat turned upside down. We could not see anyone around, and Saori was still calling for us to join her, so Drin and I dropped our bags and walked out onto the beach as well. It felt oddly exposed out there with the cliffs looking down on us all around and nowhere to hide, but I was curious to know what the sea was like. The waves came onto the shore with a quiet roar and a splash of foam before they drew back again, and Drin and I stood together at the water's edge looking out, until suddenly a bigger wave pushed further up the beach and made our feet wet. So this was the sea. I had read so much about it that it felt familiar and strange at the same time. I tasted it, and it was salty. I drank in the smell, which no writer could describe, and I enjoyed watching Saori as she cavorted around and splashed us. I had never seen her look so happy.

"We'd better look at this boat," Drin said, practical as ever, and we gathered round to check if it was seaworthy. Saori crawled underneath and tapped the planks as Drin and I watched her. Everything seemed to be in good order. With a boat like this, we should be able to sail round to Banjut in spite of the Souvian blockade. It seemed as if the goddess really was watching over us.

"Quite a smart little craft, ain't she?" said a strange voice from behind us.

We wheeled round and saw three men on the beach. Saori screamed, ran over to Drin and buried her head in his back. Her arms were clamped round his waist, and she stayed there sobbing.

"Dubash!" said Drin. "What are you doing here?"

Chapter 19

10,000 Juts

~

"It's Drin, ain't it?" said Dubash. "And you've got the girl with the golden hair. I hope you've been looking after her properly, Drin, she's a valuable bit of property, that one is."

"Dubash! I never thought I'd see you again."

"Hello, darling. Why're you hiding behind Uncle Drin? Come out and say hello to your old friends. We don't mean you no harm."

Dubash was a lean, wiry man, with deep-set, blue eyes. His body was tense and restless: some part of him was always moving, as if he was preparing to dodge some imaginary missile. He was holding a long, curved dagger in his left hand. To the right of him was a huge bear of a man, a head taller than Drin. His legs were as thick as the pillars of a temple, and his head grew out of his shoulders without any obvious neck. He threatened us with a throwing lance and an expression of stupid hostility. On the left, the third man was an archer with strong shoulders and arms, and unlike Dubash, he was perfectly still. It was uncomfortable to feel his arrow aimed straight at us. The skin of all three looked as if it had been tanned by the salt wind and the sun until it was as tough as leather.

"Where's Goollen?" asked Drin.

"You remember Goollen? Poor old Goollen, a true seafarer he was. It was the money as did it, 880 juts, that's what we got, seemed like a lot of money at the time – 880."

"I shouldn't have paid one. Not to rats like you."

Up to now Dubash had kept his voice low, but suddenly he was shouting: "Rats, is it? You're the rat, Drin, it's your fault he's dead! You should've let Nostoc buy her, that's what you should've done, that's what caused all the trouble."

"Trouble?"

"It was Nostoc's men killed Goollen and stole the money, and all because he didn't get the girl. You better watch out, Drin, you're the one as got our shipmate killed, and we end up with nothing – nothing!"

"Nothing's what you deserve."

"880 juts." Dubash was speaking quietly again. "It seemed like a good price at the time, but now we know better. She's not just a slave, Zeno wants her very bad, and she's worth a lot more. 10,000, that's what Nostoc's offering now, and since you've been so kind as to come and visit us in our little cove here, 10,000 is what we're going to get."

"No, you won't," I said. "Do you really think Nostoc will pay you the money after what he did to Goollen?"

"Who are you?" Dubash asked, as if he had not noticed me until then.

"Chaemon."

"Kymon. And what exactly is Kymon?"

"I am a scholar."

"What's that?"

"I read and write and use my brain."

"So you're the brains. Is there a reward out for you?"

"Not as far as I know."

"Not even one jut?"

"No."

"Then you'd better shut up, hadn't you? Right! We're all going to walk slowly up the beach. No tricks, Drin, or you get an arrow in your guts."

"All right," said Drin. But Saori did not move. "Come on, Saori, we'd better go."

"You are not demons after all." She was speaking to Dubash, but it was as if she was talking to herself. "When I first saw you on the holy island, I thought you were evil spirits sent to punish us by an angry god. How else could you appear from nowhere? What else would look so ugly or smell so foul? Right up to the time when you ran off after the auction, I was certain you were devils in human form, and I was frightened of you. But now, here you are again – and there's nothing to you. You have no evil power. You are not demons any more, but only men."

"Yes, darling, that's right. It's like what you say, we're just ordinary sailors trying to scratch a living, nothing to be scared of. So why don't we all go up to the cabin, nice and easy?"

"But if you are only men, how did you become devils?" Saori stood staring at Dubash, lost in her own train of thought.

"That's all a bit beyond me, darling. But we can't stand here all day, can we?"

Drin touched her arm gently, she looked at him for reassurance, and the two of them began to walk up the beach. The rest of us followed, and we were ten yards from the wooden shack when Drin stopped and said: "Dubash, you should listen to Chaemon. You'll never get the money from Nostoc."

We all came to a halt. Dubash was just behind Drin, and Saori and I were a yard or two in front of him. To the right was the giant, and to the left the archer, and they raised their weapons again.

"Shut up, Drin," said Dubash. "Or this dagger'll slice off your blabby tongue. All right, lads. Wait here while I get some rope to tie 'em up."

"That will not be necessary." The words came from a tall, slim man, who appeared suddenly round the side of the house. He was holding a bow and arrow and aiming it straight at Dubash. To my surprise, it was Elkan – how had he got here? But there was no time to try to puzzle that out: things began to happen very fast.

The pirate with the strong arms swung round to shoot the intruder, but his arrow looped harmlessly up onto the roof of the cabin, and he toppled backwards with Elkan's arrow sticking out of his chest. Drin hurled himself onto Dubash, and within an instant they were grappling for control of the pirate's long dagger. The giant watched intently for a chance to hurl his lance at Drin and save his leader, but the fight was so furious that the chance never came, and he moved heavily from one foot to the other with the lance poised to strike. Saori and I hesitated for a moment, unsure what to do. "Out of the way!" shouted Elkan, and I took Saori's hand, and we ducked and scrambled over to the house. As we reached the door there was a great roar of pain behind us, and when we whirled round, we saw the lance fall to the ground and the giant clutching his throat where another of Elkan's arrows had hit its mark. All of us now ran to help Drin, but he got the better of Dubash without us and delivered him a mighty punch to the side of the head.

It took a moment to realise that the fight was over. We were safe. We had been saved by Elkan. But why, and how?

"We'd better check inside the cabin," he said. "Back me up."

Drin was searching Dubash for hidden weapons and found a small knife, which he stuck in his own belt. I took the bow from the archer's hands and an arrow from his quiver and went over to help Elkan, who was standing next to the door of the shack. Saori was gazing into the face of the giant, and I could only guess what she was thinking – about the scene on the island, about the boat and the long journey, about what it all meant. She shuddered as if she felt some evil spirit at work, unseen, but nearby.

Elkan slammed open the door and burst inside. I slipped inside also and stood with my back to the wall. Nothing happened. No wild sailor charged at us with a whirling axe. Nothing moved at all. I had expected to find a mess, with food, clothes and gear from the boat scattered around the dark room; but I was wrong. The cooking pots were lined up neatly beside the hearth; three sleeping spaces were laid out on the sand; and all the men's belongings were hanging tidily on the walls. "Shipshape": I remembered the word from one of the stories I had read. Even these pirates kept things shipshape. But no amount of reading could have prepared me for the smell.

"Pooh! It stinks!" I said.

Elkan pointed upwards. "Fish being dried," he said.

Above our heads, on long poles, were hanging row after row of silvery fish. I went back outside for some fresh air, and Elkan followed.

"There's nobody inside," he reported to Drin, and I told him about the fish.

Saori was still lost in her own thoughts. "Perhaps even living men can be used as demons by an angry god when they have evil hearts," she murmured.

"That sounds like something Elkan's poet would say," I said.

"Yes indeed," said Elkan. "He had the same idea: 'Because their hearts were evil they could be turned into devils.'"

"Can someone get a rope?" said Drin. "We need to tie up the prisoner."

I held my nose, went back inside and found some lengths of cord hanging on the wall. I was hungry and searched for food also, but there was nothing except the fish. As I gave Drin the rope, I thanked Elkan for coming to save us. "I'm sorry we left you behind at the inn," I said.

Elkan looked hard at Drin: "Yes, that was an unkind blow."

Drin mumbled something as he tied Dubash's wrists together. It might have been "Sorry", but it might not.

"You make me sick," said Dubash. "All this carry-on, and my mates lying dead on the sand. The best mates a man ever had, and they're all dead, just me left alone..."

"Stop whining," said Drin. "You brought this on

yourselves when you kidnapped an innocent girl. Do you expect anyone to grieve for men like this?"

"Why not? It's normal, isn't it? – to grieve when your mates are murdered, to ask for a decent burial…"

"Are you saying that these are the ones who kidnapped Alamanda?" Elkan asked Drin.

"Yes."

"Then I have no regrets about their deaths, but this man is right: we should bury the dead. Let him dig the graves."

"Dig?" said Dubash. "I'm not digging any holes. These men don't belong in the ground, they belong to the sea, like any other seafarer."

"Then we'd better put them in the boat," said Elkan.

"So I should hope. Who are you anyway? Suddenly pop up out of nowhere and start killing people…"

"That's enough!" said Drin. He ripped a strip of cloth from Dubash's shirt and tied it round his mouth as a gag to stop him from talking any more.

Together we dragged the corpses down to the boat, heaved them on board and covered them with a rough cloth. Elkan told us they would float if we put them into the sea as they were, so we collected some heavy stones from the beach and tied them with ropes to the bodies. Then we took down some of the fish from the cabin, made a fire and grilled them until they began to smell quite tasty. There was fresh water coming down in a stream from the cliff, and we all ate and drank as much as we liked. I was so hungry that I lost count of the number of fish I ate. The world started to feel like a better place. We were alive and free, our stomachs were full, and with the boat at the water's edge we began to hope that we might make it safely to Banjut after all.

"Now that we've eaten," I said, "I suppose we'd better get in the boat and head out to sea."

"Not so fast," said Elkan. "The sea is not the same as a lake. Men ride it like fleas on a buffalo, as the poet said. I am afraid that it would be rash to try to make the crossing to Banjut at night. It's getting dark, this is a rocky coast, and the weather is uncertain. Far better to set off in the morning."

"Then we've got some time to spare. Please tell us: how did you find us?"

"That is a long story."

"But Chaemon's right: we have plenty of time," said Saori, whose mind seemed at last to have returned from reflection on the past.

"If you wish to know, Alamanda, then I should be delighted to tell you. Where should I start? Perhaps from the moment when the Souvians found me lying on the ground half-conscious after Drin had knocked me out? My head ached for days afterwards."

Once again Drin grunted something in reply, but I could not tell what it meant.

"Anyway, they assumed that I was on their side and had tried to stop you from leaving, and together we followed your trail until you turned off the main road onto a side-track, but once you entered the moor it was impossible to see where you had gone. Back at the inn, Belpano was in great pain from a wound in his leg, and everything was in chaos. I was able to sneak away and come to look for you. I headed for the north-south road. I figured that you would have to cross that if you were heading across the moor, but I did not know at what point you might do so. Then I had a stroke of luck because I heard from a waggon-driver that someone had dropped this on the road, and I made him show me the exact spot where he had found it." He pulled Saori's handkerchief out of his pocket and gave it to her with a bit of a flourish. "I am delighted to be able to return this to you, Alamanda. I recognised it at once: the figure of a crane is so beautifully embroidered. It was just the sign which I needed."

I felt embarrassed all over again, but Saori said simply: "Thank you for returning it."

Drin asked: "How did you find your way to this bay?"

"I know this coast pretty well. Out there is the island of Helva, and for many years it was the haunt of pirates until Banjut brought together Valosia and the other coastal states in an expedition against them. After we had defeated them, some of them fled over here. Most of this coastline consists of rocky cliffs, and it can be dangerous for ships when the wind blows onshore, but here and there are a few small coves like this one, and that is where the surviving pirates set up new bases. When we were looking for them, I got to know this coast pretty well. I worked out that if you started from the place where you dropped the handkerchief, and if you were going towards the sea, you were likely to end up either here or in the next cove along."

"We're lucky you found us," Saori said.

"Not luck. It was the work of the gods."

"There's one more question," I said. "You've never told us who you really are."

"No, I never have."

"Will you tell us now?" asked Saori.

"To you, Alamanda, I will reveal all, but not to this pirate."

Drin made Dubash stand up, and they walked a long way across the beach, scattering some grey birds, whose voices echoed across the bay in complaint. Then Drin made him lie down and tied his ankles together before rejoining us next to the fire.

"You can tell us now," he said.

"Very well. I am King Gandarel Velitankan III of Valosia, known throughout the world as the king who ran away. I took the last syllables of my proper names to make the name I use now."

"But that doesn't make sense," said Saori.

"El from Gandarel and kan from Velitankan."

"I don't mean that. I mean that I can't believe you ran away. We've seen you fighting, and you're not a coward. Tell us what really happened."

"I am sorry to disappoint you, but I would greatly prefer not to. I have never told anyone about that."

"I see," said Saori. "I don't wish to force you to speak if you don't want to, but I cannot believe that these things that people say about you are true."

"What is truth? Sometimes what people say becomes the truth."

"And you're happy for everyone to believe a lie?" I asked.

"No. For a long time I have thought that it would be best if they forgot about me altogether."

"But you can't forget, can you?" asked Saori.

"No, I can never forget. Every day, and especially every night, the memories return to torment me."

We were all silent for a bit, but then Saori said: "You might feel better if you shared the true story with others. None of us is truly alone. We all need someone who believes in us."

Again there was silence. Down by the sea the cries of the grey birds, which I thought must be seagulls, sounded as if they were mocking us.

At last Elkan said: "Perhaps you are right. Perhaps it will help to tell someone what really happened, and if anyone has the right to know, it is you, Alamanda. Even now, after so many hours of thinking about what I did, I am not sure if I could have chosen a better course. The poet said that there was a time to fight and a time to talk, a time to run and a time to die. Was this the time to talk or to fight? To run or to die? Everybody seems to think that death would have been the honourable choice, and that leaving Valosia alive was the easy way out, but the truth is that it has brought me nothing but anguish and pain. If I had known what would follow, I might have chosen to die. And yet I still cling to the hope that some day I will get the chance of revenge, and if I do, and if I use it well, then I shall have made the right decision after all. Let me tell you what happened, and you can judge for yourselves."

Chapter 20
Elkan's Story

~

"It all began when Zeno conquered Milesia, and then one after another the kingdoms between Souvia and Valosia fell to his army. There was a sense of gathering panic among our people as the Souvians came closer to us. I could see that our only hope was to find help from other countries as part of an alliance. Our little country was no match for the Souvians on our own. So I sent envoys to our neighbouring kings and drafted a treaty for all of us to sign so that if one country was attacked by Souvia, we would all come to its defence. They all said that it was a good idea and promised to sign it – but none of them did, because they were frightened of Zeno. My envoys reported that one of them secretly hoped that if he did not join the alliance, his kingdom might be spared; another feared that if he sent off his army to help his neighbour, his own kingdom would be left undefended; yet another seemed to believe that Zeno was a scourge sent by the gods and no human power could stop him. Perhaps this last one was right: we prayed for divine help, but the gods did not listen. Every single one of those kings is now dead, and all their kingdoms have been destroyed.

"As time went by and my fellow kings offered no support, I appealed to Lazadim in Banjut. He understood the danger and wanted to help, but he could not persuade the majority of the Councillors to join us in an alliance against Souvia. 'Why put Banjut at risk for a small country like Valosia?' they said. 'What threat is Zeno to us?' They preferred to carry on doing their own business as usual.

"So when the Souvian army arrived at our border, no one came to our aid. If we fought on our own, we were certain to lose: many brave men would die, families would be sent into slavery, and our country would be destroyed forever. Our only choice was to negotiate. 'A time to talk', as the poet said. Zeno sent Nostoc as his chief negotiator, and after many days of argument we reached a deal: I would acknowledge Souvian sovereignty over Valosia, I would allow our men to be recruited into the Souvian army, and I would pay a large annual tax to Zeno, and in return we would be allowed to run our own affairs in all other respects as we always had done. There were many arguments among my advisers about these terms. Some thought them too demanding, others did not trust Zeno to do what he had promised, but the majority agreed with me that we had little choice but to accept. As Nostoc went off to present the agreement to his master, he assured me that Zeno would be very satisfied with it.

"In a few days he returned, smiling and saying that everything was agreed, and we began to make arrangements for a ceremony when Zeno and I would sign the treaty together. I went to bed that night a happy man. I told my wife and children that there was no need for them to be afraid; Valosia would avoid war with the Souvians and achieve peace with honour."

At this point Elkan stopped and stared at the fire. "What a fool! What a shameful fool I was!" he murmured to himself, shaking his head. Saori and I tried to comfort him, and eventually he took a deep breath and resumed his tale.

"When I awoke that night it was still pitch-black in our bedroom. Something sharp was pressing at my throat, and my arms and legs were pinned down. I tried to dislodge the attackers but I found that I could not move. Beside me my wife began to scream. Someone lit a torch, and I could see her being dragged out of the room by force, struggling amidst a group of men. I cried out to stop them and lunged with my feet to try to free myself, but it was no good. I never saw her or my son and daughter again."

Once again Elkan stopped and this time he broke down and wept. Tears rolled down his face, and he put his hand to his forehead and turned away from us. His body shook with sobs.

"How awful!" said Saori, and she too was in tears.

"This is why..." Elkan said, gulping for breath, "this is why I never told this before..."

"Those three little figures in your house," I said. "They represent your wife and children, don't they?"

Elkan nodded, and with an effort he said: "Yes, yes, they do, and every night I prayed that I might see them again. But even if they are still alive, they must be slaves and I cannot bear the thought of..."

He stopped, closed his eyes and hung his head, and again Saori tried to comfort him. I too felt a lump in my throat when I imagined what Elkan must have felt whenever he looked at his little figures and thought of the ones he loved.

After a while Drin asked: "Was Nostoc staying in the palace?" Elkan looked hard at him and resumed his account.

"Yes, we tried to make him feel welcome. We were so trusting, so stupid. We lived in the old castle within the walls of the city, and when we let Nostoc and a few of his men stay with us, we were letting them into our stronghold. We were as foolish as babies: we made it so easy for them."

Elkan paused again and gazed for a long while into the fire.

"I'm sorry. It's painful to remember – those were the most awful moments of my life – but since I've started telling you about it, I had better go on. Well, soon after his men invaded our room, Nostoc himself came in and smiled his oily smile.

"'What is this?' I shouted. 'Where have you taken my wife? I demand that you let her go.'

"But he replied: 'You are in no position to make demands,' and he told his men to tie me up and gag me. I stayed like that for hours, unable to move my body, but nothing could stop my mind from racing to and fro. It was always the same thoughts: what would happen to my wife and children? And my kingdom? How could I have been such a fool? The only thing I knew for certain was that I myself would die. Eventually I was carried into the great hall and tied to a kitchen chair, which was on the floor in front of the throne. I was still gagged. Suddenly Zeno strode in, followed by a crowd of officers. He sat on my throne and looked down at me. I shall never forget that scene, and I can remember every word that was said.

"In his harsh, grating voice, Zeno barked out: 'Bartamis, report.'

"A stocky man with short, grizzled hair replied: 'Our men control the castle and most of the town. Some enemy units are resisting around the east and north gates. We are conducting operations to eliminate them. We hold the road from the frontier to the city. Arichi is advancing towards the port with the cavalry.'

"'Have you secured the treasury?'

"'Yes, sir, but we suspect that some items are missing. We will make the guards tell us where they are.'

"'Do that. Empty the temples as well. I want everything.'

"'Yes, sir.'

"'Make a proclamation. Tell everyone that we have captured the king. Tell them to assemble outside the walls. I will speak to them. I will tell them to rejoice. By the power of Lord Mangra, I have brought them justice. Nostoc!'

"'Yes, sir.'

"'You did well, Nostoc.'

"'Thank you, sir.'

"'You deserve a reward.'

"'Thank you, sir.'

"'I give you this king. You caught him. Now you can execute him in any way you like.'

"As I listened, I felt a furious anger stir inside me. I remembered how my father had held court in that hall, and when he died, I had done the same. We had welcomed kings, priests and merchants from near and far, entertained them with feasts and music and recitals of the poem. We had made Valosia famous as a centre of culture and civilisation – and now in that very hall, I was trussed up like a pig for roasting and this monster, Zeno, lorded it over all. That is when I made a vow by all the gods, that somehow, sometime, somewhere I would take my revenge. It was crazy. I had just been handed over for execution. What chance did I have of revenge, at least in this world? But I felt this burning anger, and I was determined never to accept defeat.

"Nostoc said: 'I have an idea, master. You could have some sport with him. You like to hunt wild boar and stags. Why not hunt a king for a change?'

"'What do you mean?'

"'The king has a hunting ground just outside the city. It is fenced all round to keep in the animals. We could set him loose in there and hunt him down with the dogs.'

"'Hunt the king?! I like it! Arrange it for dawn tomorrow.'

"'Thank you, sir,' said Nostoc. 'Now, you will be known as the hunter of kings, and all will tremble before your power.'

"And so it was that before dawn of the next day I was brought to what had been my own hunting lodge. Zeno and his whole infernal crew were there with horses and dogs, and the scene was lit up with blazing torches. I was at last released from my bonds and allowed to move my limbs, which were stiff after so many hours tied up. Nostoc had a bowl filled with water, which flowed out of a tiny hole in the base, and he said to the soldiers who held my arms: 'Let him go now, and when this bowl is empty we will release the dogs and begin the hunt.'

"But Zeno said: 'No. That is too quick. The game would be over too fast. We will start the hunt when the first rays of the sun touch the ground here, where I am standing.'

"When I heard this, my heart jumped. I knew that I had a chance. After all, I knew that place far better than any of them. I had played there as a boy, climbed the trees, bathed in the streams, hid in the bushes and carved my name on the rocks; and later, I had returned again and again, at first for hunting, and later just to enjoy the peace and quiet.

"The guards let me go, and I began to run. The hunting ground occupied a valley in the foothills of our tallest mountain. The lodge was on the flatter land at the bottom, and from there the ground rose up and became steeper as it grew higher. At the top of the valley a stream roared down in a series of waterfalls and rapids, but as the valley broadened out, the stream slowed and began to curve with tall trees growing along the banks. The boundaries of the whole area were marked by banks, on which a continuous line of hedges and fences formed a barrier.

"As soon as I was out of sight, I ran to the stream and went along it for several tens of paces. Every now and then I climbed out onto the bank on one side or the other and ran about a little in the hope of confusing the dogs. All the while it was growing lighter, and I left the water and ran up the eastern slope to a place where I knew that the fence was weak and needed repair. I threw myself at it and crashed through onto the other side. Then I ran for a while along the outside, and when I came to a steep slope I took off my night-gown, which I was still wearing, and threw it into the trees below me. It caught on a branch and fluttered in the wind. I thought that that would give the impression that I had left the hunting ground and run off; but I had no intention of doing any such thing.

"I retraced my steps to the break in the fence and headed up the slope on the inside to an area where large rocks stood up from the ground. Far below, I could hear the dogs barking with excitement as they began the pursuit. Many years ago I had mastered the art of climbing the rocks and jumping from one to another without descending to the ground. In this way I returned to the stream, which remained the best way of concealing my scent, and climbed upwards along it towards the main waterfall. Within seconds my body was chilled by the cold water, and my feet were cut by sharp stones, but I hardly noticed in my haste to reach the secret chamber.

"You see, one year, when I was a boy, Valosia was struck by a terrible drought, and in the hunting ground, the stream ran so low that the broad, rushing waterfall was reduced to a single spout of water. One day I noticed that the rock behind it contained a narrow crack. Nobody else was about, and when I climbed up to have a look, I found that, being slim, I could squeeze through into a small cave. When the stream returned to its normal amount, the entrance was completely concealed by the waterfall. I resolved to tell nobody about it and to keep it forever as my secret place. I went there rarely in case somebody saw me, but I kept some dry clothes inside and material to make a fire because it was pitch-dark inside. I had discovered, when I first made a light, that other men had been there before me and made drawings of animals on the walls, but I was pretty sure that they had lived long ago and that no man alive except me knew about it.

"It was harder than I remembered to push my way through the waterfall, and I nearly slipped and fell back down to the pool below, but somehow I got through and found the crack in the rock. I had a moment of panic when I thought I had become too big to squeeze through, but I tried another angle and scraped inside. I was wet and shivering, and I could see nothing in the dark, but I did not dare to make a fire. Because of the roar of the water I could hear nothing either. I felt for the dry clothes, put them on and settled down to wait.

"Sitting there on the hard floor, I spent a long time racked with grief, until that again turned to rage, and my mind was filled with plans for revenge, until in the end I must have slept. When I awoke, I could tell from looking at the crack in the rock that it was night-time, and I wondered whether to squeeze back out and go on my way. Would Zeno and Nostoc have given up the hunt, or might they have left men in the valley to search for me? I resolved to stay in the safety of the cave for another day, and I spent the time reciting passages from the work of the poet until I achieved a curious state of calm.

"When it was dark for the second time, I made my way out of the cave and out of the valley, and no one came in pursuit. I had evaded death at Zeno's hands, and now I needed to find help. I went to the main city of one of the neighbouring kingdoms, whose king and I had played together as boys. If anyone would understand my plight and give me the aid I needed, it would surely be him. But he did not treat me as I had expected. Without even listening to what I had to say, he told me that I must leave his kingdom at once and tell nobody I had been there. He said that Zeno was calling me 'the king who ran away' and had set a price on my head, dead or alive; that all the people believed that I had disgraced myself and my ancestors; and that if I was recognised in the street, anyone might kill me.

"Then I realised for the first time what I had done. I had never sat down and thought about whether I should die. I had been so filled with the idea of revenge that I had been determined to live. Now I found that I was dishonoured and friendless. I had expected my life to be in danger from Zeno's men, but now I learnt that anyone might be my enemy and that, wherever I went, I should have to conceal my true identity and skulk like a criminal out of shame.

"I ended up in Banjut and tried to pass a message to Lazadim, because I thought that he was the only man who might have the courage to help me, but while I was waiting for his reply, I spotted Nostoc walking through the markets, and I fled. I wandered inland, feeling more and more desperate. I could see no hope of getting revenge, and I had no desire to roam in fear and disgrace for the rest of my life. I ended up in the forest, far up the Banjut river, all alone, sitting on a rock, filled with despair, when one of the Dangoys appeared suddenly from the trees. Others came after, took me back to their village, gave me herbs and calmed my spirit. Truly I owe them my life, and ever since I have stayed among them. Until you came.

"That is my story. In my own mind I had decided not to die but to fight, but in the eyes of the world I had merely run away. What do you think? Did I do the right thing, or is the world right to condemn me?"

Saori was the first to reply: "I think the same as I thought in the beginning. You are not a coward and not a king who ran away. You tried to do the best thing for your country. But poor Elkan! You have suffered so much! To lose your family, your people, even your good name, everything. Sometimes I feel sorry for myself, but not any more, not now that I have heard what happened to you."

"Thank you, Alamanda. What you say brings me great comfort. But what of you, Drin? What would you have done?"

"Me? Oh, sooner or later I'd have got into a fight, and that would have been the end of me, I expect."

"And you, Chaemon? What would a scholar have done?"

"I don't know. I pray to all the gods that I never, ever find myself in such a situation. I've no idea what I would do if I did. But Saori is right that you're not a coward. That's for sure."

"The jury is divided. Perhaps that is the best I could expect. The poem has taught me never to hope for too much, but always to be content with what I have."

He fell silent, lost in thought.

"Talking about the poem," I said, "you have it with you, don't you? I wondered what it was – the scroll you kept hidden in your house. It must be the poem."

"Yes," said Elkan. "You are a sharp observer. It is the original manuscript written by the poet himself – the greatest treasure in the world. That at least I have kept safe with me."

"That's amazing. How did you do it?"

"What do you mean – do what?"

"You said you left the hunting ground with nothing except the clothes you kept in the cave. So how did you get the scroll?"

"Ah, that is a very good question, Chaemon. I can see that I shall have to tell you my last secret. You see, most people believed that the scroll was kept in a golden box in the Temple of the Sea God, and every year the box was taken out on the poet's birthday and shown to the public, but the truth is that the scroll inside was only a copy. Many generations ago, at a time of war among the kingdoms, one of my ancestors and the chief priest of the time feared that the manuscript might fall into the hands of our enemies, and so, in great secrecy, they had a copy made and took the original to a special hiding place in the hills. In each generation only the king and the chief priest knew where this was. When I escaped from Zeno, I feared that I might be the last person alive to know the secret, and so I took the scroll and kept it with me. I know most of the poem by heart, but it has been my greatest comfort for all these years to see the writing of the poet himself and feel his wisdom enter my mind.

"So now you know everything, Chaemon. I have nothing more to hide."

Chapter 21

Brought Low by the Waves

◠

W e set off the next morning as soon as it became light. The level of the sea was higher than I remembered – Elkan said that the tide had come in – and the boat was lifted by the water. We pushed it out from the shore and paddled towards the mouth of the bay. The waves lapped against the hull like those of Lake Kandalore on a windy day, but there was no wind in the bay, just grey cloud above and grey sea below. We left Dubash tied up at one end of the beach, and shortly before we set off, Drin put his knife in the sand at the other end and told him to roll over to it if he wanted to cut himself free. All of us hoped that we would never set eyes on him again.

We were almost at the entrance to the bay when Elkan called a halt. He said a short prayer to the god of the sea, Saori prayed to her goddess, and we pushed the bodies of the two dead men over the side and watched them sink into the cold water.

We paddled on. It felt good to be out on the sea, as if we had left behind all the complications of life on land. Here there were no Souvian escorts, no false identities and no Dubashes creeping up on us – just the wind blowing fresh, salty air. Saori was especially happy. She knew that we had yet to find the navigators, who would know how to get to her island; but she still felt as if we were sailing closer to her home across the sea, and she loved the sensation of being afloat.

The same could not be said of Drin. As we left the bay, the waves became higher, and the boat began to rise and fall more sharply in the open sea. Like me, he had sometimes sailed across Lake Kandalore, and he had not much liked that; but he had never been in a boat which pitched and rolled like this one, and he liked this even less.

While Saori held the steering oar, Elkan raised the sail and once it filled with the breeze, the motion of the boat changed again: it went much faster with the wind pushing it along, but it kept leaning to the right ("starboard" as Elkan made us call it) while continuing to rise and fall with the waves. Birds with long wings glided smoothly over them, dipping into the hollows and shooting up again over the white crests, and at one point some large fish swam beside the boat, dipping underwater for a moment and then half emerging before dipping down again. We were well out from the coast now, and above us grey clouds scudded across the sky, so that all around us was water and air in motion, and the boat seemed tiny as it raced along.

But Drin hardly noticed any of this. He was too busy concentrating on a strange sensation in his stomach. It was as if its contents were moving up and down with the boat, like someone shaking liquid in a jar to mix it – but very slowly, so that he could feel everything rise up to the roof of his stomach in a dizzying surge and then crash down again. He felt tired, and his eyes wanted to close, but when he shut them for a moment it brought no relief. Everything in the boat seemed woolly and distant, compared with the tide of movement inside him.

It seemed to help a little if he looked at the horizon, and as he stared at it, he told himself that he was getting used to the surging feeling inside him and getting it under control. He could defeat this thing – it was just a matter of willpower, he thought. But the trouble was that, even though the horizon did not move, he did; and however hard he tried, he could not ignore the endless, regular rise and fall of his stomach. Up the boat went on each giant wave until his insides were flying in the air, and down it crunched back again until they were like a heavy stone descending inside him. He gulped for air. He was hot now and even beginning to sweat, and with a great effort he took off his outer coat. Up again, and he could imagine the contents of his stomach leaving the bottom of the jar and striking the lid. Down, and they splatted against the bottom again. He wished it would stop. If only the boat would stay still for a moment, his stomach could settle and he could get back to normal. But there was no break, and no prospect of a break, and still the boat rose and fell, rose and fell, and he could feel every movement amplified inside him.

It ended as it was bound to end. He was horribly sick over the side.

"Mighty Drin is seasick!" Elkan cried out. "The strong man is brought low by the waves, as the poet said."

Drin barely heard him, but for once his tone annoyed me, and I wished he would stop quoting his poet. I clambered along the side of the boat and sat next to Drin and tried to comfort him by patting his shoulder and saying words of sympathy, although I was not sure that he even noticed I was there.

"Is there anything we can do to help him?" I asked.

"Personally I have never been seasick," said Elkan, "but people say that it helps to take a herb called ginger, which grows in the southern forests. Unfortunately I do not have any of that with me, but please do not be concerned. Even the strong man is brought low by the waves, but he soon recovers when he returns to land."

Saori handed the steering oar to Elkan and came over to sit on Drin's other side, and as I had done, she patted him and uttered words of comfort, and Drin appeared to revive a little. We were all on the same, port side of the boat so that our weight helped a little to balance the power of the wind, which was coming from the north-east and pushing us briskly along towards Banjut in the south. The sky was now blue with round, white clouds, but the sea was still dull grey and studded with countless white crests. To starboard we could see the rocky cliffs of the uninhabited coast, and to port Elkan pointed out a dark smudge on the horizon, which he said was the island of Helva, now owned by Banjut after the pirates had been expelled.

"We are lucky so far with the wind," he said. "If this continues, we shall reach Banjut well before dark. Many times in the past, when a storm has blown up from the east, ships have been wrecked on this coast, but I think that we shall be all right."

I must admit that my own stomach was feeling a bit strange and I had become a little drowsy, but by good fortune I was not attacked by sickness in the way that Drin had been. Periodically he would be hit by another attack, although by now his stomach must have been empty, and Saori and I would try to comfort him, but nothing we could do made any practical difference. Meanwhile the boat continued to race through the waves.

The sun was past its mid-point and starting its long descent towards the west when Elkan pointed out a pinpoint of light shining from the top of a distant headland. "Banjut!" he said. At first we could not make it out, but as we went on, Saori and I also saw it. Elkan said that it was a ray of sunlight striking the golden statues on the roof of the great temple which stood on the highest point of the citadel and which housed Banjut's most sacred treasure, the Golden Disc.

As we approached, we could see more details. The temple stood among other large buildings on top of a huge rock, which rose steeply out of the sea and resisted the power of the waves, which smashed against its base over and over again in huge clouds of spray. The coast on either side was lower, and we began to make out the massive city walls on the northern slope of the rock, which was the only point where it was attached to the land, and finally we saw that beyond it to the south was the opening where the river came out into the sea. So this was Banjut, I thought. I had read so much about it, and the traders had told me so much more, and now here it was before my eyes, and I was willing the boat to go faster, to speed up our arrival so that I could see if the city was really as I had imagined it.

Next to me, Drin was muttering something again and again to himself.

"What are you saying?" I asked.

"A great oath," he said. "I solemnly swear by the god of the sea that if he lets me reach dry land, I will never again bother him by trying to travel across his domain. Never, ever again."

Both Saori and I smiled at this, but Drin was in earnest and went back to muttering his oath with his eyes closed.

Meanwhile we had changed direction, and Elkan was steering the boat straight towards the rock, and I asked him in alarm if he was trying to crash it and get us all killed, but he replied calmly: "I am assuming that the Souvians have occupied the whole town below the citadel and we cannot land in the main harbour. That means that our only chance is to try to enter the seaward harbour which the Banjutis constructed on the outer side of the rock. If we miss it, you are right: we shall crash. So please stand ready to lower the sail when I give the order."

Saori and I did as he said. We could now make out the shape of a stone wall which stretched out into the sea. The boat was heading towards it at a frightening pace, with the wind pushing us along. Now we could see that what had looked like a continuous wall was in fact two walls made of gigantic stones which curved out from the land. Where they met there was a narrow opening where they overlapped and ran in parallel to each other for a short distance. This was our target. I marvelled at how the Banjutis had managed to build such a structure in the open sea and make it strong enough to survive the stormy waves.

Just when I was sure that we were going to smash against the wall, Elkan brought the boat sharply round into the wind, and ordered us to lower the sail. With the boat's momentum and a little help from our paddling, we entered the channel between the walls and escaped from the wind. I felt an immediate sense of relief, but then we saw that a new challenge awaited us: our way was blocked by thick ropes which had been tied across from one side to the other.

"Bring your boat over here!" called a voice from the inner wall, which towered above us. On top of it blue-coated archers stood with their arrows aiming down at us, and we paddled towards them. The voice had come from a large man who was standing at the top of some steps and who now called out: "Raise your hands above your heads!"

We did as we were told, trying to keep our balance in the swaying boat.

"Are you bringing food?"

"No," replied Elkan. "We have come to…"

"Are you citizens of Banjut?"

"No, but we wish to meet…"

"Then turn round and go back where you came from."

"But you haven't heard why we came."

"I don't care why you came. There's a war going on here, and I'm ordering you to leave before we shoot you all and sink your boat. Is that clear enough?"

Elkan was silent. None of us had foreseen that we might be turned away from Banjut when it had taken so much effort to get there.

"No!" Saori lowered her arms. "We are not leaving here until I have met Lady Katila again. I have her token – here!" She held up the small silver medallion, which Katila had given to Drin that evening so many months ago.

Elkan called out: "She's right. You must let us in. This is the Alamanda, and Zeno is hunting for her."

I added: "He's offered 10,000 juts as a reward!"

By chance I had said the right thing. In Banjut, city of trade, money was the key.

"10,000 juts!" said the man on the steps. "That's a lot of money."

"That's the reward," I said.

"10,000 juts," he repeated. "Let the girl come up here! The men stay in the boat."

In the shadow of the rock it was becoming darker and chillier as Saori climbed up the steps and showed Katila's medallion to the men. Her golden hair billowed out in the breeze.

After a while the man in charge said: "All right. We'll take them to the captain. He can decide what to do with them. Let the men come up one by one, and search them carefully."

We let Drin land first, and as he did so, he bent down and kissed the hard stone and thanked the god with all his heart for letting him reach dry land. Elkan and I followed, and when we were all together the men led us along the wall to a fine stone building at the base of the rock. We were made to wait in a room with desks where I supposed that in happier times scribes had recorded the cargoes which came in and out of the harbour.

A short stocky man, dressed in the usual Banjuti blue, came bustling in. The corners of his mouth were turned down, and he looked as if he was always discontented.

"Show me the token," he said, and when Saori handed it to him, he examined it carefully. "Yes, it's Katila's mark. How did you get it?"

Saori told him her story.

"So you're the slave girl that Gadim rescued. I told him at the time no good would come of it. 'Annoy Zeno,' I said, 'and he'll take his revenge on us all.' And now look what a mess we're in. Who are these others?"

Saori introduced us one by one, but without revealing Elkan's true identity.

"Well, you've chosen the worst possible time to come," said the officer, who we learnt later was Amorim, Captain of the Outer Port. "We're besieged by Zeno, there's no food, and all they can talk about is that pile of gold outside the city walls. I don't think you're going to get much help here. We'll be lucky to save our own skins, never mind yours."

"What pile of gold?" Elkan asked.

"You don't know about that? It's Zeno's work, and it's devilish clever. Just outside the city wall he's made a great heap of gold coins, and every day they add a little more, so now it's as high as a man's head."

"But why would they do that?"

"It's a trick of course. It's obvious it's a trick, but that doesn't stop men dreaming."

"What does Lazadim say?" asked Elkan.

"Lazadim? He says the same as he's always said: we control the sea and we can defend our walls, he says; no one can get through our defences, not even the Souvians. And to start with, everyone believed him. Even Zeno's met his match in Banjut, they said."

"And he was correct, was he not? In all the history of Banjut, nobody has ever captured the city by force of arms."

"That's why Zeno's trying the gold. That gold will be the end of us – mark my words. Here in Banjut we love gold. Gold on the temples, gold in the markets, even a Golden Disc. However much we've got, we always want more. So they go up, the fools, onto the walls, and gaze at Zeno's gold for hours on end."

"But surely Lazadim has warned of the danger."

"Oh yes, he warns them, all right. He warns them all the time. That's the trouble. That's why a group of them have turned against him – because he stops them getting what they want. Their leader is a fellow called Quizlim. He blames everything on Lazadim."

"But that is foolishness," said Elkan. "When the storm strikes, the boat needs a steady hand at the tiller."

"Lazadim's hand is steering us onto the rocks, that's what Quizlim says."

"Then Banjut is in real danger."

"It's not just the gold: people are tired of waiting. We thought Zeno would attack the walls and try to get in, but he doesn't. He just sits out there, with his army all around the city. There's only us blue-coats left inside now. Our women and children have been sent to Helva, and everyone else ran away when we lost the outer town. The markets are closed. There's no food. Days, weeks, months, we've spent like this, waiting for something to happen."

"All this is terrible," said Saori, "but we've come a long way to see Lady Katila. I know you have other problems, but could you please take us to her? Only she can help me find my way home."

"Yes, you've shown me her token, and I've a duty to honour it. I'll send a message for her people to collect you."

"Thank you. I hope things will turn out better than you say."

"No, no chance – and my advice to you is to leave this place while you still can. Banjut is done for, finished."

With these gloomy words Amorim left us to wait in the darkening room with the empty desks.

Chapter 22

The Gods Abandon Banjut

~

fter a while two men came in and said they had been sent by Katila. They led us at a fast pace up a long staircase cut into the rock and into the town along narrow streets which sloped steeply upwards. We stopped breathless outside a small gate in a low wall, which I guessed must surround the summit of the hill. We could hear men shouting far off. Our guides spoke briefly to the soldiers guarding the gate, and we were allowed through. The ground was flatter here, and the buildings bigger and taller, and we glimpsed grand colonnades and marble walls. But the route we took went round the back of the buildings through empty alleyways, until we were led through a courtyard with storerooms and into a huge kitchen. The servants working there never looked up to see us pass, and I supposed that we had been brought in round the back so as to avoid the curious eyes of watchers at the front. Our guides pressed on through the house and showed us into a grand room, well-lit by candles. The walls were painted with scenes of ships offloading goods in harbour and of a battle at sea, and in front of us was a huge but empty fireplace. There was little furniture, just a table with chairs around it to our right, and on our left two more comfortable chairs, in one of which Katila was sitting.

Saori fell to her knees in front of her and, just as she had done with my mother, raised Katila's hand to her own forehead. Katila drew her up and embraced her, then greeted Drin, who responded shyly, and then turned to me, and I had to explain who I was.

Elkan said: "Do you remember me?" and Katila stared hard at him before nodding and replying: "I wasn't sure after all this time, but it *is* you, isn't it, King Gandarel? How have you been?"

"I have survived," said Elkan. "I found a place to hide away, and I survived, until this young lady came and brought me hope."

"That's what we need in Banjut – hope – and a bit more courage. Each of you must tell me why you have come here at a time like this, but first we must make you welcome. Have you eaten?"

"Not for a week," I replied, "except for some dried fish, and Drin threw up…"

Drin's glare made me stop just in time.

"Bring them food," ordered Katila.

"But we heard you were short of food yourselves," said Elkan.

"That's one of the many lies put about by our opponents. If we ration our stocks sensibly and catch plenty of fish, we can feed ourselves for many months, if not years, and we can certainly entertain our guests."

A servant scurried out of the room, and Katila invited us to be seated around the table. "I'm sorry that Lazadim is not here to greet you," she said, "but they are having a foolish debate and he has to make sure that common sense prevails."

"About the gold?" Elkan asked.

"So you've heard about the gold. It's so obviously a trap that you wouldn't expect grown men to think twice about it, but it's become a kind of obsession. They talk about nothing else except how rich they would be if only they could get their hands on it. You wouldn't believe the crazy plans they've dreamt up."

"Amorim mentioned someone called Quizlim," said Elkan.

"He's the worst of the lot. Years ago Lazadim caught him cheating in the grain market, and he's had a grudge ever since. Now he's got together a band of idiots who say they want to rush out of the gates, fill their pockets with as much gold as they can carry and rush back in again."

"Those whom the gods wish to destroy, they first make mad," said Elkan, and this time I recognised the quotation.

The servants brought in plates of bread, slices of cold meat, hot grilled fish and dried fruit, and placed them on the table. We sat down and with a hurried prayer began to eat. I was so hungry that it tasted like the finest banquet ever prepared.

We were still eating when the door opened, and a tall figure with a neat beard and a long blue cloak swept in and embraced Katila. Other men and a few women followed him in until the room was full of people, and we had to stand up to make space for them. Most of them were talking earnestly to each other, but I could make no sense of what they were saying. They were so wrapped up in their own affairs that they ignored us completely, but they kept looking towards Lazadim and Katila. I remember thinking that by pure chance we might be present at a historic moment, and I inched my way forwards to get a better view.

Lazadim and Katila stayed in each other's arms for what seemed a long time, but finally Lazadim drew back and began to speak, and everyone in the room fell silent: "Once a cheat, always a cheat. I will not let Quizlim destroy this city with his lies. It is the Council that rules Banjut, and I will have him arrested as a traitor."

He was tall and grey-haired as Drin had described, but his face was lined with age and care, the corners of his mouth trembled slightly, and although the words he uttered were full of anger and fire, it was clear that he had suffered an unexpected defeat.

Katila said: "Gadim, tell me what happened."

"It's a long story," said one of the men, whom I realised must be the same official who had helped to save Saori in the slave market. "But the short version is that the meeting voted to allow Quizlim and his volunteers to make a dash for the gold."

"But that's ridiculous. Why didn't they listen to the Council?"

"President Lazadim gave a fine speech…"

"I told them not to fall for Zeno's trap. The gold was of no value compared with the safety of our city. They had only to be patient and stick together, and Banjut would remain free and independent forever."

"It was a fine, eloquent speech," continued Gadim, "but unfortunately Quizlim had organised men at the front to heckle and interrupt."

"An absolute disgrace!" said Lazadim.

"Then Quizlim spoke. He said that President Lazadim was right to be cautious: it would be dangerous to leave the safety of the walls, and no one should be ordered to do so; but if a few volunteers were willing to take the risk and have a go, why should anyone stand in their way?"

"Shameless! He even had the cheek to suggest that such men would be 'courageous'!" said Lazadim.

"The President said that the Council was unanimous in opposition to such an attempt and tried to call the meeting to a close, but Quizlim shouted that the Council was divided and pushed Morishim forward."

"Morishim! That snake!" cried Lazadim. "I should have kicked him out long ago."

"Anyway, Morishim said the people should decide and he read out Article IX, that a decision of the Council can be overruled by a vote of all the citizens in an open meeting."

"I told them that I refused to allow it," said Lazadim.

"But, well… the vote went ahead anyway," said Gadim, and his shoulders slumped.

"Totally irregular!" Lazadim fumed.

Katila said: "We must make sure that the guards on the gates don't let Quizlim and his crew go through. Gadim, take some men there at once and make sure that no one is allowed out!"

"What if they have gone already?" asked Gadim. "They

could be helping themselves to the gold while we speak."

"Then they must not be allowed back in."

"But the Souvians will kill them," said someone behind me.

"If a few of these greedy fools end up dead, that's their own fault," said Katila. "Don't you agree, Lazadim?"

But Lazadim's mind was not on the gates but on his own position. For 20 years he had ruled Banjut. For 20 years, with Katila at his side, he had defeated every challenge to his rule, and the people had looked up to him as their leader. It had been his duty to maintain order and keep the city safe, and he had grown used to that responsibility and the power which went with it. Now, suddenly, his authority had gone: whatever the laws might say, the President had no power to lead if the citizens did not want to follow. He had felt their mood change in recent days and weeks, and yet he had still believed that he could keep control. He was looking anxiously round the faces of his followers to gauge their support when something caught his eye: "Is that someone with golden hair?" he asked. "There, where the light falls."

"Yes," said Katila. "She arrived while you were at the meeting."

"The girl with the golden hair! How astonishing that she has come back to Banjut at a time like this!"

Saori went up to Lazadim, knelt and placed his hand against her forehead.

"No need for that. Please stand up. But is it true that you are the Alamanda?"

"Yes," said Saori. "I came to seek your help, and Lady Katila's."

"But we're the ones who need help now."

"Gadim! Why are you still here?" said Katila. "We must make the gate safe. There's no time to lose."

But as she spoke, the door slammed open, and a young man pushed his way in. He was panting deeply as if he had been running at full speed.

"President Lazadim, sir!" he cried. "The Souvians are coming in! Lots of them! They've captured the gates."

"Then we're too late," said Katila.

"We must fight them!" cried Lazadim. He seemed suddenly filled with new energy. "Sound the trumpets. We must get our men together. There has been treachery here tonight, but we will defend the city."

A cheer went up at the back of the room, but Katila shook her head: "No, it's no good. The city is lost. Just as you told them so many times: once the walls are breached, it's all over."

"But men must fight for their country. Didn't the Valosian poet say there was a time to fight and a time to die?"

"But you must not die. As long as you live, Banjut is not dead."

"I am not afraid to die for the city I love."

"But the city needs you to live," Katila said. "You must lead us to Helva. Hasn't that always been the plan? If we had to leave Banjut, to fight back from Helva?"

"Do you want me to run away? Like Gandarel did all those years ago. I would rather stay and fight. Then I can die an honourable death."

Lazadim looked around at his followers once more, and his expression changed. He pointed to the corner of the room: "Wait! Gandarel! It's strange, but I think I see his ghost over there. Has he come to haunt us?"

"Not a ghost," said Elkan. "I am here in flesh and blood."

"This room is full of strangers. First Alamanda and now you. But why? What are you doing here?"

"I came with her. She is our only hope. The gods have sent her to save us."

There was a loud banging on the front door, which must have been securely locked.

"The Souvians!" said Katila. "Quick! We must get to the harbour!"

But Lazadim did not move. He appeared lost in thought.

"Come on!" said Katila. "Please, Lazadim! We must go!"

"What's that sound?" he asked. He had an air of concentration, like someone trying to identify the song of a bird far off in the woods, but I could hear nothing except the banging on the door and shouting in the street outside. "Do you hear that music?"

"No," said Katila, and others shook their heads.

"Am I the only one who can hear it?" Lazadim said. "Then only I know what it is. The melody of the soul, the perfect harmony. There is no human music like this." He was smiling, old age and tiredness had gone, and his face was lit up with joy. "But it is moving, away, down towards the harbour. The gods are abandoning Banjut, and we must follow."

With that, Lazadim's expression became grim once more, and he strode through the door, and everyone streamed out after him. The four of us were left behind in the painted room with the candles flickering.

"I wish I could have heard the music of the gods," I said.

"No time for that!" said Drin. "Let's go!"

So we hurried out and followed the Banjutis down into

the cellars, past rows of barrels and storage jars, through a narrow door into a tunnel and eventually up some steps into a deserted alleyway. We ran down the back alleys, passed quickly through the little side gate and carried on down between the houses. It was dark outside now, though the sky was still light, and we had to be careful not to slip on the uneven paving stones as we raced down the narrow streets until we came to the rock-cut stairs and the harbour wall. A large boat with two masts and cabins was moored now by the sea wall, and Lazadim and his party hastened aboard. We were about to follow, but Drin stopped.

"It's no good," he said. "You'll have to go on without me. I swore a great oath, and I can't go on the sea again."

"But, Drin!" Saori cried. "We can't go without you."

"I'm sorry to part like this," said Drin, "but you'll be safe now on Helva."

Saori was still protesting: "No! You must come!", when Elkan grabbed Drin's head and neck from behind, and clung on in spite of Drin's efforts to shake him off.

The fight did not last long, because Drin's legs gave way and he fell to the ground. Elkan stood over him, breathing heavily.

"What have you done?!" Saori screamed, and she and I bent down to see if Drin was all right.

"I'm frightfully sorry," said Elkan. "but he's only sleeping. He'll be fine when he wakes up. It's just a powder I keep with me that puts people to sleep. You didn't want to leave him behind, and this seemed the best answer."

"Are you sure it's safe?"

"I swear it does no lasting harm."

An arrow zinged over our heads. We looked up and

found Amorim and his men grouped round us firing back at unseen enemies. With their help we bundled Drin onto the boat and into a cabin. The crew cast off, and within moments the boat had set sail for Helva.

So ended our visit to Banjut. It had not gone quite as we had expected – or hoped.

Chapter 23

Helva

It was still dark when we arrived in Helva, and there was much confusion in the harbour when our boat arrived, so that although everyone disembarked, the four of us had nowhere to go and ended up sitting by the sea wall. As it grew light, an apologetic official found us and took us to a stone castle which looked out over the harbour and where we again met Katila, this time in a cold, empty room. She said that she wanted Saori to stay with her and told the official to find quarters in the town for Elkan, Drin and me. We were invited, however, to meet Saori for the evening meal in the great hall of the castle, where Katila and the senior Banjutis came together at the end of each day. Quite quickly we settled into a daily routine. We were no longer on the road or in enemy territory, and we had time to settle down to a more regular way of life while we waited for news about the navigators. Each of us found something different to do during the day, but we would get together in the evening to chat and share information.

To begin with, Saori was happy with this new turn in our affairs. She was treated with great respect by Katila and the other Banjutis, and given a comfortable room and a place to bathe. Katila's role on the island was all the more important because Lazadim had fallen sick and nominated her to take charge in his place. The loyal Banjutis who had fled with them to the island did not question this, and Katila proved an able leader even in Lazadim's absence. Saori felt it natural to have a woman in command of the island and was filled with admiration for the way Katila managed things at such a critical juncture. She was flattered too to become Katila's chosen companion, to spend every day at her side and even occasionally to be asked for advice. Above all, on the subject which mattered most to Saori – how to contact the navigators – Katila admitted that she herself did not know the answer but promised to make urgent enquiries of Lazadim and anyone else who might be able to help.

The top priority for Katila and her people was to improve our defences in case the Souvians launched an attack against the island. Its low hills provided no natural fortress, and although there was a ditch and wooden wall around the town, it would not hold up the Souvians for very long. The best defence therefore would be to prevent them from landing, and Katila organised a major exercise in which half the Banjutis would board their boats, sail round the island and try to land on one of the beaches at night and the rest would try to defend it. Drin found himself caught up in this on the defending side and helped to devise barriers to block the enemy boats from reaching the shore, though what he really wanted to do was to go out into the fields and help with the animals. He was happiest of all when one of the local farmers let him make friends with his sheepdogs and round up his flock with them.

Elkan too became involved with the island's defences, though in a much more shadowy role. A few days after we arrived, he had a long, secret meeting with Katila, which no one else, not even Saori, was allowed to attend. After that, he seemed always to be busy but never revealed to us exactly what he had been doing. Drin and I concluded that it was some kind of espionage. He always had the latest information on what was going on in Banjut; and there the news was grim. Zeno had made all the surviving Banjutis into slaves, and anyone who resisted had been killed. Their first task was to pull down the mighty walls which defended their own city so that it could never again be used to resist the Souvian army. The pile of gold had disappeared, and all the money in Banjut's treasury, as well as the riches in the temples and private houses, had been carried off.

As for me, I have to admit that I had discovered a kind of paradise. Yes, it was a library. For several years Lazadim had employed scribes to copy the finest texts in the Great Library of Banjut, and as Zeno's siege took hold, he had sent some of the scribes and their documents to Helva as an insurance policy. The Great Library was one of the wonders of the world, and although it made me sad to think what Zeno might be doing to it, at least the most important texts would not be lost. The chief librarian, Mallabim, was a man of exceptional intelligence with keen eyes and a high, domed forehead, and when he spoke, he chose his words carefully so as to convey precisely what he meant. That was a problem for me when Katila first introduced us because Mallabim habitually used complicated Banjuti expressions which had never featured in Marcon's lessons, and I found myself again and again having to ask him what he meant. I was afraid that he was not at all impressed by my scholarship. I thought I even overheard one of the other librarians mutter something about my "being only a boy".

By good fortune, however, I spotted a curious document hanging on the wall and recognised the script as Palaeo-Quadratic. The characters were written in a spiral, and I had never seen anything quite like it before. When I mentioned it, Mallabim suddenly became very interested and asked me a series of questions. The Quadratic script was commonly used in the plains to the west of Akond in the age when four great cities competed for influence and wealth there. "Palaeo" meant only that this was the older form. When I had explained all this to Mallabim, I asked why he was so interested.

"Because this is no ordinary text," he replied. "This is a copy of the symbols inscribed upon the Golden Disc. Many generations of scholars have studied it with mathematical, semiotical and cryptographical techniques with reference to all the languages known to us and their linguistic variants, but no one has ever been able to read it. Can you do so?"

"Maybe," I said cautiously, and I settled down to look at it more closely. I wished now that I had paid more attention to my teacher Rokuron's lessons, but I had found the Quadratic texts rather dry and uninteresting, and I had to cudgel my brain to remember what each squiggle stood for and what the Quadratic words meant. But after the first twenty or so characters I realised with great relief that the text itself was familiar. The Paradoxes of Cambient, as it was known, had become one of the basic texts of our own religion in Akond, and even children were taught to recite it. Since I knew the words so well, it was not too difficult to translate them from Palaeo-Quadratic into Banjuti:

"*Life is short, and yet Life is everlasting.*
Life fears death, and yet Life has no fear.
The sun rises and sets, the moon waxes and wanes,
    the sea rises and falls, and yet Life is always the same.
Living things are born and die, they move and change, they
    grow and decline, and yet Life is always the same.
Stay true to your true nature, for that is the way to Life."

When I read this out to Mallabim and the other scholars, they surprised me by clapping. One or two even gave a discreet cheer. Mallabim said that this was the greatest advance in Banjuti scholarship since his own work on the city's history. Everyone was full of praise for me, which made me feel embarrassed and pleased at the same time.

That evening I reported this triumph to my three friends, and they shared my joy, although I am not sure they fully grasped the importance of my discovery. Saori smiled broadly and said how clever I was, but went on to ask why the text was so contradictory and full of opposites. Elkan said he was impressed I had been able to read it, but the text lacked the elegance of the great poem. Drin simply shook his head and muttered: "Scholars!"

Soon after, the community on Helva was shocked to hear that Lazadim had died. Katila organised as grand a funeral as she could in the circumstances, and everyone turned out to mourn the former President as his coffin was paraded slowly round the little town and buried in the cemetery outside the walls. She announced that a monument would be built at the top of the highest hill in Helva, and work began on the design. Meanwhile she continued to govern as she had been doing before, and the military exercise went ahead as planned on the beach. Many lessons were learnt from it, according to Elkan, but there was no sign of a Souvian invasion even though Zeno continued to keep most of his army in the area around Banjut.

As the time went by, Saori became increasingly frustrated by the lack of any news about the navigators. Katila continued to treat her in the same way as before and often said how pleased she was to have such a dear friend beside her, but Saori began to have doubts about her true intentions. Whenever she asked her about the navigators, Katila gave only vague replies, and Saori began to suspect that she was not actually making any effort to find them but was keeping Saori beside her for some other purpose of her own.

Meanwhile, I had become a hero to the scholars in the library, and they were keen to help me in any way they could. I said that the main thing I wanted to discover was why Zeno was so desperate to capture Saori: could anything in the library offer a clue?

This led to an animated discussion among the librarians, and one after another they rushed off to consult their favourite texts, but all came back shaking their heads to say that they could not find the answer. I noticed that one of them had remained silent throughout and asked if he had any ideas.

"Serapim cannot answer you," said Mallabim quickly.

"From childhood he has been unable to hear or speak, but you are right to ask him, because he is our greatest expert on oracular responses."

I wrote down my question, and Serapim's face lit up. It turned out that the other scholars had checked the answers given by the great oracle at Hoxxkorn, but Serapim knew that the Souvians had always distrusted Hoxxkorn and preferred their own oracle at a place high in the northern mountains called Extopi. He had brought a selection of the Extopian responses with him from Banjut and ran to get it. When he opened the scroll, I could only understand a small part of it because most was written in languages other than Banjuti, but this was no problem for Serapim, and he whizzed through it at great speed until he came to one particular answer which the oracle had given and looked up at me with an air of triumph.

"This is written in Souvian," he wrote. "Unfortunately the question is not recorded, but it was asked by Zeno the Great, and the oracle replied:

'*A girl will come with golden hair,*
With spirit pure and beauty fair,
And she alone can cause him pain,
For she alone can end his reign.

For she must judge if it is right
To bow her head before his might,
Or to reject him and to fight.
The choice she makes will not be light,
For if her judgement causes strife,
The weaker one may pass from life.'"

"That's it!" I cried out in excitement. "You've done it! That explains everything!"

Serapim beamed at me, and I hastened to write down for him my everlasting thanks.

That evening, when we met for our usual meal, I reported what I had discovered, and this time everyone immediately understood its significance. Elkan was delighted: "It is just as I always believed," he said. "You were sent here to destroy Zeno."

But Saori's reaction was the opposite.

"What a stupid verse!" she said. "Is that why Zeno has been chasing me all this time? It's all nonsense! I wish you'd never told me."

"I'm sorry," I said. "I just thought you should know."

"And another thing," Saori went on. "Day after day passes, and Katila pretends she's helping me, but I don't think she's doing anything at all. I wish now we'd never come to this place. There must be some other way of finding the navigators and getting home. I'm tired of sitting around here wasting time."

"You're right," said Drin. "We should go and tell Katila to stop her games."

"Or else we'll leave and find the navigators for ourselves," I said.

"I too sympathise," said Elkan. "Believe me, I do. But, with great respect, I think you are being a little harsh towards Katila. I believe I am aware of most of the information which is coming into Helva from sources outside, but I have never heard any news of the navigators. If I had, I should have reported it at once, whatever Katila thought."

"That is all the more reason for us to leave Helva and try

something else," said Saori. "We'll never find out anything when we're stuck in this place."

"Perhaps we should try Hoxxkorn," I suggested; and we had a long discussion of alternatives. In the end, we resolved that, as soon as we awoke the next morning, we would go together to see Katila and demand that she either find the navigators or let us leave so that we could try to track them down somewhere else.

We were still filled with this resolve when dawn broke, and after further discussion over breakfast, we went together to Katila's room for what we thought would be a difficult meeting. As usual, Elkan acted as our spokesman and, with a fine mixture of firmness and tact, explained why it was so important to find the navigators quickly.

Katila's reaction caught us all by surprise: "I was just going to ask you to come and see me about the same subject. I have some excellent news. After all these weeks of trying, we have finally succeeded in finding them."

It took me a moment or two to take in what she was saying, but Saori reacted immediately. "That's wonderful!" she cried, and for the first time in weeks she was smiling her radiant smile. "You found them? Where are they? Are they coming here?"

"They're staying at a small island further out to sea. One of our fishing boats saw them sailing back from Banjut yesterday and managed to make contact."

"Do you think they'll take me home?"

"I expect so, and I certainly hope so, for your sake, but I don't know what their plans are. Apparently they went to Banjut to sell their goods, but of course that's now impossible."

"How can I meet them? Will they come here? Or can I go to the island where they stay?"

"That's no problem. The fishermen are waiting in the harbour and will take you there as soon as you're ready. I'm so glad that we found them for you after so much waiting."

"Thank you, Katila. Thank you so much. I don't know how I can ever thank you for everything you've done."

Saori was bursting with joy and energy again, just like when we had first seen the sea and she had rushed down to splash about in it. All the doom and gloom of the evening before had vanished, and her enthusiasm cheered me up too, and soon both of us were laughing and joking together.

But Drin looked as sad as I had ever seen him.

"I really will have to say 'Goodbye' this time," he said. "I can't go over the sea, not on a long voyage like that. Elkan has no powders to knock me out that long. You'll have to go home without me, Saori. At least I brought you safely this far, and the rest is in the hands of the gods."

"Oh Drin!" Saori had changed in an instant from bright happy smiles to floods of tears, and she was hugging Drin as if she would never let him go. Elkan and I quietly left them. Both of us knew that Drin had become Saori's rock, the one dependable source of comfort and protection in a hostile world, and that to be parted from him was like leaving a father; and that for Drin Saori had become the dearest person in the world and that without her everything would seem empty.

When we eventually assembled in the harbour and Katila came down to see us off, she was surprised that we looked so miserable after the joy which we had expressed earlier. Elkan inevitably quoted his poet, who had said that to part was to come a little closer to death; but I did not feel any closer to death, just sorry for Saori and Drin and sorry myself to be leaving Drin and Elkan after all our experiences together. As the boat set sail for the open sea, Saori and I waved to the people on the harbour wall as long as we could see them.

Then at last I began to think about the voyage we were about to make and which would take me to a new country which hardly anyone had ever visited. It was an exciting prospect – fresh adventure and new people and places. Saori was still downcast, but I tried to comfort her and to get her too to think about what lay ahead, and every time she began to talk about Drin and the events of the past, I switched the topic to the future and how we could persuade the navigators to take us to her home. Gradually I could feel her mood becoming a little brighter. After all, she was the one who had been so keen to leave Helva and head home, and that was exactly what we thought we were now doing.

Chapter 24
Soft Cushions and Hard Words

~

As the boat ploughed through the waves, Saori began to think of home. She was desperately sorry to be parting from Drin after all that he had done to protect her and look after her, but now at last she was on her way to meet the navigators. For the first time since she had been abducted from her island she would meet people who knew it and who could even speak her own language. She was sure that they would agree to take her home, and then she would be reunited with her mother, her family and her friends and return to the peaceful, happy existence she had always known. She was sure too that I would soon fit in and learn their language and be made welcome. It was a bright, sunny day with a light, southerly breeze, and the boat was heeling over on the starboard tack. Behind it Helva was gradually growing smaller until we could barely make out the harbour and castle in the distance. For a while a few gulls followed the boat, but eventually they settled on the sea behind us.

Saori wondered idly when the crew would change course. As it was, the boat was heading in the direction of the coast, and since the navigators were staying on an offshore island, we would soon need to change tack and head out to sea. She asked the steersman, and he gave a long story about currents and winds, but none of it made much sense. So she asked him again, more sharply this time. Instead of replying, he called out to the captain, and the whole crew gathered around us. When we had boarded the boat, they had seemed like normal sailors, but now they drew out their knives and cutlasses, and the captain warned us not to make any trouble.

Saori warned me not to try to resist. We both realised that we had been tricked: the story about the navigators had been a lie from start to finish. The truth was that we were being taken back to Banjut, where Nostoc would be waiting for us. The sailors tied our wrists together, and two of them stood guard over us. The boat did not change its course: it carried on towards the coast.

Saori was shocked and downcast. All her hopes of reaching home had been dashed. Worse than that, we had been captured by Nostoc – the one thing we had made so many efforts to avoid. She wished that we had not left Drin behind: this was just the kind of crisis he was used to dealing with. Our best hope now was that, when they found out what had happened, he and Elkan would come and rescue us.

Saori began to pray to the goddess for help. She was sure that ever since she had been kidnapped from the holy island, the goddess had been watching over her. How else to explain Drin's actions in the slave market, the many other occasions when she had been saved from disaster, and the appearance of the goddess herself to me on the moor? But the more she thought about the predicament we were now in, the more Saori began to worry. She had gone from safety on Helva to capture by Nostoc and Zeno. How could the goddess have allowed that to happen? Was an evil god, Mangra perhaps, more powerful than her? Or – and this was a wholly new idea – was this in fact a part of the goddess's own plan?

At first she dismissed this as absurd. The goddess could not have wanted her to be kidnapped from her own island, and so she must want Saori to go home as soon as possible. But was that right? Suppose that the goddess did not want her to go home just yet. Suppose that she had some mission that she wanted Saori to perform here on the mainland. That would explain why we were now heading back to Banjut. She began to think through what this might mean. Up to now her aim had been to return home as quickly as she could, but if the goddess did not want her to do that, there was no point in persisting. But in that case what did the goddess want her to do? What might be the mission waiting for her to perform? She had no answer to that.

She wished she could talk to me about this, but the sailors would overhear, and so she sat in silence and watched a dark seabird near the port bow, which dived to avoid the approach of the boat. She resolved to give up trying to go home and instead to go along with the flow of events until it became clearer what the goddess wanted her to do.

The boat did not stop this time at the outer harbour but rounded the southern tip of the rock, and for the first time I saw the huge port along the northern shore of the estuary.

It made our city of Kandalore look like a small village: there were so many jetties coming out over the water and so many storehouses and other buildings behind. And yet, although I had often read of the noise and bustle of this city, now it was quiet except for the sound of distant marching and shouted orders. There were plenty of boats tied up at the jetties but very few moving on the water.

We landed at one of the piers and were marched briskly through the streets to a large and well-guarded compound, which might in happier times have been an inn for travelling merchants. We crossed a courtyard, entered the main building and climbed a broad wooden staircase to an upper room, which was filled with soft cushions and the scent given out by a burning stick of some exotic perfume.

"Alamanda, welcome back to Banjut. It has been too long since we last met." Nostoc looked and sounded just as Drin had described him – soft and sleek. He was wearing loose orange robes, and his round body made them look as if they were padded out with pillows.

Saori simply stared at him.

"And you too, Chaemon, Prince of Akond – scholar! You too are most welcome. I have been hearing so much about you."

I took my cue from Saori and stayed silent. How could any man's head be so smooth and shiny? I wondered. It looked as if it had been polished. And such long ears...

"Please be seated. I hear that both of you have become quite fluent in the common language, and I have been so much looking forward to having a nice, long conversation with you."

His voice was like his head – smooth and oiled. It

reminded me of the slow, deceptive dance of a snake as it prepares to strike its victim and inject its deadly poison. We remained standing.

"I must admit, Alamanda, that when Lazadim stole you from me, I never imagined that it would take so long to get you back. But here you are now, safe and sound, and with a young friend too."

"What do you want with us?" Saori's voice was cold. "I was not stolen by Lazadim or anyone else. I was set free. Why can't you leave me alone?"

"Ah, I can sense that you are angry at the little trick I played to get you here. I am sorry to have disappointed your hopes, but you have had a troublesome habit of disappearing just when I was sure you were within my grasp, and I could not afford to let that happen again. Please forgive my little deception."

"I forgive you nothing. Ever since the demons first brought me here, you have pursued me, you and your horrible master. Why?"

"Now, now. I advise you to be careful with your language. People have died painful deaths for saying such things about my master. It is not wise to get on his wrong side: even now the blue-coats of Banjut are paying for their arrogance towards him. I warned Gadim, when they stole you from me, I warned him that they would be punished, and now you can see for yourself: Banjut has fallen to our heroic soldiers, and its citizens have become slaves, forced to destroy the walls of their own city with their own hands. Be careful, Alamanda."

"You cannot frighten me. I will say what I like."

Suddenly, without warning, Nostoc slapped me hard on the side of the face. In spite of myself I cried out.

"No!" cried Saori. "Stop that!"

Nostoc smiled by turning up the corners of his mouth without showing his teeth. His eyes were as cold as ever.

"I promise that I will do you no harm, Alamanda, but your young friend here is different. The fact is that we have no particular need of scholars, and my master will not care what I do with him. But you care, don't you? I can tell from the way you reacted just now. You care very much. You have perhaps also heard that I have certain skills in the art of inflicting pain on different parts of the body without actually causing the subject to die. I should enjoy carrying out some experiments on someone so obviously intelligent and sensitive."

"Don't worry about me," I said, trying to sound as if I meant it, even though Nostoc's words had made my body tingle with imagined pain.

Then Nostoc slapped me again without warning, and I had a flash of anger: if he hit me, I would hit him back. I lashed out at him and tried to punch his smooth nose – but he had read my thoughts and I was too slow. He moved surprisingly quickly, blocked me with his fat body and ducked, and I was still trying to regain my balance when the guard, who had been waiting by the door, rushed over and knocked me to the ground. I got to my feet, but there was no point in trying to carry on the fight.

"Such a brave young man," said Nostoc, "or so he wishes to appear, but that will not last long. I will not have to hurt him very much. His imagination will do my work for me."

"All right," said Saori. "Don't hurt Chaemon. In future I will not say hard words about Zeno. Is that what you want?"

"Good!" said Nostoc in his smoothest of tones. "Very good. Now we are making some progress. You are beginning to understand. Please do take a seat: I promise you they are extremely comfortable."

We sank into the soft cushions. Nostoc sat opposite us.

"The most important thing for you to understand," he said, "is that you will obey my master's orders. There is no point in trying to resist: it is your destiny to serve him."

"I'm not afraid of you. Chaemon and I have many friends outside, and they will rescue us."

"Friends?" Nostoc was smiling his cruel smile again. "Which friends are they? Perhaps you are counting on the former President of Banjut, but Lazadim cannot help you now, I'm afraid. Or perhaps you mean his agent, the bold trader Asterballudrin, who dared to insult my master. If so, you will be disappointed again: within the next two days he will walk into the trap I have set, and then he will receive the punishment he so richly deserves."

"Don't be so sure about that. Drin will never fall into your trap."

"I caught you, and I shall catch him."

"No, you won't. And don't forget Elkan."

"Ah yes. Elkan, as you call him. Gandarel, the king who ran away. If I were you, I should not count on help from him. Shall I tell you why?" We did not answer, and Nostoc continued: "I will have to let you into a very big secret."

"What do you mean?" Saori asked.

"I mean that the former king of Valosia has been one of my finest secret agents for many years."

Saori paused for a second to take this in, but then shook her head.

"I don't believe you. Elkan hates you. You destroyed his kingdom and killed his family. How can he be your agent?"

"The human heart is mysterious. I have had many agents down the years, but if you asked me why each of them agreed to enter the shadowy world of espionage, I should find it hard to reply."

"But Elkan told us how you betrayed him."

"He is so good at telling stories. I wonder which one he told you. I wonder if you asked him how he came by the scroll he carries around with him? I am sure that Prince Chaemon, being such a great scholar, noticed the scroll."

"I did ask him," I said. "It's the original manuscript of the Valosian poet. Elkan said that one of his ancestors and the chief priest had hidden it outside the city and he took it with him after he'd escaped from you."

"And you believed him? I am surprised that someone as intelligent as you did not spot the difficulties with that version of events. Would nobody, through so many generations, have noticed that the scroll was a copy? Could the king and the chief priest really have slipped off to its hiding place without being seen? And where was this wonderful hiding place, where they could feel sure that their priceless treasure would be safe? No, the story is unconvincing, but I must admit that Gandarel would tell it well. He has such a natural talent for deception."

"So how did he get the scroll?"

"As a matter of fact, I gave it to him. It was a reward after his first successful mission. Gandarel – and in my experience this is very rare – had no interest in gold or precious stones, and so I rewarded him with something which to him was far more precious. Ever since, I am happy to say, I have never had the slightest reason to doubt his loyalty."

"I still don't believe you," said Saori. "From the time we

first met him, Elkan always helped us to avoid being captured. He is on our side, not yours."

"Are you so sure? It was a stroke of luck for us – or perhaps I should say that Lord Mangra looked kindly upon us – when you walked uninvited into the Dangoy village which Gandarel uses as his hideaway when he is not on a mission, but after that he seized his opportunity well. The way in which he got you away from the Dangoys and gained your trust was very clever, but his master-stroke was when he persuaded Drin and Chaemon to pretend to be soldiers escorting a prisoner and then got a real escort of soldiers to bring you all to me."

"Drin got us out of that."

"Your Drin is indeed a troublesome fellow, but Gandarel recovered well from that little setback, and when you escaped to Helva in the company of Lazadim and his scheming wife, he was able to gain access to their secret intelligence operation, which has been most productive from our point of view. So you see, the truth is that at every stage you and your friend Drin have been outwitted, and that is why you are now my prisoner and you have no choice but to serve my master."

"You're wrong: Drin will never give up until we are safe."

"Such obstinacy! What about you, Prince Chaemon, do you share Alamanda's faith in your friend, Drin?"

"Yes, of course," I said. "He is a true Akondian."

"Oh yes, that reminds me. I have some good news for you about Akond. As a prince of that country, I am sure you will be delighted to hear that my master has decided to add it to our magnificent empire so that your countrymen can benefit from the power and glory of Lord Mangra."

"But no… you can't… the mountain…"

"The mountain is indeed the greatest obstacle, but no task is too great for the heroic Souvian army. We will build a proper road to replace the primitive track which has existed up to now. Once the blue-coats have completed their present task, they will be sent with thousands of other slaves to accomplish this project, and as soon as the road is completed and our forces are on the other side, they will sweep away all opposition and win another glorious victory."

"I wouldn't be so sure of that. We have plenty of brave men in Akond."

"Led by your brother the king, I believe, whose tactical ability appears to be somewhat questionable."

"What do you mean?"

"I mean that the Guards are the finest soldiers in the Souvian army. Did your brother really think that he would be able to ambush them in such an amateurish way? Only a few days ago I heard the Guard commander telling my master how his men had spotted the trap and reversed it, how they caught your fellow countrymen by surprise and drove them down the hill, and how they would have carried on killing them if they had not discovered that you, Alamanda, had already left. A man told them this in the common language, and when they were sure that he was telling the truth, they returned home in accordance with their orders. My master has declared them all to be Heroes of the Souvian Nation."

"Marcon!" I said. "It must have been Marcon. Is he still alive?"

But Nostoc ignored my question.

"People act out of greed and fear, but there is one other thing which makes them stubborn: and that is false hope.

I have seen men bring quite unnecessary suffering upon themselves when it would have been wiser to accept reality. I urge you not to make the same mistake. You are my prisoners, surrounded by the Souvian Guard. You will not escape, and no one will rescue you. The man you put your trust in is working for me. Banjut is finished, and Akond will soon be ours. That is the reality. If you accept it, if you give up your foolish struggle, everything will be easier for you. Please think about what I am saying, and understand that you have no other choice."

"No," said Saori. "You and your master will never win. Evil will never win. My goddess, the Goddess of the Peaceful Sea, will save us."

"Still you resist, but look around and you will see that you are mistaken. The victory belongs to Lord Mangra, who has given such strength to my master that he has conquered every country and city North and South, even Banjut. Soon he will cross the mountains and conquer every country there too, so that all mankind will be his subjects and all mankind will worship Lord Mangra. Your goddess has abandoned you. Lord Mangra rules supreme."

"No, never!" Saori responded, but Nostoc merely smiled at her.

"Guard!" he cried. "Take them away and lock them up. They need some time to reflect on what I have said."

Chapter 25

Sorrow and Anger

~

When the boat had left the harbour at Helva and Drin had waved farewell until he could no longer see us waving back, he found an old fish-box and sat on it and watched the boat sail away. Saori had gone, and he knew he would never see her again. Sadness welled up inside him: his throat ached, his brain whirled, and his eyes begged him to let them cry. He stared out to sea, straining to see where she had gone, but the boat became smaller and smaller until it was only a dot somewhere among the waves. She had left, and he was alone again. She was going home, to see her family and her friends just as she had always wanted, but this gave no comfort to Drin.

For months he and Saori had spent at least part of every day together, and the thought that they would never meet again was almost impossible to bear. Images flitted through his mind – images of Saori when she was laughing and splashing in the sea, when he had first seen her in the tent, when she had refused to have her hair cut, when she had groomed the horses, when she had sung her song to the Dangoys, when... There were so many scenes, and as he saw each one in his mind's eye, Drin wished that he could go back and live that moment all over again. But he could not. No one could bring back the past, and now there would be no more scenes to file away in his memory. Nothing could be added. The future was empty.

He had so much enjoyed looking after Saori for these few months that he wished now that he had had a daughter of his own. He could have watched her growing up and shared her joys and sadness, and there would have been no need to part like this. But Drin had never found a wife and never imagined before that he might enjoy being a father. It was too late now to regret the might-have-beens: all he could do was to sit on his fish-box with a lonely gull crying above his head, and feel waves of misery breaking over him.

It was Elkan who found him there, who put his arm around his shoulder and sat with him and gazed at the sea by his side. In the end Elkan persuaded him to walk along the quay back to the town, took Drin into the tavern and bought him a drink and something to eat. But for a long time Drin sat in the noisy, smoky room without showing any sign that he knew where he was. Only when the landlady's puppy escaped from its place behind the bar and ran up to him with its tail wagging and barked did Drin pay attention to his surroundings. He picked up the puppy and stroked it, and when it tried to bite him with its sharp little teeth, he pulled his fingers out of the way just in time. In this way, at last, he found some escape.

Drin drank too much that evening. Elkan kept him

company, talked about unimportant things to help keep his mind off the things which mattered, and, later, helped him stagger back to their lodgings, put him to bed and watched him fall asleep before doing the same himself.

Nostoc's back room had a small window high up, but it was barred and offered no possibility of escape. There was no furniture, and Saori and I sat next to each other on the wooden floor. We spoke in whispers out of fear that we might be overheard. I was filled with admiration for the way that she had stood up to Nostoc, but what he had said, especially about Elkan, troubled me, and I could not work out if we should believe him or not. But Saori did not want to talk about that: far more important to her was to share with me the idea she had had on the boat, that the goddess had some mission for her to perform on the mainland before she could go home. As soon as she explained it, I saw that she was right, and even that I must be part of it since I too had been chosen by the goddess. But how did this fit in with the curious oracle, and what could be our mission?

We were still talking about these things when the door opened abruptly and two female guards took Saori out of the room. They left some stale bread and water on the floor for me. There was hardly any light now at the little window, and after eating and drinking, I lay down on the hard floor and tried to get some rest, but for most of the night my mind was racing and I could not sleep. When the first light appeared, the guards took me back to Nostoc's room with its soft cushions and mysterious scents. To my relief Saori was already there. She looked drawn and tired but gave a quick smile when she saw me come in.

"Good morning," said Nostoc in his normal oily way.

"I trust that you have had plenty of time to reflect on our little conversation of yesterday. Please come over here and sit down, and have some breakfast. You must be hungry."

We sank down on the cushions, and a low table was placed in front of us with many different kinds of food.

"Do help yourselves. These little cakes are very good, and the plums from Coroscania are excellent this year."

We both hesitated but then began to eat.

"I suspect that some of the things I said yesterday may have come as rather a surprise to you, but I am sure that you are intelligent enough to recognise the truth when you hear it. Events are not always as they seem, and neither are people."

Neither of us responded.

"I hope that my words have helped you to understand the reality of your situation. You are completely under my master's power, and there is nothing you or anyone else can do about it."

"We understand well enough," I said.

"I see. So Chaemon will do the talking today."

"Why did you tell us all that yesterday? What do you want from us?"

"From you, Chaemon, nothing. As I told you, you are of no value, except that the young lady cares about you."

"Then what do you want from me?" asked Saori.

"All in good time. You will find out when the time comes, and when my master gives you his orders, do not imagine that you can resist. Even the Alamanda must obey the orders of the Great Leader. Is that understood?"

We were silent.

"Alamanda?"

"Yes, I understand," Saori replied.

"And you, Chaemon?"

"Me too," I said.

"Good. That is much more satisfactory. I will introduce you to my master later this morning, Alamanda. He has become impatient to meet you after so much time. If you will excuse me, I must go and report to him now, but you may remain here and finish your breakfasts."

Elkan had expected Drin to be upset. He had not rushed to give him the news; he had let Drin sleep on, well after sunrise, and get up slowly, have some breakfast, and begin to think about the day ahead, before he told him. But it made no difference. Drin was furious. He could not have been angrier if he had been woken in the middle of the night.

"There is no doubt she and Chaemon are now in the hands of Nostoc. I am as sorry about it as you are, but that is the fact."

"Then tell me who betrayed her!" Drin bellowed so loudly that everyone in the room where they had been eating turned to look.

"I do not know," said Elkan quietly.

"Someone on this island is a traitor, and when I find out who it is, I'll kill him!" Drin paused, as a thought struck him. "Or was it her? Was it Katila? She's the one who told them to go on the boat. She's the one who tricked us with all those lies about navigators."

He got up and headed for the door.

"Where are you going?" asked Elkan.

"To see Katila and get the truth!"

A man tried to block his path, but Drin pushed him out of the way.

"Wait!" cried Elkan, but Drin was through the door and

heading up the street. Elkan followed as fast as he could. Drin headed into the castle, where the guards recognised him and let him in, and climbed the stairs until he stood outside Katila's chamber, where more guards asked him what he wanted. He pushed them aside and hurled open the door. Katila looked up in alarm. An old priest, who was the only other person in the room, shuffled out by a side door.

"Was it you?!" Drin cried with his finger stabbing the air. "Did you fix this up? It was your boat, wasn't it? You're the one who told Saori to go in it. Answer me! Was it you?"

"How dare you come in here like this?" Katila responded. "Guards, seize this man!"

Soldiers rushed in and tried to grab Drin, but he fought back. He punched one, threw another onto the ground and grabbed a spear to protect himself.

"Wait!" Elkan stood in front of him. "Wait! Drin, calm down! Stop fighting! Put down the spear!"

Drin stood panting with a ring of soldiers around him. "Then tell her to answer my question!"

"Drop the spear first!"

"Not till I get an answer!"

"Lady Katila, please forgive him. The news about Alamanda has temporarily driven him insane. He has got it into his head that you might in some way be responsible."

"What nonsense!" said Katila. "Do you think I wanted Nostoc to get hold of Alamanda? I'm just as angry about it as you. Now throw down the spear!"

Drin flung it on the ground and glared round at everyone in the room before turning and heading for the door.

Katila called over one of the guards and whispered in his ear. He rushed off after Drin.

"What are you going to do?" Elkan asked.

"No one," Katila said in a cold and steely tone, "no one comes into my room without warning and behaves like that. That man is a dangerous lunatic. He will be tied up, taken over the sea and dumped on the beach outside Banjut. The Souvians can deal with him as they please."

"But…"

"You too may go now."

Elkan left the room, and as he went out, he smiled quietly to himself.

Chapter 26

The Great Leader

~

Zeno. We had heard so much about him that I had formed an image in my mind, but when at last we came before him, he did not look at all as I had imagined. His voice was as harsh as Elkan had described, but whereas I had supposed him to look like a demon with an ugly, misshapen body and a face twisted with evil, he did in fact look as strong and athletic as a champion wrestler, and his face with its clean-cut, regular features might even have been called handsome. But as I looked more carefully, he began to remind me of a stone sculpture when the outline of the body and head has been chiselled out, but the soft details have yet to be carved and none of the shapes has been rounded or polished; or of a drawing where strong lines show the outlines of the limbs, muscles and features of the face, but the artist has yet to add shading and detail. His forehead was square and flat, and his eyes deep-set under straight eyebrows. Between them his nose rose in a long, straight triangle, and below that were narrow lips and a square jaw. He wore only the simple tunic which the Souvian soldiers had as their undergarment, but his belt was wide and made of gold and he wore thick, gold bands round his bare arms, wrists, legs and ankles. A large, circular golden disc was hanging from a gold chain around his neck.

We had been brought by our guards outside the walls of the town to a wooden hall in the centre of a well-guarded army camp. Inside it, spears, swords and shields had been hung on the walls as a kind of decoration; above the height of a man's head there were windows to let in the light, but otherwise it was bare. At the far end Zeno was sitting on a large throne, which was decorated with fittings of gold; it was placed on a low wooden platform, which stretched from one side of the hall to the other. At each corner of the platform stood a fully armed guard, and I was sure that the one nearest to me was a woman. Beside Zeno, on his right hand, stood a huge upright stand, made of a dark wood, on which was mounted a large flat circle of gold. This could only be the Golden Disc, which he had taken from Banjut's great temple: it gleamed dully in the shadows. Thirty or so men in Souvian military uniform stood in three rows in the body of the hall, facing Zeno, and in front of them, close to the platform, were Nostoc and a tall man with a long grey beard and yellow robes. On entering, we had been led past the rows of officers and made to stand next to Nostoc.

"So this is the girl?" Zeno said after a while. He spoke slowly as if every word he grated out should be treated as precious.

"Yes, sir," Nostoc replied. "This is the one. You can see the colour of her hair."

Zeno came down from his seat and strode to the edge of the platform. His arms and legs had bulging muscles, and his chest was built out like a massive barrel. Even without the platform he would have towered over Saori. Two of the guards came and stood on either side of him with their spears lowered, but it was hard to imagine how she could pose any kind of threat. Zeno looked as if with one blow he could squash her flat as someone might swat a fly.

After staring down at her for a while, he ordered: "Tell her to turn round."

Saori did so at once, and Nostoc explained: "While she has been here, sir, she has learnt the common language. You can speak to her directly, sir, if you wish."

"Turn back to the front," Zeno ordered, and Saori obeyed.

Without warning, he squatted down and looked straight into her face. Surprised, Saori took a step backwards.

"Frightened of me?" he asked.

Saori said nothing but stepped forwards to her original position and stared back at him. She was determined not to let him bully her.

Standing next to her, I could see his eyes now: they were not brown or black like ours, but white, and as cold as the mountain snow, with no sign of any human feeling. I shivered as a chill ran down my spine. That was the answer, I thought: it did not matter whether a man's body was strong or weak, dark or light, straight or twisted. What mattered was the spirit inside and whether it was drawn to the truth or felt only the power of evil.

"What is your name?" Zeno asked.

"Alamanda."

"Where is your home?"

"An island, across the sea."

"Why did you come here?"

"Demons brought me."

"Demons?" Zeno straightened up and turned towards the man with the grey beard. "Farragon, what do you say?"

"With the greatest respect, sir, may I ask her a question?" Zeno grunted.

"Why did you run away to Akond? Why not come at once to meet the Great Leader?"

"Because he wanted me as a slave. I am not a slave to anyone and never will be."

"She has such spirit, master," said Farragon. "This is the one we were warned about."

Zeno returned to his throne and said: "Then tell us, Alamanda. Which is it to be? Reject me or obey me? Death or life?"

"What do you mean?" asked Saori.

"It is the choice foretold by the oracle," said Farragon, "that if you submit to our master, you will live; but if you refuse, you will die. Choose wisely, Alamanda."

No, I thought, the oracle said only that the weaker one might die, but there was not much point in arguing about that now.

Everyone was looking at Saori, expecting her to reply, but she remained silent.

"Come, Alamanda," said Nostoc. "Remember our little conversation. Obey the Great Leader – and live!"

But still Saori did not speak. She had no wish to die, but she would never obey Zeno.

"You must answer the question," Farragon pressed her. "The Great Leader is waiting."

Saori's lips were moving in silent prayer, but still she said nothing aloud.

"Answer now, or you die anyway!" came Zeno's grating voice.

And then I had a truly brilliant idea and the words tumbled out: "She cannot reply here in Banjut, but only on holy ground, only in a place chosen by the gods."

All eyes turned to look at me. The guards came over with their spears. Nostoc clicked his tongue and shook his head. I suddenly felt very hot.

"Who is this?" Zeno exclaimed.

"I am Chaemon, Alamanda's assistant."

"I have never heard such…" began Farragon.

But Zeno ignored him. "Holy ground. Is this correct, Alamanda?"

"Yes," she replied simply.

"Then so be it. We leave tomorrow for Hoxxkorn. Banjut has fallen. It is time to thank Lord Mangra and dedicate his new temple. In Hoxxkorn this girl will give her judgement and decide her fate. Gorbanya, take charge of her."

The female bodyguard came over and stood beside Saori, and Zeno began to issue orders. A general called Bartamis was told to stay in Banjut with a part of the army and oversee the prisoners while they completed the destruction of the walls. Another general was told to take his unit to the foot of the mountain, take charge of building the new road to Akond and "speed it up". One or two others had to take units to other parts of Zeno's territory. But almost all those present were commanded to accompany him to Hoxxkorn, and so were the Souvian Guards. In addition, each unit of 250 men in the whole army was ordered to send one officer to take part in the ceremony there. All these men had to have food and drink, and Zeno ordered supplies to be delivered, since Hoxxkorn lies on the edge of the southern desert.

When he had finished, he came again to the platform edge, squatted down in front of Saori so that his face was level with hers, and said: "Obey or fight." He began to laugh, "Ha! Ha! Ha!" as if this was some kind of joke, and all the others in the room pretended to laugh too. Then he stood up and shouted: "Life or death!" before sweeping out of the hall.

Chapter 27

Hoxxkorn

~

At dawn on the next day, the whole camp was packed up, and a long column of marching soldiers, cavalry, carriages and waggons began the journey to Hoxxkorn. In ordinary times I should have been delighted to go there, for this was the most sacred place on this side of the mountains, and until Zeno had turned everything upside down, it had been visited by a stream of pilgrims seeking cures for their illnesses, oracles about the future, and the general blessing of the gods. According to what I had read, the heart of Hoxxkorn was a huge rock, which stood in a lake in a green valley. This rock was like a stretched cube in shape, taller than it was wide, and its sides were as smooth and vertical as a plastered wall. No one could climb it, and everything which was taken to the summit, even the priests themselves, had to be lifted by a complicated system of pulleys and weights. Only the four chief priests were allowed to set foot on the top, where some wooden buildings gave them a place to live and protected Quafteq's copper sheets and other sacred texts and objects. Some of these had belonged to the hero Tenjin, whose epic journey began and ended at Hoxxkorn.

Saori and I were split up as soon as we left the hall, and she was taken off by Gorbanya for special treatment. I was thrown among the male prisoners, and to my surprise found that most of them were well-educated scholars and priests. Some had already suffered terrible treatment from the Souvians and were sick and weak, and those of us who were younger tried to help them along the road. Our guards delighted in beating us whenever they could find an excuse – and sometimes without one – and we did our best to protect each other. With soldiers all around us, it was impossible to escape. Every day became a simple battle for survival, and I had little time to think about our situation, and no chance at all to talk to Saori about it.

For the first day or so, we crossed a wide plain where the crops were growing tall and green; but as we went on, the land became drier, and though green fields still spread out on either side of the rivers which we had to cross, there were long stretches in between where nothing much grew except thorny bushes and brown tufts of dry grass. It was mid-summer now, and around the middle of the day when the sun was high in the sky, the heat became intense, and water was in short supply. High above, vultures circled as the hot air rose and lifted their broad wings. On the eighth day, we did not cross a single river, and the earth was soft and sandy: we were entering the great desert where no man or animal could survive the heat and drought. The mountains, which we had always been able to see far off to our right, now rose up in front of us as well, and the road began to slope upwards towards them. This made the journey more difficult for the animals pulling the heavy waggons, and as we toiled up the hill, the column had to stop regularly to rest them and give them water; but there was little or no water for us, and several of my fellow prisoners collapsed by the road and we had to half carry, half drag them up to the summit of the ridge.

When at last we reached it and could see the land beyond, I had hoped to find the green valley of Hoxxkorn, but there was no sign of that. Instead, a large expanse of sandy desert sloped away from us towards the sea, which came in from our left and formed a narrow bay reaching inland in front of us. Beyond that was more desert, and nowhere could we see any mark made by man except the road curving round to our right. We plodded on, downhill now, round the foothills of the mountain, until suddenly there it was – the upper part of the rock, square and black against the pale sand. How many pilgrims had rejoiced on that same spot to see the end of their long journey before them? We too stopped for a moment, but it brought no joy to us.

The guards drove us forwards, and eventually we reached the edge of the long valley which the rock dominated. The old scholars had called it the stepping stone to heaven, and I could see what they had meant. The rock was enormous, and when they stood on the top, with the wide, dry sky of the desert open around them, the four priests must have felt that they had risen halfway to the world of the gods. But though the rock was as I had expected, its surroundings were not. I had read of a lush, green valley, a river carrying water from the mountains down to the sea, and a lake which encircled the rock. Over many generations people had built terraces on the slopes of the valley and made channels for the river water so that fruit and crops could be grown in little fields. It should have been like a magical garden in the middle of the desert. But when we looked at the valley now, there was no water and nothing green, just a few sad weeds trying to cling onto life on the dry terraces. Instead of willows weeping along the edge of a lake, a few dead stumps rose out of the dry soil. Even the river had vanished. All the beauty and mystery which had drawn people to Hoxxkorn for so many generations had been destroyed, and in its place had come the dead world of Zeno and Mangra.

Almost all the soldiers were ordered to make their camp on the nearest, eastern slope of the valley, but we were taken down to the bottom and made to climb the slope opposite. This was when we made another unwelcome discovery: an enormous ramp of sandy earth had been piled up on the far side of the rock, and along the ridge of the ramp a path reached up from ground level to the summit. When they saw this, many of my fellow prisoners fell to their knees and began to wail and pray to the gods, for their holy rock had been desecrated. Contrary to their ancient laws, anyone at all could now climb up the ramp and reach the summit. The stepping stone to heaven was open not just to the four priests but to anyone who felt like going for a walk. The guards forced everyone back onto their feet, and we were driven into a wooden stockade at the foot of the ramp on the western rim of the valley. Further on, we could see a scruffy camp, where the slaves who had built the ramp, together with the soldiers who guarded them and forced them to work, lived in temporary shelters out in the desert.

It took me a long time to get to sleep that night – too many thoughts were whirling around my brain – and when I finally did, it was already time to wake up. The morning was dark and cold, and the guards needed lamps to see their way round. No one spoke. Across the valley the army camp was coming alive. Soldiers were gathered round fires eating breakfast, and even they were speaking in hushed tones. The gate of our compound opened, and the guards pushed in an elderly man and a middle-aged woman before closing it again. They were dressed in simple white smocks and looked ordinary enough, but they were greeted with great reverence by my fellow prisoners. One of them whispered to me that these were the two Hoxxkorn priests, Tadashi and Masako, who had been captured by the Souvians. The other two priests had left the rock beforehand and taken with them the copper plates and other sacred items so as to keep them safe; but these two had remained to the last in order to warn the Souvians to obey the gods and not to set foot upon the summit. But the Souvians had swarmed in regardless, destroyed the sacred buildings and started to lay out designs for the new temple which Zeno had ordered to be built on top of the rock in honour of Mangra.

Suddenly a woman's voice barked an order to our guards, who straightened and stood to attention. The gate opened again, and this time I was the one who recognized the person entering. She was dressed in rich red robes and wore a simple, white crown. Her golden hair had been parted in the middle, and each side brought forward so that it spread out over the front of her dress.

"Saori!" I was so happy to see her alive and well after so many days that I ran over and would have hugged her, but she did not respond.

"It's me! Chaemon!" I said. "How are you?" But Saori showed no emotion in response. "Ah, yes, Chaemon," she replied, but she seemed to be repeating my name because I had said it, not because she knew who I was. I felt a sudden chill of fear: Oh no, what have they done to you? I thought; and then, even worse, came the sense that I might have lost her, that they might have sucked out her spirit and left her as an empty shell, and now I felt like crying – but Masako asked: "Who is she?", and I began to tell the story of Alamanda, until the guards came in with their sticks and made us all keep silence.

It was a little less dark now, and though the sun was still below the horizon, the sky was light enough to see blurred shapes even without the lamps. Suddenly horns blasted out, and there was the massive figure of Zeno standing at the base of the ramp, surrounded by his bodyguards. Drums were beating a steady rhythm, and when the horns sounded again, he began to move up the slope with giant strides, followed by a line of dark shapes and bright torches marching breathlessly, trying to keep up with him. When he came to the top, Zeno did not hesitate for a second but strode straight across to the eastern rim of the rock and looked out over his soldiers, who were gathered on the terraces below as if they were in a theatre or a stadium. Most of the people who had followed him up the ramp stopped when they reached the top, but a small group advanced onto the rock and stood a few paces behind Zeno. I thought I could see the shapes of Farragon and Nostoc among them.

A gong sounded as the eastern sky became a glorious mixture of red and pink and orange, and for a moment I forgot our troubles as I drank in its beauty. An eagle glided overhead with a pointed fish in its talons, and in the silence I thought I could hear the faint whispering of the sea. The edge of the red sun rose just above the horizon, the summit of the rock was bathed in gentle, orange light, our faces were brightened by the fresh sun, and gradually the colour of the slope below us changed from grey to a soft brown. It should have been a moment of pure delight in the beauty of nature, except that the dawn of the new day also lit up Zeno standing atop the holy rock with his legs apart and his arms raised in a gesture of triumph.

"I am Zeno!" he cried. "Ruler of the World!"

A loud roar from the soldiers greeted him, and they began to chant "Zee-no! Zee-no!" as the red disc of the sun emerged from the dark horizon behind them. As they looked up at him, they would have seen the light reflecting from a man made of gold: for he was wearing a golden crown on his head and golden armour on his body, and behind him stood the frame containing the face of the Golden Disc. High up on the mighty rock, he must have looked to them more like a god than a man.

The horns blared out again, and Zeno signalled for silence. He stepped back and took his seat on his throne, which had been set up beside the Disc; and Farragon came forward.

"Today," he said in a loud, quavering voice, "we are gathered together to dedicate the foundation of a new temple for Lord Mangra, here on the holy rock of Hoxxkorn. The old gods whom men used to worship here were false gods. Their priests were false priests. Lord Mangra has driven them from his holy rock. Only one god is true, and he is the one we serve. O Lord Mangra, we pray to you to give us the strength and skill to build for you the greatest temple which the world has ever seen!"

Farragon then recited a series of prayers in honour of Mangra, and between each one the soldiers sang hymns of praise. Meanwhile, our guards opened the gate again and ordered us prisoners to follow them up the ramp, with Saori in the lead, and onto the summit. Many of the prisoners at first refused to set foot on the holy rock, but when the guards began to beat them, the Hoxxkorn priests encouraged them forward and said the gods would forgive them. All except Saori and me were forced into another enclosure at the top of the ramp, but we were held by two bodyguards each just outside the enclosure, and our wrists were firmly tied together.

Farragon said: "Now listen to me! Lord Mangra has sent our Great Leader to punish the wicked and bring justice to all men through fire and the sword. Today we give thanks to Lord Mangra."

"Thanks to Lord Mangra!" cried Zeno, who had jumped down from his throne. "He has given us victory. Tell me! Did we conquer Milesia?"

"Yes!" roared the soldiers.

"Did we kill the king and all his sons?"

"Yes!"

"Did we crush Basutia?"

"Yes."

"And Coroscania?"

"Yes!"

"And Valosia?"

"Yes!"

Zeno went on naming the countries which the Souvians had conquered, and after each country was named, the crowd roared "Yes!" more loudly than before, until he reached the last:

"And did we smash Banjut?"

"Yes!" they cried.

"Here is their greatest treasure, the Golden Disc!", and Zeno pointed to it shining in the sun. "And their leader Lazadim is dead and buried!"

The soldiers gave a great roar when they heard this, and they began again to chant his name "Zee-no, Zee-no!" until he signalled for silence and returned to his throne.

"All these things," said Farragon, "are the blessings given by Lord Mangra to our Great Leader. But why? Why has the Great Leader been favoured above all men? Why has such great power been bestowed upon him? Listen and I will tell you. It is because he is no ordinary man. He has no ordinary father. No. He is not the son of a mortal man. He is the son of the god himself! His father is Lord Mangra! He is the son of Lord Mangra!"

Zeno had come forward and was standing again on the rim of the rock. He raised his arms in salute, as Farragon cried out: "Hail to the Son of Lord Mangra!" and all the Souvians took up the cry. From all the terraces the sound of men's voices echoed into the sky, and all were hailing Zeno as the son of Mangra. This was the moment of Zeno's greatest triumph, and he stood with arms upstretched and legs apart, glorying in the chants of the crowd. To them, he had ceased to be a mortal man – he had risen to a higher state. They were worshipping him as a divine being, the son of their god. Soon their chanting turned to song: they were again singing the hymns glorifying Mangra, but this time they honoured his son as well. "Glory to Lord Mangra!" they sang. "Glory to his Son!"

The sun had risen well above the horizon now, and for everyone lined up on the platform facing eastwards, it was too bright to look towards it. But from the soldiers' point of view, the sun made the Golden Disc shine out like a golden star; and there, beside it, on top of the towering black shape of the rock, stood a golden figure, flashing with reflected brilliance, high above them, master of the holy rock, halfway to the heavens.

I looked across to Saori to see if I could catch her eye. I wanted desperately to know that she was well, in spirit as well as body, but she stared straight ahead. Even when I whispered "Saori", she did not turn her eyes towards me. She seemed to be unaware of what was going on around her, as if she had entered another world. Perhaps, I thought, that was for the best, because if her mind stayed like that she might avoid fear and pain – but I myself felt all the more alone.

The chanting and singing went on a long time, but in the end the moment I had been dreading arrived. Zeno signalled for silence, and Saori was led across by her guards to a position next to him, where she stood stiffly in her red dress with her golden hair, and looked straight ahead. Farragon began to tell the crowd about the oracle and the choice that Saori had to make. Looking at her slight figure beside Zeno's enormous bulk, it was hard to believe that she had the power to harm him as the oracle had claimed.

"So, Alamanda," Zeno's grating voice cried out. "Which is it to be? Will you obey me? Or do you choose to die?"

All around was silent. The soldiers below were hushed. Far off a crow croaked in the mountains. But Saori did not speak.

"Come," Farragon said. "You must reply."

"The time has come," said Nostoc. "You cannot avoid it now."

But still she was silent. I wondered what was going through her mind.

"Tell them!" said Zeno. "Tell them you will obey me, the son of Lord Mangra!"

Saori turned slowly and looked up to his face, and as at last she gave her reply, her voice shocked with its intensity.

"NO! I will never obey you or your god! Never will I join in your evil murders! I will fight you until my dying breath!"

"So be it!" responded Zeno. "Your fight will be short, because you will die here, now. My father, Lord Mangra, thirsts for blood, and I will sacrifice you to him."

A great cheer went up from the soldiers, and the guards grabbed Saori's arms again. I was dragged over to stand near her, while a wooden frame like a low gate was brought over and placed in front of her on the very edge of the rock. Saori was made to kneel and bend her head forward so that her neck was resting on the top rail. She offered no resistance.

"And now," announced Farragon, "the Great Leader will sacrifice this girl to his Father in return for everlasting life. Once she is dead, nobody can end his reign or cause him pain."

A huge axe with a golden blade was handed to Zeno. The horns blared out, and there was a long roll of the drums. Then everything and everyone was silent again. Nothing moved: even the air was still. Zeno slowly raised the axe.

I could not watch. I could not bear it. I could hardly breathe. I closed my eyes. I waited for the roar from the crowd when the deed was done. Tears were trickling down my cheeks. After all we had done together, this was the end.

Chapter 28
Bloodstained Dagger

~

B ut the roar of the crowd never came. Instead, I heard someone shouting behind us, and when I opened my eyes, Zeno had lowered the axe and was looking towards the ramp where two horsemen were riding at full speed up the slope. When they reached the top they dismounted, and for a moment the guards held them up, but now all of us could hear what they were calling out: "Flash message for the Great Leader! Flash message!"

One of them passed through the guards, came running towards Zeno and threw himself on the ground face down in front of him.

"Great Leader, sir, flash message, sir, from General Bartamis."

Zeno called over one of his officers: "Arichi, read out the message!"

The messenger got up onto one knee, pulled out a square wooden tablet from the bag which hung across his body, and gave it to the officer.

"The seal is unbroken, sir," Arichi said. He broke the seal himself and opened the folding tally. "It says: '*Great Leader, Lazadim and his forces came in the night from Helva. They have freed the slaves and retaken the citadel. My men have resumed the siege but need reinforcements. It was a great honour to serve you. Farewell. Bartamis.*'"

Among the Souvians around us there was a buzz of surprised murmuring.

"What is this?" said Zeno, who appeared as surprised as the rest. "Lazadim? But he is dead. Have you betrayed me, Nostoc?"

"No, no, master." Nostoc appeared unnaturally calm. "We have all been betrayed. How could Bartamis with so many men lose control of the citadel? I beg your forgiveness, sir: I never imagined such treachery."

"Do we go to Banjut at once, sir?" asked Arichi.

"No," said Zeno. "We finish the ceremony. Then we go. I will kill Lazadim with my own hands. But first the girl. Give me the axe!"

Zeno looked round, and as he did so, the kneeling messenger hurled himself forward and tried to stab him with a long dagger with an S-shaped blade. But Zeno was too quick: he dodged the blade and threw the messenger to one side so that he was left sprawling on the ground. At once the bodyguards ran over and thrust their spears into his body, so that what had been the form of a tall, uniformed soldier was turned into a bloody, mangled mess.

"Are you all right, sir?" Arichi asked.

"Who was he?" asked Zeno.

"There's blood on your arm. We must tend the wound."

A bodyguard tore the hem of his tunic and tried to wind it round Zeno's arm as a bandage, but he pushed him away.

"Only a scratch. Take off his helmet!" he ordered.

The guards who had been holding Saori and me had rushed over to help Zeno, and another soldier had come over and was cutting the ropes round her wrists with a short knife. Saori turned and smiled – she smiled for the first time: "Drin!" she said. Where had Drin come from?

Meanwhile the guards were pulling off the attacker's helmet to reveal his face.

"It's Gandarel," someone said. "The king of Valosia. The king who ran away."

"I thought he was dead," said someone else, and everyone crowded round.

It was Elkan: there was no mistake about that, and there was no doubt now about his true intentions, no doubt that all along he had wanted only one thing – revenge on Zeno – and had gambled everything in one last, desperate attempt to achieve it. But it had all been in vain, because Zeno was still alive, and Elkan himself lay there, dead. Saori gave out a little cry, ran over to the mangled corpse and closed the staring eyes. Tears were pouring down her face as she cradled Elkan's head on her lap. Drin cut my wrists free, and I went over to kneel beside her.

Zeno had returned to the edge of the rock. A guard handed him the axe, he straightened his shoulders and looked out towards his faithful soldiers.

"Even here, my enemies sent an assassin to kill me!" he cried. "But look! They failed! I am Zeno, son of Lord Mangra! I will rule forever! I will never die!"

"Yes, you will," said Saori. Her voice was colder and harder than I had ever heard it before, and she spoke with a calm certainty. She was standing very straight and absolutely still. The power of the goddess flowed through her and she knew exactly what the goddess wanted her to do. As Zeno turned to face her, she looked straight into his cold eyes. "You will die, and your evil god will die with you."

Zeno raised the axe with one hand to threaten her, and his mouth opened to make his reply, but then the strangest thing happened. His arm slackened and fell, and he appeared to be struggling for breath. The axe slipped from his grasp and dropped over the side of the rock down to the ground far below with a clatter and a thud. Now both arms were hanging limply by his side, his neck bent forwards as if the weight of his head was too much for it to carry, his shoulders slumped, his legs sagged at the knees, and very slowly, ever so slowly, his whole body crumpled, until at last he overbalanced and toppled silently over the side and followed the axe, to land with a thump on the ground far below.

Such was the shock that for a moment no one moved: they could not believe what they had seen with their own eyes. But then the Souvians on the top of the rock – generals and bodyguards, Nostoc, Farragon, everyone together –pushed forward to the edge and looked over the side. "Is he alive?" one cried, but from the men down below the only answer was a long "No-o-o, no-o-o", not so much replying to the question as expressing their horrified grief. All of them were trying to take in the enormity of what had happened. A moment before they had been prepared to believe that Zeno was the son of their god, that he would live forever, that he was superhuman – and now he had fallen to his death, right in front of them.

The man they had served, whose every command they had obeyed, the man who was never mistaken, who had led them to victory after victory, for whom they had been ready to lay down their own lives, had lost his. How could this be? It was as if the sun had risen in the West or the rivers flowed uphill. For a long moment they appeared frozen by the shock as they struggled to accept the evidence of their own eyes.

I felt the exact opposite: delighted to be freed from Zeno. But I realised that we were still in great danger: it would have looked both to the men below and to the people on top as if Saori had killed Zeno with some kind of magic spell, and as soon as their shock and grief turned to anger, they would seek revenge. I do not know why, but an idea popped into my mind: that perhaps it was not Saori's words which had killed Zeno, but Elkan's dagger. Suppose that he had covered the blade with Dangoy poison so that he had only to cut Zeno's skin and a few moments later the poison would do the rest. If so, the dagger might still be deadly. It lay on the ground about ten paces away after being knocked by Zeno out of Elkan's hand, and I ran over to pick it up.

But I was not the only one to have had this idea. Nostoc was after the dagger too, and he was closer to it than me but moved more slowly. We reached it at almost the same moment, and Nostoc pushed me away. I ended up rolling onto my back on the hard stone, but in the split second before he had pushed me, I had managed to get my fingers round the hilt of the dagger and I was still holding it in my right hand as I lay on my back. Had I cut myself with the blade as I rolled over? I had no time to check: Nostoc was on his feet and standing over me. I rolled onto my knees and slashed at his bare legs, but he dodged with surprising speed. He turned to grab a spear from the hands of one of the bodyguards, and in that second I got onto one foot, lunged upwards and plunged the dagger through his robe and into his soft belly. He jabbed at me with the spear, but I dodged it and got onto my feet and out of his range.

"Over here!" a voice called, and I saw Saori sitting on Zeno's throne and Drin standing in front of her with a spear. I ran over to join them. The prisoners had broken out of the stockade and were grouped around the throne too.

One by one the Souvians turned and saw us, and Farragon shouted: "Revenge! Revenge for the Great Leader!" Others took up the cry, and they came slowly towards us with swords drawn and spears levelled. "Kill the murderers!" shouted Arichi.

Saori descended from the throne and stood in front of our group with the two Hoxxkorn priests on either side of her. "Stand back!" she said. "I am Alamanda, and the power of the goddess is with me. Stand back!"

The Souvians hesitated. "Lord Mangra seeks vengeance for his son," cried Farragon, but Masako the priestess replied: "Mangra did not protect Zeno, and he will not protect you."

"Did you not see the power of Alamanda?" said Takashi. "Did you not see Zeno die at her command?"

Nostoc pushed his way through the crowd. He had dropped the spear and was holding up the blood stained dagger instead. He was limping, and the bottom of his robe was stained red. "No," he said. "She did not kill him. She has no power. It was this dagger…"

"Watch!" I said. "Nostoc will be the next to die."

And then he slowly collapsed, just as Zeno had done, and toppled onto the ground, and lay there, a mass of flesh, dead.

"Zeno and Nostoc were punished by the gods for their pride," said Masako. "Who will be next?"

The Souvians inched backwards, away from us. Even Farragon looked less confident. We were winning the battle of wills, but I could see that that would not be enough to save us. The Souvians on the rock might be too frightened to attack us, but they were not our only problem. Down below thousands of other Souvians were in a state of grief at the death of their leader, but very soon that would change to anger, and they would storm up the ramp to avenge him.

"Lord Mangra will protect us," Farragon said. "Avenge his son!" But he himself had no weapon and made no move.

"Stand back!" said Saori. "If you fear the goddess, stand back!"

The men below were leaving the terraces and crossing towards the western side of the valley. We could hear their shouts coming closer, but at the same time I noticed a new sound – a distant rumbling far off in the mountains. Saori and the priests took a step forwards, and the Souvians in front of us backed off a step. But at any moment I expected the mass of the Souvian soldiers to reach the top of the ramp, and then it would all be over for us. In the background the rumbling was becoming louder: it sounded like thunder, even though the sky was blue and cloudless. Drin had his sword drawn, and I decided to go over to Nostoc's body and pick up the knife. I looked round first, and as I expected, a horde of Souvians were on the ramp, but, to my surprise, they were not rushing towards us. They were standing still, looking towards the head of the valley, pointing and crying out in alarm.

Then, suddenly, every sensation was overwhelmed by the

deafening roar of a huge wall of water, which came crashing down from the hills and into the valley. It was as if a giant had emptied an enormous bucket or overturned a massive bath, and the valley formed the only channel for the water to escape. Nothing could stand in its way. This was not water as I had known it before: it was a crushing, monstrous, thundering force of destruction. The river of the Dangoys had flowed quickly over the rapids but it was no more than a trickle when compared with this. The water smashed into the great rock, and the spray was hurled far, far above our heads before crashing down and drenching us all. On one side of the rock the flow was held up by the ramp for a second or two until it crumbled and the sand was carried off in a churning fury as the water forced its way down to the sea. On the other side there was nothing to slow the passage of the current, which filled the valley and washed away everything in its path. Such was the speed and volume of the water that for the men on the ramp and on the ground there was no possibility of escape: they simply vanished into the foaming torrent.

The rock itself held firm, and we were lucky it did, because otherwise we too would have been carried off downstream and out to sea. Without any doubt, the rock of Hoxxkorn saved our lives that day. Drin gathered Saori and me together away from the edge and made us crouch down with our backs to the danger. Our ears were battered by the noise, we were constantly soaked by the splashing spray and our bodies were shivering with the cold and damp. There was nothing we could do, nothing we could say, and no point even in thinking, for none of us had any strength compared with the raw power which had been set loose around us. So we stayed huddled together, comforted only by each other's presence.

Just staying alive was all that mattered then, while the waters surged, foamed, bubbled, roared, smashed, gouged, swirled and scoured their way past.

Finally, when it felt as if the flow of water would go on forever and end up flooding the whole world, the noise began to lessen a little and the spray stopped splashing onto us so heavily. Then at last we gained the courage to look up and see what was happening around us, and found the priests and Souvians – those who had survived – doing the same. The stream of water continued to flow past, but we could see the level going down and the flooded area gradually shrinking. The storm was past, and we were safe. Relief swept over us. Saori, Drin and I hugged each other out of pure joy. We were still alive. The raging torrent had somehow passed us by.

Down below, as the water receded, it revealed a scene of devastation. The terraces, which men had toiled to build over so many years, had gone, leaving the sides of the valley smooth and even. The massive ramp, which so many slaves had laboured to build under the baking sun, had been reduced to a low mound at the foot of the rock. But the greatest, and most shocking, change was that the thousands of men who had thronged the terraces had disappeared. They had camped there, sung hymns to Mangra, celebrated the glory of Zeno, his supposed son, and mourned his death, but now there was no sign of them. There was no risk that they might come storming up the ramp. They were gone, and it was as if they had never existed.

Chapter 29
Aftermath

⁓

L ike us, the former prisoners were embracing each other and thanking the gods for saving them from the giant wave. The remaining Souvians, however, looked dazed and shocked. There was no sign of Farragon: he must have fallen into the torrent and been carried away. But Arichi had survived, and instead of threatening us, he came over and lay flat on the ground in front of Saori, in the same gesture of submission that Elkan the messenger had adopted before Zeno, and one by one Gorbanya and the other Souvians followed.

"The victory belongs to you, Alamanda," Arichi said. "Our master is dead. Spare us, and we will obey your orders."

Saori thought for a moment, and then said: "Then these are my orders. Pay good attention. There will be no more fighting and no more killing. You will set free all the prisoners and slaves and let them return to their homes. There will be no more slavery ever. You will destroy every statue of Mangra; and you will send all your soldiers back to their homes and destroy their weapons. The cities, towns and villages will be rebuilt, and everyone will return to their old peaceful lives. Will you do all of this?"

"Your orders will be obeyed," Arichi said.

"We'd better write them down," I said, "so that there's no mistake. We should do that as soon as we can get hold of writing materials."

"Chaemon is right," Saori said, "and I have one other order. You must obey the priests of Hoxxkorn, and I will ask them to check on my behalf that you are doing what I have ordered, because the task which the goddess gave me has been accomplished, and I am now free to leave here and go home."

This order too was accepted by the Souvians, and when the soldiers who had guarded the slaves who had built the ramp came to the rim of the valley to see what had happened, Arichi duly ordered them to set the slaves free. For their part, the priests approved of Saori's orders but were sorry to hear that she would leave so soon; but when she mentioned the navigators, it turned out that the priests knew them well and could easily make contact with them. There would be no more obstacles to Saori's journey home.

Or at least there was one: we had to find a way to get down from the rock. The old ropes and pulleys had gone, and the ramp had been swept away. The solution was to shoot onto the top of the rock an arrow with a long string attached, and we would then be able to pull up a rope tied to the other end of the string; but it took a long time to make a string and rope long enough and to fire the arrow successfully. While we were waiting, we did what we could to put things in order on top of the rock. We rolled Nostoc's body over the side, but we wrapped Elkan's body in a cloth and made sure that it was treated with respect. I had a long talk with some of the priests about the Golden Disc and the Extopian oracle.

While we were occupied with this, a group of people came down from the hills and hailed us from the eastern bank. Among them were two figures dressed in white, who turned out to be the other two Hoxxkorn priests; but Drin, Saori and I were far more surprised to see Marcon and the mountain traders from Akond with them. We yelled and waved to each other, and late in the day, when we finally descended from the mountain, we sat round a fire together, had an evening meal from the Souvians' supplies and told each other what had happened since we had last been together.

With help from Saori and Drin, I went first and explained everything as simply and quickly as I could, from the moment that we had parted from Marcon on the mountain up to the arrival of the flood. Then we pressed Marcon to tell his story.

"There's not much to say really," he began, "except that, to be honest, we caused the flood."

"You?" asked Saori. "But how?"

"I suppose I'd better go back to the ambush. Except that it turned out not to be an ambush because somehow the Souvians got wind of it, and it turned into a messy fight instead. Many of our men fought bravely, but the Souvians had the advantage. As you know, I'd been following them down the mountain, and I managed to find their commander and after a bit of argy-bargy I persuaded him to call off the attack because Saori had already crossed the mountain. So they went back up the track, and we looked after our dead and wounded. Even the king had been hit by an arrow, though fortunately his wound was not serious.

"When they heard what had happened, everyone in Kandalore started worrying that the Souvians would attack again, and I suggested to the king that he should send us traders over the pass to give early warning of any more Souvians coming, and he agreed. But before we left, the queen gave us an extra mission. She was worried about you, Chaemon, and she asked me and the lads to see if we could find you. She kept saying you'd never been out of your library before and asking what chance would you have with the Souvians, though I think you may have just answered that by killing Nostoc. Anyway, we promised to look for you and bring you home, and it's true that if the king's injury had been more serious, Akond would have needed you to take charge in his place."

I did not know what to say to this. I had no wish to go back to Akond, whatever my mother might have said: I wanted to go on with Saori to her island. So I looked at the fire and said nothing.

Marcon resumed his account: "Well, when we got to Gate B we saw that the Souvians were digging up the mountain, so we left four men there to watch them and report to the king if they made any move up the track. The rest of us, the five you see here, decided to look for you. We thought that if we tried to follow you to Banjut, we were likely to be captured; so we decided to come to Hoxxkorn and ask the priests because they pick up all kinds of information. But when we arrived, we found that even Hoxxkorn was full of Souvians, and we weren't sure what to do. That's when we had a stroke of luck. We sent Golodin here to climb a hill and spy out the land, and when he was halfway up, a woman dressed in white appeared out of nowhere and asked him who he was. He thought she was a goddess and started praying like he's never prayed before – isn't that right, Gol?" Golodin looked embarrassed. "Anyway, after a bit he understood she was one of the Hoxxkorn priests, and he brought her down to us with her partner, and we had a good talk about the Souvians, but they didn't know much about you, Chaemon, except that Zeno was looking for Saori and you might be on Helva.

"While we were talking, they mentioned the river. Apparently, it was only a small stream in the autumn when the Souvians first turned up. They wanted to drain the lake, and they decided to build a dam up in the gorge to stop the flow of water. The trouble with that was that in the spring the river was swollen by the melted snow from the mountains, and the Souvians had to keep making the dam bigger. The priests wanted to ruin Zeno's construction plans by breaking it, but they didn't know how. Well, we've built quite a lot of dams in Akond, and as it began to grow dark, we went down and had a good look at this one. We could soon see that it wouldn't take much to make it collapse.

"There were a few guards and a work party of slaves trying to shore it up, but this morning, just before dawn, we crept up on the guards, put them out of action and set free the slaves. Then we got to work on weakening the dam. The hardest bit was not getting ourselves drowned when it finally broke and the water went storming off down the valley. Good job done, we thought; that'll make a mess of the Souvians' building project. But until we came down here, none of us had the faintest idea that Zeno himself had come, and if we'd known that you were here, we'd never have dared to break the dam in case you came to harm. We're very lucky it turned out the way it has."

"Not luck," said Saori. "It was the will of the goddess."

Only one mystery now remained, and that was how Drin had come to Hoxxkorn. He was as shy as usual, but when Saori urged him to speak up, he told us what had happened after we had parted on Helva. After his argument with Katila, he had been put on a boat, been sick all over again on the crossing and dumped on a beach on the mainland. He had quickly been found by Souvian soldiers and locked up for four days in a small underground cell.

"I began to dig a tunnel. It was the only way I could see to get out, but I hadn't got far when Elkan appeared in a Souvian officer's uniform and spoke to me through the hatch in the door. You know what he was like: full of apologies, all his usual palaver, but I didn't want to hear his excuses: I just wanted to strangle him.

"Anyway, in the end he persuaded me to listen to him, and he told me, so quietly that I could hardly hear, all about his dealings with Nostoc, how he'd pretended to serve him as an agent in the hope that if they trusted him, they'd let him get close to Zeno and he could get his revenge, but that moment never came. Now he had a new plan. He said it was the only way to save you, Saori, and he needed my help. For the first time since we met him, I thought he was telling me the truth, and anyway I couldn't see any alternative, so I said I'd do it, and he let me out.

"He'd been feeding reports to Nostoc and Bartamis about Lazadim's death and how the Banjutis on Helva were terrified of a Souvian attack, but he knew full well that Lazadim was alive and well – actually I'd seen him when I burst into Katila's room – and planning to attack Banjut that very night. He made me dress up again as a Souvian in a large uniform he'd brought with him. As it was getting dark, we headed off for the Souvian camp, and with the help of a pass he had, we were able to go right up to Bartamis's HQ. There were lots of men going in and out, and we waited out of sight for a while. We could hear the sounds of fighting and see a fire blazing up, all from the direction of the citadel. A group of about 20 officers rushed into the HQ, and Elkan thought he saw Bartamis among them. Soon even more men were running in and out, there was confusion everywhere, and Elkan and I hung back in the shadows.

"An officer came out and shouted: 'Where are the duty messengers? Quick! It's a flash.' That's what we'd been waiting for. Two young soldiers ran into the building and almost immediately came out again and ran straight past the spot where we'd been hiding. It took only a second to trip them up and knock them out; then we tied them up and dragged them behind some barrels in a dark alley. Elkan took their bag with the message in it, and we hurried off to the stables to get horses. Someone said we weren't the usual messengers and I was too big for the horse they kept ready, but Elkan showed them the flash message and asked if they wanted to argue about it with Zeno, and that shut them up. Just as we were leaving, a soldier ran in and said Bartamis had killed himself.

"That's about all really. At every stop on the road we were waved through, and whenever we needed fresh horses or food they gave us the best. Then we arrived here, and you know the rest."

"You were only just in time," I said. "One minute later, and... well, Saori wouldn't still be with us."

"Elkan was worried about that. We hardly got any sleep, he was in such a hurry to get here."

"He saved my life," said Saori, "but he lost his own."

"He must have known he would die?" I asked.

"Yes, we talked about it on the last night," Drin said. "He said it was his time to die, and he was glad of it. It would be a kind of relief after everything that had happened. I said that, now I knew his true nature, I was sorry for the way I'd treated him in the past, but he said he didn't blame me. He said it wasn't revenge he was after – not any more: it was too late to help his own family, but he wanted to stop Zeno from bringing any more misery to other people. He still had the little figures he'd made of his wife and children. He had those with him when he died."

"What did he do with his scroll?" I asked. "He loved that poem so much."

"Yes, he made me promise to look after it after his death if I survived. We ought to go and get it tomorrow. I know where it's hidden."

"It's a tragic story," Marcon said, "and the saddest part is that after he'd stuck to his aim over all those years, even cooperated with his worst enemy, and when he'd finally managed to scratch the poison onto Zeno, he himself died before he knew it had worked."

"Without him none of this would have happened," said Saori, wiping away her tears. "Without him the goddess could not have triumphed. We should send his body back to Valosia and make sure it is buried properly with his ancestors."

"I'll make sure of that," Drin said.

"Then all the people of Valosia will know that their last king was a clever and brave man, and he never ran away."